Gamma Glamma

Gamma Glamma

Kim Flores

KENSINGTON BOOKS
http://www.kensingtonbooks.com

KENSINGTON BOOKS are published by

Kensington Publishing Corp.
850 Third Avenue
New York, NY 10022

All Kensington titles, imprints, and distributed lines are available at
special quantity discounts for bulk purchases for sales promotion, pre-
miums, fund-raising, educational, or institutional use.

Special book excerpts or customized printings can also be created to fit
specific needs. For details, write or phone the office of the Kensington
Special Sales Manager: Attn. Special Sales Department. Kensington
Publishing Corp., 850 Third Avenue, New York, NY 10022. Phone: 1-800-
221-2647.

Kensington and the K logo Reg. U.S. Pat. & TM Off.

ISBN-13: 978-0-7582-2242-8
ISBN-10: 0-7582-2242-4

First Printing: February 2008

10 9 8 7 6 5 4 3 2 1

Printed in the United States of America

Dedicated to Michael Swenson, Amelia Flores, and Brad (B-Dawg) Walk.

Acknowledgments

Special thanks and *muchos besos* to most amazing DNA inventions ever created:

My family: Dr. Juan Flores, Jackie and Steve Engels, John, Christy, Mingo, Felix, Fred, Dante, and Isa Flores; the one and only Nicholas Roman Lewis—AKA Literary Wonder; Ms. Stacey Barney for believing in *GG*; my talented writing partner-in-crime, Rodney Stringfellow; my gifted cousin and fellow novelist, Annette Gonzalez-Morgan; Margie, Luna, and Camille Aguilar for sharing their talents and the spirit on the cover; and Joe Riley for your graphic greatness.

Felix Flores for your artistic endeavors.

Owen Hannay, David Coats, Ned Bryant, and the webwonders at Slingshot.

Bronwen O'Keefe who, unbeknownst to her, helped me on my writing path in the literary world; my "Choo Chi" Yvonne Wagner, world's most amazing stylist; my daily partner-in-crime, Elizabeth "EA" Hammond for her endless amount of encouraging spirit and love; Darrell Hammond for his support and kindness; and Miss Mia for letting us take over your bedroom!

Paula Chase Hyman for her words of wisdom; the talents of Selena James and Kristine Mills-Noble and all the other cool kids at Kensington; and, of course, to Mike Swenson, who is the coolest and most creative person on the planet and who jumped into this experiment with me. *Tu es mi vida.*

"No one was ever great without some portion of divine inspiration."
—MARCUS TULLIUS CICERO

Chapter

1

A mass murder was about to occur. So, I did what any red-blooded American Latina would do. *I went shopping.* To be more specific, I went shopping for a frog. Courtesy of Bart Marquez. I knew that if I didn't get that chemically preserved frog out in time the formaldehyde would soon turn those little fishes in that tank into toxic sushi.

I had witnessed this *muy grande* drama before at Atwood Jr. High in the eighth grade. That fateful day another pickled amphibian had landed in another tank and lived—okay, not *lived* but was stuck and hiding behind the pink artificial coral. By the time Mrs. Jones had discovered the new specimen in her tank, that school of fish was doomed and so was that eighth-grade biology class.

And then to make matters worse, when none of us said nada, Mrs. Jones had announced that since we were all "accomplices to mass murder," she would give everyone Fs for the six weeks.

By threatening us, I think she thought one of us would crack and finally fess up. I never heard silence so loud in a classroom before. It was terrible and even more terrible was trying to explain my grade to my parents, especially since science is not only my *mas favorito* subject but it's what I live for. It's my fashion accessory. It's *almost* my best friend.

History would *not* be repeated. At least not in this science class. After hearing the splash of water, which was particularly loud since I sit by the aquarium, I also heard Bart's stupid laugh. Instinctively, I knew exactly just what had happened and would have given him a few choice words but didn't since I was totally in a fight-or-flight response.

Just for the record, Bart is both a jock and a jerk. Fortunately for him, he's been blessed with really great shaggy brown hair and Hershey chocolate dark eyes. And as a bonus, he has broad shoulders, chiseled abs, and a basically overall hotness. But it's not nearly enough to compensate for his really big mouth and braces.

When he laughs, not only does he blind people with all that metal but he also makes sounds like a donkey on steroids. It's enough to make me want to shove pencils in my eyes—oh, and my ears. And then there's *my nose*. Did I forget to mention the sea of cologne he swims in daily?

His tragic story is that the teachers only passed him into his freshman year so he would stay eligible for varsity football at Gamma. *Whoopee.*

But back to the current drama. Bart was spinning his frog by its leg when he should have been dissecting it and discovering some glorious vital organ. And that's when frog body detached from frog leg (I know—ew) and flew into Dr. Hamrock's fish tank.

Determined to be a hero, I jumped up on a chair so pronto that I didn't stop to even think if I was flashing my fellow classmates with my new denim flared mini. I plunged my hand in the icy cold water and every time I tried to grab he would jump—okay, not really *jump*. I mean *he's dead*. The frog would kind of squirt away from me.

With each uncomfortable second that passed, my heart pounded louder and louder. But, unfortunately, not loud enough to cover up Bart's constant braying.

That's when my science partner, Jimbo Billimek, came to my rescue, helping me navigate through the murky tank. But since there were so many gaudy fish decorations and gadgets, it was all I could do to keep my hand from getting stuck. This tank was in need of a serious aquatic makeover.

By the time my hand turned blue, victory was finally mine and I tried not to squish too hard what was left of Mr. Frog. It was really important not to get frog innards under my nails, since I had just had a manicure a day ago.

Before I could climb down and do my celebration dance, someone yelled, "Dr. Hamrock!" Someone *always* yells when Dr. Hamrock comes, because we all know he's just waiting to catch us in some awkward situation so he can conduct some evil scientific experiment on us.

For the most part, Dr. Hamrock is tall, dark, and lanky but not in a cute way. Much to the contrary, he looks like a stretched-out Elmer Fudd. His glasses magnify his pupils so much that they resemble two big burnt-out fajita skillets. This effect only gets worse when he pierces you with his eyes as he scolds you. It's so intense you can almost smell your flesh burning, I swear.

And since Dr. Hamrock also teaches science to college kids, I'm pretty sure he considers teaching our class glorified babysitting, and he has very straightforward rules when it comes to his apparatus in his classroom. Touch them and you *die*.

So, now, with my arm fully submerged in his precious tank, I was obviously taking my turn in a sick little game of science class Russian roulette.

Just as the lunch bell rang, everybody else in the class scrambled and scattered as Dr. Hamrock walked in and noticed me right away.

Not because I'm five feet with superstraight shiny chocolate hair and kinda curvy but more because I was standing on a stool in my Frankenstein platform shoes smiling nervously like the last two contestants waiting for their name to be called on *America's Next Top Model*.

Unfortunately, all my visions of greatness evaporated rather quickly when he barked "Luz Santos!" and I knew that *my* dissection was about to commence.

And for the second time in one day, Mr. Dead Frog startled the school of fish.

After class and after again fishing out the frog, this time managing to get my ponytail wet with water, I was so over science and I was so over the lecture that was about to begin.

Only one brave soul came to my rescue—sorta. Swinging the door open only for a nanosecond, my lab partner, Jimbo, coughed, "She didn't do it." Then he disappeared into the sea of Gamma High. I decided to be my own superhero and stay for the entire duration until I was fully rescued.

"I didn't do it," I said, making sure I had a clear pathway to the door.

"Then who did do 'it'?" asked Dr. Hamrock, reminding me that "it" was a really terrible thing.

"I don't know."

"Miss Santos, what is the first lesson of science?"

"To be *observant . . . sir.*" I added in the "sir" because I was hoping to cut the convo short so I could leave. I had *observed* that my stomach was growling.

"Well, then, I know you can help me find out who was responsible for this," said Dr. Hamrock with a laser-beam stare.

I just nodded and observed my flesh starting to blister from his heat.

"And while you're researching that problem, I'd like you to propose a project for this year's science competition."

I knew this was more than a suggestion. As he walked to his desk, I began my appeal. "But I'm only a freshman. How can I compete with the upperclassmen?"

"Miss Santos, you came to Gamma to develop and expand your skills in scientific inquiry and reasoning, and it's my job to make sure you apply them. I like to see participation from every grade level. You had the highest math and science scores coming into the cluster, and I'm certain you'll maintain those standards as representative of your class."

I was right. This was more than a suggestion. It was a death threat.

Dr. Hamrock continued, "I have no doubt you'll sail through the school competition and make it to Regionals."

A light bulb exploded in my head. "*Regionals?* Isn't that during Homecoming weekend?"

"Yes, I believe so. Do you have a problem with that?" He raised his eyebrows at me when he finally looked up.

I shook my head and didn't say a word because I thought I was going to vomit. He finally scratched out a hall pass and handed it to me. Taking it, I stumbled out of the classroom. *Science competition, Regionals, missing Homecoming?* With all these crazy events swirling in my brain, I ran to lunch with my clammy hand and my fishy smelling ponytail.

When I entered the toasty cafeteria with only twenty minutes instead of thirty, I felt like I could breathe again even if it was the unappetizing smells of cafeteria food. I soon found my way to my table and sat down next to my best friend, Bridge (short for Bridget), who wrinkled her nose in disgust.

"I stink. I know."

"I didn't say that," Bridge said.

"No, but your nose did." Bridge was taken by surprise, as if I had told her that her pink Izod and her matching Pumas were off colors.

"Did you know I was held against my will by Dr. Hamrock?"

Bridge pulled back her long wavy hair with a clip on top of her head as she pushed her Polo glasses on her cheek.

"Yeah, I know. Jimbo told me. That's why I bought you lunch." Bridge pulled out a plate from the empty seat next to her and pushed my free lunch closer to me.

I carefully examined the specimen of greasy orange ooze on a bed of wilted lettuce.

"It's taco salad day," Bridge sang, unfolding her napkin in her lap and inspecting the cleanliness of the school's utensils.

"Thanks, B."

I don't know what's more amazing about high school—the daily lunchroom experiments or the fact that news travels faster than the speed of light. "What else did you hear?" I asked, picking at my hot lettuce.

"Well, I also just overheard Bart telling Venus that he gave you something *special* and how much you *loved* it."

"I hate him."

"And then he started caressing Venus's face with his leftover frog leg," Bridge said.

"Okay, now I love him."

"Wait, it gets better. Then she hit him hard in the stomach with her *Gucci* clutch."

"Red or silver?" I said.

"Silver," Bridge replied.

"I love the silver. It's so hi-tech looking. Then what?"

"Then he apologized and tried to flirt with her. Isn't that gross?" Bridge asked, looking for approval.

"Ew, grosser than this salad."

Ew isn't for Bart. Ew is for Venus Hunter—who, like Bart, is blessed in the looks department but can't be trusted. (More about that later.)

"Okay, whatever. But did you hear about how the rest of the frog ended up in Dr. Hamrock's aquarium and I tried to get it out?" I smelled that memory on my hand as I unsuccessfully lifted a bite of salad from my plate.

"Yeah, only fifteen people from your class told me." Bridge began to dip her carrot stick carefully in her little tub of hummus.

"Were they all laughing?"

Bridget laughed. "Yes, *all* of them."

"Well, here's something that I know you didn't hear from Gamma's gossip line. Hamrock is totally forcing me to enter this year's science competition so that I will be eligible in Regionals."

After Bridge's carrot fell out of her mouth (hummus and all), I realized that that particular factoid hadn't quite reached her yet.

"*Omigod!* Shut up! You're *kidding*!" Bridge leaned closer to me.

"No, I'm not."

"Then you're officially the luckiest freshman girl in the world! I'm so jealous! But not *really*. I mean, you know I totally support you, right?" Bridge said, then went back to polishing off her carrots.

Now, let me explain before it sounds like Bridge is a total mental case. Ever since my parents sent me away to Camp Copernicus, a science camp, I have been jazzed about science and Bridge, whom I met there.

I mean, I love to discover what makes things tick (people included), and I'm truly *obsessed* about inventing things, all kinds of things. For me, science is like supercrafting. And now with Bridge as my BFF and science partner for life, we've made it our sacred duty to change the face of science by giving it a makeover. So, we apply our scientific methods to improve our grades, our clothes, and basically our whole world at Gamma High. It's a way of life for us. We call it our "Gamma Glamma" calling.

So, it's totally understandable that Bridge would think I would jump for joy when asked to represent our school (as a freshman even) in the region wide science competition but (a) I don't like to be told I have to do something and (b), more importantly, it lands on the same weekend as our *first* big school dance—Homecoming. And being that this is our first year at Gamma, this, of course, is the opportunity of our lives, y'know, a chance of a lifetime. In other words, I don't want to be stuck with geeks that reek during Homecoming weekend.

"So, what are you going to do?" asked Bridge as she turned on her periwinkle lip-gloss flashlight (her personal invention she aptly named the "Glowkissa") to rummage through her bag. As Bridge looked up at me she noticed my attire of the day.

"My, my. Is that my polo shirt *repurposed*?" Bridge wrinkled her nose.

"I just amped it up. Besides, you didn't want it anymore. Remember what happened after our *nail enamel experiment*?"

"Hmmm. Oh . . . right, right. *I forgot*." Bridge looked around to make sure that no one was noticing us. No one was. *Bummer.*

Bridge had "forgotten" about our nail enamel experiment because we both almost passed out from the noxious fumes filling my room as we attempted to create the "ultimate hot pink nail polish." Her shirt had one itsy-bitsy stain on it and she was ready to give it to Goodwill.

So, I decided to embrace her goodwill for myself. I cut it up and added a bit of black fabric to it so it would match my black mini tutu skirt and my black-and-pink steel-toed Mary Jane platform shoes. These are the ones I carved out and installed mini tape recorders in. Pretty much my everyday school uniform shoes, because I don't have to worry so much about taking notes *and* I can keep track of promises and overheard gossip. I call them my "Chica Speakas."

Anyway, this particular outfit was my *Pretty in Pink* meets punk look. I loved it. However, Bridge had other opinions.

"Now, do you have any idea what you are going to do?" Bridge asked, resuming to my dilemma.

"You mean about the science competition?"

"No, I mean your lunch," Bridge said, rolling her eyes. "What's going to be the focus of your project?"

I swallowed a large lump of ground beef. "The focus of the science experiment is to see how Miss Luz Santos can get out of this without being burned alive or failing the science cluster." I stabbed my plate for more pieces of greasy lettuce as Bridge's eyes widened.

"*What?*"

"Bridge, don't you get it? If I win, I have to go to Regionals, which under normal circumstances would be my dream. But because it lands on Homecoming weekend, it has easily evolved into my nightmare."

"You *can't* miss Homecoming. This is our first one," Bridge said, finally realizing my dilemma. "Does the competition count as a grade or extra credit?"

"Hamrock didn't say, but if I bomb the competition, I'm sure it will affect my grade somehow."

"*Omigod*, Luz. That sounds more like a science experiment for a painful dissection of your social life," Bridge said, shaking her head at the table. She looked more worried than I was.

"Well maybe I can get Dr. Hamrock to dissect me after Homecoming," I said, trying to find the courage to smile.

"With your *corsage* on?" Bridge smirked back.

"*Exactly.*"

After examining my predicament, I was no longer hungry and shoved my plate away from me. Just in time for dessert came our friend Adam, who was ready to serve a heaping pile of Gamma's daily dirt. Oh, my. What can I say about Adam Bellows? What can I *not* say about Adam Bellows? Bridge and I both love Adam, because if he were a girl he would so be a third sister. Even if he does appreciate our scientific efforts in a Trekkie/nanu-nanu way (which is barely tolerable).

But the most fascinating thing about Adam is that he knows

everything that is going on in this *escuela*, from when we are having a pop quiz to who is about to get dumped as well as the really vital info like how to score the freshest Tater Tots at lunch. He has really been the best ambassador to our freshman year since Bridge and I started here at Gamma.

The only bad thing about Adam, if I had to mention it (and I will), is that he is in love. Uh, strike that; he's *obsessed*—with Bridge. He is a superprep like she is and sometimes I think he even tries to outprep her. I mean, por favor, how many times can you have the same logo dripping off you? Polo, Lacoste, Puma, Adidas . . . *y mas y mas*.

And not only that, but occasionally (okay, lots of times) Adam will know *exactly* what outfit Bridge is going to wear for the day. And then he makes sure to be color coordinated with her so that everyone at school will think they're a couple. Bridge and I both agree it's a bit stalkerazzi, but deep down, and I mean deep down like to the earth's simmering core, she thinks it's kinda cool.

In total Adam fashion, Adam leaned in between Bridge and me.

"Wanna know what's hot?" he whispered.

"Hotter than the grease on my taco salad?" I said.

Adam rolled his eyes, stood straight up, and glanced around the cafeteria very dramatically to make sure he *was* being watched as he grabbed a nearby chair and created a wedgie in between Bridge and me. As all six-four of him sat down, he brushed his shaggy blond hair from his eyes and peeked over his glasses, glancing first at Bridge and then at me.

"It's *big*. . . ." Adam said, taking a dramatic pause.

"Is this about the frog?" Bridge had no interest in old news.

"No."

"Is this about Luz having to enter the science competition?" Bridge continued, zipping up the last of her lonely carrots in a plastic bag.

"No," Adam said while making a scrunchy "as if" face.

Bridge stopped altogether, in desperation. "Is this about the dance?"

"Yes, *finally*. *Thank you*, Miss Joiner. This year's dance is going to be ostentatious, to say the least."

"What do you mean 'ostentatious'?" I asked, not sure what he meant with his word of the day.

"Flashy, splashy, and over the top, girls, because it's going to be *televised*!"

"No," I said.

"*Yes!*" Adam said with his Hollywood-ready smile.

"Shut up," I said with a mouth full of orange taco salad.

Bridge made a face at me. She was hooked. "Luz, *you* shut up. Go on, tell us, Adam."

"Okay, here's the deal. There's going to be a film crew from *High School Rules* that's going to shoot *only* the finalists for the Homecoming Court. And then, at the dance when the winners are announced to the plebeians, they are going to keep filming the new Homecoming regime to see how this type of status affects their lives," Adam said, now sounding like a news reporter.

"So, it's like a total science experiment," I said, wiping the orange grease off my mouth.

"Yeah, *weird* science." He motioned that I had missed a spot.

I had to agree with Adam that it was kinda weird—not the grease—but the experiment. And I also hoped one day to have my own TV show. Kinda like *Oprah*. You know, live your best life and all, but accessorizing it with science and glamma!

"Do you think we should do it?" Bridge asked, hesitantly nibbling at her thumbnail.

"Do what? Get nominated? *Absolutely*. If we become nominated, then people will get to know us. And if we get on TV, then this could change our lives forever. This is exactly what we need."

Bridge searched the table for something to calm her fear of our potential celebrity.

I leaned in front of Adam to get my point across. "Bridge, this is great!"

"Yeah. But what happens if we *lose*?"

"Nobody would notice." I leaned back.

"Ow," Adam said.

I know it sounded harsh, but it had to be said. You didn't have to be a rocket scientist to realize where Bridge and I linked into the school popularity chain. I turned away from Bridge as she was still gasping for air from my last comment.

"How do you get nominated?"

"Somebody just has to put your name down. Over there." Adam pointed across the lunchroom to the Student Council table by the doors. Behind it a large poster proclaimed "Homecoming Nominations."

"Okay, Bridge, I'll nominate you and you can nominate me."

"What about me?" Adam bellowed.

"Get Mason to nominate you," I said.

"I don't know if he can spell. He's very *rudimentary*." Adam turned his head toward the line that was starting to form at the Student Council table.

I had to agree. Mason's talent was in art, not spelling. And he had real talent, like God's gift, and that had brought him to Gamma High, which is the supermagnet school of Dallas.

It was here at Gamma that we have the best of science, best of drama, best of art, even the best of sports. Standing out here was a bit tricky to do, especially if you were a freshman. However, Mason Milam had that something—something that not everybody had. And that was utterly, outrageously fabuloso artistic talent.

First of all, let me say I am such a big fan of all of Mason's homemade T-shirts. I love them because they are crafty, but I also love them because they are really smart.

For helping Mason with his science homework, Mase (as we called him) created my all-time favorite T-shirt. It was a shirt that read "Scientific Eleganz" in way-cool Gothic lettering. Now, I really didn't question his spelling abilities because it was like, art, y'know?

And the pink test tubes that he painted around the collar really rocked, because it could have come out all stupid crafty like the crafty crap those folks at the craft store make with slick paint and glitter. But this was *muy differente*. And I loved it.

And when I stepped out into the foyer at Gamma High, people couldn't stop raving about it. It was so cool that I decided to give Mase my favorite pair of chunky black sci-fi superhero boots to have him paint more test tubes on those, too. I know it could have been a bit much and matchy-match, but when I wear that outfit, watch out world!

But as far as Mase and his world, he would prefer to live in solitude or, at most, in Adam's shadow. Mase was brought into Bridge's and my little inner circle—or I guess that would be a semicircle—by Adam.

Adam, who was funny and ambitious, was sometimes such *a mouth*! Plus, since he was in journalism, his vocabulary was, like, so vast that he could be totally cutting you down and you wouldn't even know it unless you had a dictionary handy. And when he was really in a mood, his sarcasm could emotionally scar you for days, like a pimple that hasn't quite festered yet you still keep picking and squeezing at it.

However, Mase didn't mind that aspect or hadn't verbalized it thus far. For the most part, Mase doesn't talk.

He's not mute or anything. He just prefers to let his green eyes hide in deep sockets under his long, dark brown bangs. However, when he's done something clever or if someone comments on his amazing work, Mase just kinda eeks a little smirk. It's very cute.

So, that's where Adam comes in and speaks on Mase's behalf or on their behalf. It's a partnership that's worked since junior high. And now, having both been accepted to Gamma, Adam for journalism and Mase for art, they just continue the same routine but in a new locale.

"So, if he can't spell it, then why don't you have him draw your big ole *cabeza*," I said as I leaned my head on Adam's shoulder.

"Yeahhh," Adam said as he flashed his "whatever" face.

And with that, our little threesome gathered our trays and rolled over to the Student Council table to nominate ourselves out of our social class and into the uber-social universe.

Chapter

2

"Whr RU?" I texted Bridge on my cell phone. My parental unit had given me this phone to use only in "emergencies." But when the emergencies of my daily life became too excessive (in their opinion), they read me my rights and decided it was time to come to some type of arrangement.

They told me that if I wanted to keep my phone I would have to find a way to make the extra money to pay for it. This was really a bummer at first, because I hate babysitting and I'm only fifteen and so my job ops are, like, limited.

But thank God for science! I made extra cash by tutoring, and for an extra nominal fee, I helped kids rock their gadgets with their wardrobe. I called it my Gamma Glamma "Geek Chic" calling.

"am hre. OPN SZ ME:)" Bridge hit me back. She was outside my bedroom door. I didn't hear her come up, because I was sitting on my bed hooked up to my iPod trying to find out if the song I was listening to was really worth the ninety-nine cents. Bridge came up from behind me and pulled one of my ear buds out. She was wearing her light blue Adidas tennis skirt with a matching shirt. In classic Joiner style, she had also matched her pale blue Havaianas with her eyeshadow. She flipped her low-hanging ponytail out of the way as she set down her backpack and duffel bag.

"Hey, what's up?" I said, detaching myself from my iPod.

"We're on the list!" Bridge twirled around with a crumpled paper in her hand. "Adam snatched me a copy of all the nominees."

"I *know*, Bridge. I was with you when we nominated *each other*. Remember?"

"Yeah, but did you know that they cut off nominations today because the Student Council didn't want to have to deal with too many people?"

"And . . ."

"Well, right now there are only fourteen girls and fourteen boys in our category."

Bridge said "category" because she didn't really like saying "freshmen." Secretly, she felt it was beneath her. I love her like a sister, but she does have a tendency to visit Snobville a lot. *Whatever.*

"So, I just wanted to let you know that our probability of becoming two of the five girl finalists and winning has just increased immensely. Isn't that exciting?" Bridge continued.

I had to admit that the logical probabilities were exciting, but I also had to admit that now we were going to have tons of work to do.

"So, are you ready to start some hard-core planning?" I asked.

"Planning what?" Bridge asked as she pulled out her books and Tupperware of study snacks.

"Everything. From what are we going to wear to how we can get the rest of our peers to vote for us? And how I'm going to get *out* of this science contest."

There was too much to think about. I jumped off my bed and sat on my beanbag to do some serious brainstorming.

"Yeah, I wonder if I can create a serum to accelerate the growth of my nails in time for the dance? Because you know the press-on nails look so low rent," Bridge said as she gazed at her short-nailed hands.

"I told you, I already have a formula for a shampoo to make hair grow faster, so nails shouldn't be that hard to figure out. Can you spend the night tonight?" I asked, ready to get to work on the formulas in my own personal laboratory—the one that also doubled as my bedroom.

"You want to start *tonight*?"

"*Exactamente!*"

"Okay . . . but what are we going to do about dates?"

Bridge's eyes drifted across my poster-covered wall of movie star hotties, waiting for them to magically reconfigure their DNA molecules and jump down.

"Dates? Oh, I forgot about that part. *Not*."

There was only one crush at Gamma High who secretly made me melt and sizzle away like sitting in a hot tub of hydrochloric acid, and that was Eric Swenson.

At school, everyone just called him Swen, and he was just so . . . *chemical*. That's the only way I can describe it. When I get like ten feet from him *mi corazón* starts racing from the large amounts of adrenaline pumping through my body. Then my eyes start rolling to the back of my head and I think I'm about to faint due to the lack of oxygen to my brain, because he takes my breath away. Literally. Fortunately, with the counterweight of my Chica Speakas, I don't tip over from my upright position.

"Oh, what? Are you waiting for Swen to buy you a corsage?" Bridge asked.

"It could happen," I said, believing in my own fantasies.

"Yeah, but why would you *want* it to?"

"*Bridge!*"

"Just kidding! I mean, I know he's your dream luva and all, but c'mon, you guys are like polar opposites. He doesn't even look like he's into science or anything."

"That's probably because he doesn't have time since he's an amazing writer who works for the paper *and* annual staff." I felt my face heat up.

"Okay, Defensive. What about his clothes?" Bridge quizzed.

"Well, I guess I could *tamper* with that a bit," I said, looking at the posters of hotties who were all lacking wardrobe. I mean, they weren't *naked*, they were wearing swim trunks!

Basically speaking, Swen dressed, like, really subdued—I mean, *really*. He wore a pair of old Levis, a button-down white shirt untucked with the sleeves rolled up, and then set if off with an old skool pair of white Adidas. And that was it.

He wore white. I wore black. He was Mr. Clean Jeans and I thought distressed was best. I love metal and gadgets and his daily uniform was really vanilla compared to mine and what all the other candy sprinkles of Gamma High wear.

First, there were the superjocks, who wear kicks in every color imaginable and probably costing more than some folks' cars. I'm talking big bank.

Next came the drama freaks (aka the Dramaticas), and if you don't wear the mandatory "back in black" uniform then you were guaranteed to be stuck as an extra on the next production of *The Crucible*.

And finally, there were the techie science folk, which was my tribe. Most of them were a bit Bill Gatesish and could totally stand makeovers, except (a) they don't think they need one and (b) they wouldn't see the point of it.

Despite their poor fashion sense I still love them, because they're my peeps and they're brilliant. To me, they totally feel like bad *familia*. You know you couldn't really stand them on a day-to-day basis, but for, like, holidays—and, in my case, midterms—they're okay.

Bridge butted back in. "And what about that he's a sophomore and doesn't even know your DNA exists?"

"Simmer down, Factoid. Just for the record, we've smiled a few times at each other."

"Yeah? Exactly how many times?"

I started chipping the deep purple orchid polish off my nails. "Okay, maybe only twice. But the first smile lasted half a second and the second one lasted a second *and a half*. I know this because I timed the second one. But anyway, he's the *only* one I want to take me to Homecoming."

Bridge just let me enjoy my fantasy a little longer as she continued to look at the potential suitors on my wall.

Maybe he *was* just a fantasy. And I'm not even sure we have anything in common. But when I'm near him, he's like a tall glass of *agua*. No, strike that. I *hate* water. He's a fudge brownie. Not that he's thick, dark, or nutty. To the contrary, he's slender, blonde, and smart. But really, he is *muy delicioso*.

He also has the most amazing blue-gray eyes. To be more specific, they're actually blue with a speck of yellow. And he's not really tall but he's not shrimpy either. He's just *so* right. And his arms are vascular and sinewy (I borrowed those words from Adam), and I find that so cool, because most guys who aren't into sports are usually pretty mushy.

He's not. I think he runs or something. And he has strong-looking *manos*. I love a man with strong hands (unlike Adam, who has softer hands than mine—ew).

When I just think about Swen I can feel all my DNA molecules unravel and wind back up. Like I said, it's totally chemical. I get it and I dig it.

However, Bridge and Adam do not. Bridge thinks he's too vanilla for my punk Gwen Stefani flava. And Adam is just totally jealous of Swen's talent and power.

"And who do *you* want to go to the dance with?" I asked, already knowing the answer.

"Brad Walker."

"Well, he's hardly the carbon copy of you, Miss Joiner."

Brad Walker, aka "B-Dawg," like Swen, was also a unique specimen. As a sophomore, he was known as being an extremely outrageous student who not only was the captain of the wrestling team but also played the cello—and he played it extremely well. He was definitely everything that Miss Bridget Joiner was not—which was white and stocky with blue eyes.

Again, Bridge and I decided this was simply chemical. There was no other rational explanation. It all went back to this science experiment that had a hundred women sniff a T-shirt that various men had been wearing. Time after time, the scent that each woman preferred was one that was directly opposite of her DNA chemistry. Scientists say that this little gift is engineered in our systems so that we can produce the healthiest offspring and not have any inklings to date our siblings. Ew. I know, but thank goodness for smart DNA.

So, the fact that a Latina like myself who digs science could totally crush on a blonde, blue-eyed, Nordic-god writer makes as much sense as my BFF, bite-size Beyonce, uber-preppy, Petri-dish scientific sidekick princessa falling head over heels for a wild, wrestling cellist. It was chemically reactive romance.

Now, all Bridge and I had to figure out was how to get these cute little chains of reaction to ask us out, especially when they hadn't discovered our existence.

"Mmmmmmm." My nose hollered at me after smelling something delicious. Bridge had popped open her Tupperware.

"What did you bake for me today, Igor?" I said, ready to devour anything that Bridge brought over.

She may be a li'l science whiz in school, but at home, my girl can throw down a mean and amazingly lean (read: low-fat, low-sugar) biscuit, biscotti, or even cupcake. She's a micro Martha, I swear.

Well, today her latest cupcake creations not only were fat free and contained no sugar or dairy, but were megacute with little smiley faces. As we ate and did our homework, I couldn't get over how adorable and tasty these little morsels were.

"They are cute, aren't they?" said Bridge as she bit off the eyes of one.

"Yes, I totally am in love with them and want to marry them," I said in midbite, spewing crumbs.

"Have you thought about what you are going to tell Dr. Hamrock?" Bridge asked, with her mouth full of not-so-natural blue frosting.

As the nutritionally correct complex carbs rushed to my *cabeza*, I could feel the electrons in my brain just bouncing around. Then it came to me—the perfect idea for a science experiment, or rather, the perfect idea to ruin it.

"I've got it. I'm going to propose an idea so hideous that Dr. Hamrock will have no choice but to annihilate it."

"Yeah, but you know he's going to ask you to come up with something else," said Bridge.

"Yeah, I know. But if I stall enough before I present him with some crazy idea and then he kills it, then I won't have time to come up with another hypothesis and test it out, *especially with my freshman load of homework*. You know?" I smiled at my own brilliance.

"Well, what happens if you miscalculate Dr. Hamrock's reaction or he's desperate and he makes you do it *anyway?*"

"Good question."

"I know, that's why I asked." Bridge smiled, now enjoying her own brilliance.

"Even if I had to do it, then surely it wouldn't pass Gamma High's own science competition, which I'd have to enter and win before moving on to Regionals," I said, trying to be practical.

"Okay, so what kind of invention are you thinking about?"

"It's more of a *re*invention than invention," I said, jumping up from my beanbag as if I'd discovered some wild scientific breakthrough like electricity.

"Do what?" Bridge asked as she systematically pulled out her highlighters and pens in order to get down to the business of the project.

"You know how you transformed those cupcakes and made them better, cuter, and healthier? I'm gonna do the same thing for Dr. Hamrock."

"Are you going to cook for him or poison him?"

"I'm going to present an experiment where I take something—or better yet, someone—and make them *extraordinary*," I said, seeing the word *extraordinary* in flashing Hollywood lights.

"Now you're sounding a bit freakish." Bridge made a scrunchy face like something stunk in my room.

"That's great!" I felt the thrill of my own genius. "If *you* hate it, then surely Dr. Hamrock will too."

"*Yeah*, he will." Bridge rolled her eyes.

"My plan," I informed Bridge, "is to take three subjects, uh, students, and transform them by simply adjusting their appearance, their voice, even their scent."

"That sounds kinda infantile," Bridge remarked, as if it were one of those hideous science ideas like Styrofoam balls attached to a papier-mâché sun.

I sank back in my beanbag. I had to agree with her at first. But when she said that, my competitive streak kicked in and then I kinda wanted to do the experiment and make it successful.

But reality set in again to remind me that I needed to have some kind of theory that would be demonstrated and grounded in science. It was very important that when I talked with Dr. Hamrock my experiment didn't sound like I'd just farted it out.

"How about this?" I said confidently as I stood back up from my beanbag chair. "Okay, take, let's say, three students, and basically we're performing makeovers."

Bridge nodded. She was with me so far.

"Anthropologically, we would term this an 'alteration in their self-presentation,' and the resulting social dynamic would be to elevate their position in their given social group. That way I'll prove that the social order (in this case the high school food chain) is established on the basis of *perception* and can be manipulated easily through *superficial changes*." With that mouthful, I felt proud of myself again (or at least less like a loser).

"But what's the point of the experiment?"

"My point, which matches the one on the top of your pointy head, is this: if we can promote an understanding of how to quickly change the factors that determine acceptance by our peers, we can help the less fortunate members of our student body get through high school with less trauma." I hoped she would now begin to understand my brilliance.

Bridge rubbed her eyes and yawned. "Trying to use science to trick people to like unpopular people sounds like herding sheep to slaughter."

"It's not. It's science with a *conscience*."

"Well, I just *love* science with a conscience," Bridge said, opening up her history book, ready to move on.

"Good, then you'll let me put you down as one of my subjects." I patted her on the head.

"What? Do you think I'm that much of a loser?" Bridge jumped up from my bed and walked to the mirror to gaze at her reflection. I followed her.

"No, Bridge, just listen. I just want Dr. Hamrock to think that I have given this project a great deal of thought and that I have people already involved in it. Then, when he wants me to change my project, it will be too late and, voila, I can *finally* go to the dance and double-date with you *and* B-Dawg."

As I waited for Bridge to finally grasp my scientific grand scheme, she sucked in her stomach and patted her imaginary tummy as she continued to stare into the mirror. Since it was taking her a while for her to chew on this idea, I decided to hand her another one of her smiling cupcakes.

"Bridge, it's just for pretend. It's a stupid science experiment. You said it yourself," I said, trying to calm her down as I sat back down on my purple shaggy rug.

"Okay, but who else are you going to say is in the experiment?" She fixed a level gaze on me as she sat down. Now I had to put my thinking cap on.

"Well, you and . . . well, probably Mase," I said, feeling my neck muscles clinch.

Mase just came to the top of my head because he wouldn't turn me down. He might make an angry painting or drawing but he wouldn't physically say no.

"You should really make it more believable, Luz, and find some-one who really, really needs a transformation," Bridge insisted as she licked the frosting off her next victim.

That was Bridge's way of saying I needed to find a big fat loser. *Aye caramba!* Did I just say that? I mean somebody who has a lot of *challenges*.

Okay, honestly, I *needed* a big fat loser. And I needed to try to find someone like a freshman, because no upperclassman would go through with this ridiculous experiment even if it was for pretend.

I decided I should find a girl, because we *chicas* love makeovers of any kind. And unless you live under a rock, it's not hard to find a magazine that has a section on some makeover. Bedroom makeovers. Hair makeovers. Boyfriend makeovers.

So, this would just be one more makeover but one that's done for a school project, that's all. It would be easy. Bridge and I started to go through a short list of names of possible candidates. I stared at the ceiling as Bridge searched the floor for answers.

"How about Nuria Chopra?" Bridge offered up.

"Naw. She's an exchange student and I think things would get lost in translation."

Bridge paused for a brief moment to check to see if there was a hair or something on her cupcake. "How about Traci?"

"Armstrong? Traci would totally beat me up just for talking to her," I confirmed.

Traci Armstrong was cute but a totally standoffish blonde who didn't hang within the confines of any one clique. She was also an Angelina Jolie in training, and already had her black belt in stuff I couldn't pronounce. Girls. Girls. Girls.

As I gazed around my room (which totally needed its own make-over, but that wouldn't happen this year with all my allowance and tutoring income already going toward my cell bill).

Then Bridge's squinting eyes met mine as if we were sending telepathic messages to each other. We both screamed in unison, "*Jabba!*"

Jabba's real name was Susan Seamus (pronounced "shame us"; I know, *what a shame*, right?). Susan had made the move from Jr. High to Gamma High based on her well-honed talent with the French horn. But regardless of this thankless talent, Susan was considered a fashion nightmare and total high school prey. Her hair was stringy, always a bit greasy and, unfortunately, it wasn't like greasy cool in a TIGI Bed Head fashion model kind of way.

On good days, Susan's complexion was ruddy. On bad days, her acne was so bad that it was her only companion at lunch. *Pobre gordita*. To make matters worse, she was a bit on the heavy side (thus the name Jabba, aka Jabba the Hutt, from the retro *Star Wars* movies) and had outdated everything—clothes, glasses, and bags.

There were rumors that Susan came from a really rich family, but given her outer appearance, it didn't make any sense that she came from blue blood. And when she spoke, she kind of had an irritated tone, like she had a sticker in her foot or something.

The only positive thing I could say about Jabba (and I hate even saying that name, but after being around her for years, it just sticks like a bad piece of food in your teeth) was that she draws these really fantastic imaginary characters on her lunch sacks. It wasn't a lot but it was still pretty cool.

So, as my head swirled with the essence that defined Jabba/Susan, Bridge broke the silence.

"*Omigod*, she's on the list."

"What list?" And then it sunk in to which list she was referring. "How in a million years . . . ?"

"Hey, you don't think Dr. Hamrock will make you actually *do* this experiment?"

"Por favor, Bridge, don't be mental about this. He'd never go through with something that crazy. What do you want to start on first? Your nail growth serum or my hair harnesser shampoo?" I was getting a strange, uneasy feeling about Dr. Hamrock and this scientific makeover so I had to change the subject.

"And if you want, I can finally get started on your camera purse tonight."

For fun, I had promised Bridge that I would make her an itsy-bitsy purse that would house either a Polaroid sticker camera or her digital camera so that we could record the memories of our lives or cute crushes.

But I still felt a crushing feeling of "what if." What if Dr. Hamrock *did* like my pretend experiment and made me do it for real? Surely that couldn't be possible. *Could it?*

Chapter

3

Mase was in bad shape. I mean, generally speaking, Mase is the Tony Hawk of Gamma High. Bruises and scabs are pretty much his calling card, along with his beat-up brown backpack.

But today at his locker, it was a completely different story. A *horror* story. He was missing some teeth and some hair, and it looked liked someone had pulled out that hair. He also had a cut with a brown scab near his eye.

It was a horrific scene and I wanted to look away except I was fixated on and fascinated by the group of Care Bears who were huddled in the corner crying. Okay, so what I really mean is that this was Mase's latest self-portrait, the artistic expression of his current state of mind, including a posse of depressed Care Bears (with who knows what intended symbolism).

It was Mase's way of telling us that he was livid, felt betrayed, or worse—*both*.

"Wow. That's wild and messed up," I said, holding up his picture and inspecting it from all angles.

Mase just smirked.

"You're not mad at *me*, are you?"

Mase shook his head. Just then Bridge walked up to us and I handed her Mase's latest creation.

"Is it Bridge?" I asked, still curious.

"Is what me?" Bridge sounded confused until she had a moment to soak in Mase's pictorial rendition of his mental and emotional state.

"Oh, no!" Bridge said after a closer viewing. "I'm definitely not *that* evil."

Ahhh. Then it came to me. "Is it Adam?" I asked.

Mase confirmed by wincing, then reached into his backpack and began pulling out all kinds of show-and-tell items: skateboard wheels, a wrench, a leftover sandwich, tons of really short pencils. Finally, when he got to the bottom of the bag, he pulled out a newly crumpled piece of paper.

It was the list of the Homecoming nominations, and on the freshman boy list at the bottom was Mason Milam's name except it was misspelled with two *l*'s.

"Isn't this fabulous? All four of us! I'm so excited! I hope we all make finalists, and when we do, we can have a congrats party at my house and wear all white, you know, like they do in the Hamptons? And then I could invite Brad Walker. Maybe he would perform a song for me on his cello," dreamed Bridge.

"You nominated Adam, didn't you?" I said.

Mase nodded and took a deep breath.

"Did you want to be nominated?" I asked, knowing this was a dumb question. For a dude that has skateboarded over fiery BBQ pits and could pull off a ten-inch scab without flinching, Mase shot me a terrified look.

"So, you think Adam did this?"

Mase just shrugged, and as if on cue the bell rang and we all scattered. As I ran to my science class trying to figure out just what had taken place in the hall, I ran smack into . . . Swen. *Hard.* I just wanted to die.

"Hey, are you okay?" Swen asked, holding my arms to help me not drop any of my books or vital organs.

Omigod. I don't know what I was feeling or experiencing first. Was it embarrassment, pain, or *love*?

Diga! Diga! Say something! Anything! my brain said.

"Yeah, I'm good," my voice eked out painfully like I was doing a Jabba impersonation.

My brain started racing. What was he doing here? And then there was Venus. What was she doing there standing by my crushable?

"Hey, watch it, Santos. Don't damage my potential Homecoming merch," Venus said as she made her rapid exit down the hall in a too-tight pair of Seven Jeans.

Swen just rolled his eyes and smiled and went to the back of the science classroom. Was she serious? Was that rich witch indeed taking my chemical reaction Romeo to Homecoming?

Normally, I react with tingling all the way to my DNA when I'm in that close contact with Swen, but this time my genetic material was in an immune response to a virus named *Venus Hunter*. It had already been a rough morning with Mase being upset, and now with this nightmare invasion of my dreamworld, I was about to flip out.

Por favor, calm yourself, chica, my brain commanded.

What I needed to do was sit down—and I did, to the tune of Dr. Hamrock's "Pop quiz." I wanted to cry. Is this the kind of pressure I would be feeling on a daily basis being in high school?

If it was, then this sucked. And this pop quiz on pressure differentials and the properties of a vacuum, sucked. Just then, an angel spoke. Okay, it wasn't an angel; it was Jabba and she asked if we could use our notes. It sounded like a ridiculous question to me, but I was still curious enough to want to hear the answer.

I couldn't believe it. *It was a miracle!* Dr. Hamrock said *yes*, but only because this was our first semester with him. *Yippee!* I thought as I pulled out my earbuds and plugged them into my Chica Speakas to listen to Dr. Hamrock's last lecture.

Fortunately, I was so caught up with Bridge and her adorable snacks the other day that I forgot to change the tapes. *Miracle number two*. Maybe my luck was changing.

It was a very long and tedious quiz, and when it was over, I wanted to take a nap but I couldn't relax remembering that Swen was in the back of the room.

What was he still doing here? As I turned in my quiz, I was anxious to bolt out the door. But just then my sixth sense reminded me that Dr. Hamrock wanted to talk about my proposed project.

The bell rang and all my peers scattered like cockroaches. I wanted to be one of those little cockroaches. But I knew I couldn't avoid Dr. Hamrock's impending bug bomb.

"Miss Santos," Dr. Hamrock said with the undertones of *"You can't escape from me, my little pretty."*

"Yes?" I said, acting like I was in quite a hurry.

"Have you by any chance found out who was responsible for killing my fish?"

Darn that dead frog. By trying to do the right thing, I got caught and was forced to enter the science competition and was about to lose my *prince*. Was there no justice? Could it be any worse?

Oh, yeah, it could and it was. That's when I looked at Dr. Hamrock's fish tank. It was like a really bad car crash. You know when you really don't want to look because you think you shouldn't, yet some uncanny force makes you look anyhow to see just how much gruesome you can take in a moment's notice? It was pretty gruesome.

The tank was there but it was totally empty with a bit of a residue of where the water used to be. My stomach felt sour. Poor fishes. *Lo siento*. I'm sorry. I tried.

"Uh . . . no. I haven't found out anything—*yet*."

I added the "yet" to give him some hope. But I couldn't dare tell him it was Bart. My high school years would be endured in endless torture if I busted Bart, because he was the type to never let me live it down.

"Alright then, on to other things," Dr. Hamrock said.

I couldn't tell if he really meant it or if he was really sad and did one of those guy things to avoid any type of emotions. Or maybe, he just really wanted to win Regionals. I don't know. It was too early in the day and in the game for me to figure out his m.o.

"How are you coming on your winning project idea for the competition?"

I shifted uncomfortably. Now, here was my big chance. This is when I wished I had taken drama so I could lie effortlessly and pitch him my doozy of a project. And then when he rejected me fiercely, with a flip of an emotional switch I could change from scientifically supercharged to utterly devastated. And pull my hair and scream, *"Aye Dios!"* just like they do in the Mexican soaps my grandma watches. And then as a topper, I could start doing that totally annoying girl thing and start bawling my eyes out.

But I didn't get chosen to come to Gamma High for my drama skills. So, instead, I directed myself very quickly to just act from a place of certainty.

I was certain I wanted out of this project. I was certain I wanted to go to Homecoming and I was certain I wanted this whole discussion to end very quickly.

So, I explained Project Gamma Glamma to Dr. Hamrock. My hypothesis was that if I could alter a few critical elements of a student's self-presentation—in other words, clothes, voice, mannerisms, even their smell—then through that I could alter how they would be received by particular social groups.

I told him I had three participants for the project even though I hadn't asked Mase and Jabba directly. Okay, I hadn't asked them at all. But I figured I would see them at lunch and I also figured if the project was dead it wouldn't be necessary to ask them. Right?

Now that I had vomited out my proposal as fast as I could, I froze and waited. And waited. And waited. Dr. Hamrock didn't seem to show any emotion, but then he never really *ever* shows emotion, so what am I saying?

Seconds seemed like hours and I knew I already was going to need Dr. Hamrock to write me a hall pass since I was super late for lunch.

"That's *unusual*." Dr. Hamrock lingered on the word *unusual*. "What would be the benchmarks to determine the success of this experiment?"

This new loop I was now being thrown for only made the acid in my stomach churn faster. "Umm . . . I can observe who they start to hang out with, where they sit in the cafeteria, if they get dates to the Homecoming dance. Maybe I can even get them selected to be finalists for Homecoming Court." *Ooops*. I realized too late that I might be overpromising.

"What do you think about this proposal, *Eric*?" Dr. Hamrock tossed to the back of the room.

Eric? You gotta be kidding me. *Mi Dios!* Eric was still in the back of the room, and even after surviving the embarrassment of our collision, I would now have to endure *him* witnessing the grand rejection of my proposal. Dang, I didn't have a chance to respond to *anything* today—Mase, Venus, pop quiz, being "unusual."

"I like it," Eric said.

I wanted to scream. My nervousness started showing when I kept accidentally hitting my heels on the floor and the tapes in my shoes kept rewinding and fast-forwarding.

I would have bent down to fix the tapes except I had been in a rush to modify my miniskirt and I'd kept trimming and trimming this morning and it pretty much was a mucho micro-mini right now.

It was probably breaking school policy but I'm pretty short, so it didn't look that skanky. Nonetheless, the last thing I needed to do was flash my science teacher and my crushable. Not that it would be that big of a deal. I mean, I was already feeling pretty exposed at the time.

"I like it . . . because it combines a social theory and applies it in a way that a student audience can appreciate," Swen said.

I cocked my head like my dog Señor Shortie does when he hears a familiar Fritos cellophane bag sound. I tried to nod in agreement. But I'm sure I looked like a freakin' groupie.

Swen closed his laptop. "This is a great story to follow to help boost the science cluster."

"And bring up our numbers," added Dr. Hamrock.

"Yeah, it couldn't hurt to even things out against the drama population," laughed Swen.

That I could understand and I had to agree. Gamma High was supposed to be a supermagnet to represent all the types of folks, but the sea of Dramaticas was pretty deep.

At the first of the school year, people sometimes used to think I was one of the drama folks because of my love of black clothes. But with my repurposed Polos, Izods, and my geekspeak it's pretty clear which tribe I come from. But I have to tell you, it's really fun to cause a bit of confusion between cliques here from time to time. Who knows, maybe I am a bit of a Drama Mama myself.

"Luz, why don't you come up with a more detailed plan on how you expect to demonstrate your hypothesis. Once you've done more research, I'll help you organize the data for our competition. And then we can tweak it even more for Regionals."

Wake up, Luz! "That's if I *win* Gamma's competition first," I reminded him.

"Oh, you'll win," Dr. Hamrock said, almost sounding ominous, as he looked for something in his desk drawer. "And, Eric, thanks for helping cover this experiment."

I didn't know what to do during all this dialogue, so I just looked at my backpack and thought about when and how I could modify it with a video camera. Dr. Hamrock must have noticed—I mean *observed*—my anxiousness.

"Oh, don't you two know each other?" Dr. Hamrock asked with a bit of surprise.

"Not really," I said.

Eric walked right up to me. He was less than a foot away from me. "Eric Swenson. But you can call me Swen," he said as he extended his hand out to me (love those hands).

I reached out my hand. "I'm Luz Santos," I said, then tried to recall if I'd said my own name right.

Everything was happening so fast that I didn't have time to put on my cute voice or to talk to him with *mis ojos*, my eyes. (You know, like all that advice that sounds really good when you're reading *Cosmo*, or in my case, *Cosmo Girl*, because it's Saturday night and your overprotective Latino parents forbid you to date until you're sixteen.)

"Eric, I'm just going to call you Swen, too," interrupted Dr. Hamrock, trying to be cool. *Gross.*

"Now, why don't you guys exchange numbers or e-mails or whatever it is you do, so Swen can keep a record of your progress, Luz. We need all the press we can get out of this," said Dr. Hamrock, totally busting my love groove.

"No problem," said Swen.

For a second I observed that Dr. Hamrock sounded almost human but he also sounded nervous like he could lose his job or something. It was weird but I didn't dwell on it, because I wanted to hug him and thank him for making all my dreams and nightmares come true at the same time.

And then my dreams and nightmares slapped this chica into this reality.

"Luz, let me write you a pass," Dr. Hamrock said, sounding like himself again and digging around trying to find the pass forms.

"And let me get your number," said my dream lover.

Of course, reaching down into my backpack for pen and paper set off all types of things, like my iPod, my lipstick radio, and my home-made talking key chain, which said on cue, "Aye Papi!"

I was so tragic and then the only piece of paper I could find was the crumpled paper that Mase had given me with all our names on it as freshman nominees for the Homecoming Court. I ripped a piece off of that and scrawled my digits and gave it to Swen. I'm sure he thought it was gross that I was handing him a now warm and wet (read sweaty palms) piece of trash with my number on it. He proba-bly thought I was Señorita Basura. That's brown trash, y'all. Whatever.

My stomach acid kept churning and now I was on the verge of throwing up. It was coming. And I knew I had to outrun it. When I turned around to grab my pass from Dr. Hamrock, I knocked a book out of Swen's hand called *Elements of Style*.

I quickly picked it up from the floor and gave him a weak smile. He said he liked my shoes and made some comment that I should make him some.

I couldn't tell if he was being sincere or totally feeling sorry for me. I didn't have time to break it down. The bile volcano was send-ing seismic waves toward my mouth.

I ran and ran faster. I finally got to my destination, the girls' bath-room (upstairs and farthest from any classroom), and promptly bowed to the throne. Acid. Nothing like reflux.

But truly for me, it happens when I get nervous. And then right when I came out of my stall and decided to at least wash my face and bravely carry on, my nightmare returned in a sequel when I heard a familiar voice.

"Santos, that's so very Hollywood of you. Y'know, I was thinking about writing a report for health class about eating disorders and how it affects teens. Maybe you could help me?" Venus hissed sweetly.

"Eat it, Venus," I said.

I was so proud of myself. Courage under fire. *Miracle number three.* Right on!

Normally, I would have said something stupid, and then later in the privacy of my own bedroom/laboratory, I would have overanalyzed the episode. And then that's where the useless perfect words would have made themselves known to me.

Crawling back to lunch after missing twenty minutes of it, I tried to review the reality that would make up my near future.

First of all, I had to now go through with the experiment. Bridge wasn't going to believe this, much less like it.

Next, I had to also convince Mase to be my lab rat. Maybe I'd tell him that I would motorize his skateboard or create a video of his latest stunts that he could carry around on an iPod and show everyone.

Or maybe I could create a paint that could be eaten so that when he was done creating his masterpieces he could munch down. The possibilities were endless.

The next step of my once-fake-but-now-real science experiment was talking to Jabba. Would she trust me? Would she go through with it? I had no idea.

I mean Bridge and Mase were average to above average in the looks department. It wouldn't look like a giant step for studentkind if these two inched up the social ranks.

But for Jabba, it was a whole different story. If I could make *her* popular, she would make me *famous.* And I needed to be famosa, especially now that Swen was going to follow and cover my project.

This challenge I was about to face was going to be the mother of all challenges for me. How do I get my closest friends and schoolmates to trust me enough to change their looks? And *what* exactly was I going to change about them?

How could I make my science project look hot in the paper but not hot enough to win so that I wouldn't be at Regionals and I could still go to Homecoming?

And then there was more. How could I get kids to vote for me for Homecoming Court? I wanted to be a part of that TV documentary, and in order for that to happen, I had to be a finalist.

And if any of my grand schemes failed, what would be the worst that could happen? Failing in the science cluster? Losing my best friends after they are ridiculed by the evil masses?

Okay, maybe failure *wasn't* an option. Just then, as I opened the door to the cafeteria, Jabba quickly shuffled out. I noticed that someone had taped a sign to her back that said, "I brake for snacks."

I would have pulled it off, but I had low blood sugar and needed a snack. Something in my neurons snapped. *That's it*, I thought. *I'll just make all my science participants "Snackables." Everyone loves snacks, don't they?*

Chapter

4

In the cafeteria, my stomach somewhat settled down after my morning's trauma-rama. However, my head was racing more than ever. But I was ready for anything that might come next, now that I had strapped on my equipment, which today consisted of a small pen that was actually a microphone that transmitted to my Chica Speakas, and also my "Pic Purse," a modified shoulder bag with a small digital camera for discreet snapping, a bigger version of the one I had been promising Bridge. I was totally set to make my way across the cafeteria.

On any other day, I would have planned to bring my lunch and accessorized with the cutest little lunch box. And with Bridge by my side, we would have sashayed together, completely ignoring everyone and giggling secrets to ourselves while trying to appear cooler than we really were.

I know, we're sad. But for God's sake, we're freshmen and you just have to deal with the first semester any way you can.

But today was different. I was on a scientific mission. Lives depended on it. Social lives. If I wanted to influence the masses, the groups, the subgroups, the cliques, the outcasts, I had to win their hearts. And as the old saying went, it didn't hurt to go by way of their stomachs.

Casually, I strolled down row by row and observed what flavors of the day the students at each table were digesting. I whispered in my pen to record all my findings. I also grabbed some snaps for reference with my Pic Purse. And if anyone dared asked what I was doing in their undeclared official cafeteria zone, I would do the honest thing and lie.

"Oh, I lost my phone," I said to one table. Or sometimes it would be my wallet, iPod, notebook, anything I could invent that seemed appropriate at the time.

From my initial observation, the band kids seemed to like carbs and lots of them. Mac and cheese, rolls and butter. Real Dr. Pepper. Lay's Potato Chips. The only thing near them that was green was their band T-shirts. Woo-hoo! Let's hear it for team spirit!

On the other end of the cafeteria, the Dramaticas had marked out downstage center for themselves. They shared trauma for lunch. Lots of energy drinks called Viper. Lots of gum chewing. I hypothesized that they were jonesing for cigarettes, and since they couldn't smoke in the cafeteria (and really shouldn't be smoking at all), chewing gum was second best.

I quickly scanned this fascinating bunch. A crowd scene painted in shades of black. Faded black. Blue black. Brownish black. Silver and metal helped accent their so-called badness.

Some of these guys were post-punk styling after The Cure (you know, that band from the 80s). Others aligned their blackness with a rockabilly pose. There were also a few hints of Gothic color in the crowd. A bit of purple here, a bit of crimson there, these guys definitely weren't trying to blend here at all. This was also "body mod city"—given the extent of all the piercings around. They obviously love the taste of metal. "Must remember this," I said in my pen.

The Jocks and Locks table was easy to remember. And most visible, planted smack in the middle as if they were placed at the top of the pyramid. Which I guess metaphorically they were.

The J+L table brought the hottest and most popular athletes from football, basketball, baseball, soccer, and wrestling (Bridge would kill me if I forgot her beloved B-Dawg!) together with the girls with the biggest hair of Gamma High from cheerleading, the drill team, and Student Council. And when these groups congregated with the boys, it was no surprise that the table reeked of perfume, cologne, and soap opera.

The Jocks ate meat and truckloads of it. And protein shakes, too. Most of the Locks ate or—more often than not—*drank* diet drinks or shakes. And there were bottles and bottles of designer water.

And finally the sci-fi table. My tribe. It felt like home because they were a welcoming group and they were tidy—like my house, not my room. And boy, did they have a wide assortment of flavors on their plates. Sushi, hummus, taquitos, and corn chowder.

I never realized what such an eclectic palate my peers had. Quite frankly, I was surprised. Given the no-brand-name polo shirts tucked into khakis with a poor choice of belt and white sneakers (that showed no sign of street wear), you wouldn't know they lived on the wild side when it came to teen dining.

It made me laugh. So did seeing Bridge pull out an amazing spread while Mase dug out a malformed sandwich from his backpack, sniffing to determine whether it still had a shelf life or any sort of life, for that matter.

My Peeps. Even though Mase didn't look like he was from the science quad, no one questioned him, because he hung out with Bridge and me and we also happened to be on the farthest end of the cafeteria.

The only way anyone would really notice us is if there was a fire, but then they would have to trample over us since we were by the fire exit.

I dropped my bags at the table and bought whatever brown and greasy substance the school was serving today. As I headed back to our table, I looked at Bridge as she pulled out a Ziploc bag of edamame and another bag for her shells. Exhausted, I plopped myself in my chair across from Bridge. "Where's Adam?" I asked.

"He's sitting over there at the J+L table and, FYI, he and Mase aren't on speaking terms."

I tried not to laugh at them, because I knew this was a serious situation. Since Mase doesn't say two words to any one person in a year, it was the understatement of a lifetime to say they weren't speaking. Given how tight these two peas in a pod were, I knew there had to be some major hurt feelings.

Since things were delicate around the ole friendship circle, I decided to bring up an important matter as delicately as I could.

"You look nice today." I smiled at Bridge.

"*Omigod*, what's *wrong?*"

"Nothing," I said with my forked tongue.

Bridge squinted her eyes at me. "Then why am I smelling more smoke here than when I conducted my accelerated oxidation experiment?"

I had to put away my smoke and mirrors. "He loved my idea."

"Who?"

"Hamrock. He's forcing me to go through with the experiment."

"What?!" Bridge shrieked, then almost choked on her raw soybean.

"Bridge, it's not *that* bad."

"Are you kidding?" Bridge said in between sips of water. "Have you been trying to make nail polish again?"

"Look, I'm not living *la vida loca* here. I *do* have a plan to make this work. I swear. And I promise I won't do anything that jeopardizes your status here." (Which, to be honest, wasn't that high, and neither was mine, for that matter. I mean, c'mon, we're freshmen and we've only been here for, like, three months. We haven't even built traction, much less status.)

But to be respectful of Bridge's biggest fear of losing any potential status, I had to walk a fine line.

"Bridge, you're the only one who can help me pull this off, but I'll need your brain and your cooking."

"*Cooking?*" asked Bridge.

"Yep. It will be a vital part of the success of this experiment."

And then, as if she needed help to add on to her already 4.0 GPA, Bridge asked, "Will I get extra credit for helping?"

"Well . . . yeah," I promised. "And you might even make it as one of the five finalists." Bridge beamed for a nanosecond and then frowned.

"What if this experiment doesn't work?" she asked, remembering our current lack of social standing, then used her X-ray vision to pierce through me to make sure I was telling the truth.

"Then I'll be sure to take your name off and no one will have a clue that you were part of an experiment that bombed. Or see any pictorial records. Right? *Es verdad, Señor Mason?*"

I shot a look at Mase, knowing how mighty his pen or, in his case, his little stubby charcoal pencil could be. Mase gave me a crooked smirk in return.

Good. Bridge was in. Now, I just needed to convince my next two victims—I mean, *subjects*.

Next on the list was Mr. Milam. Casually, I pulled my chair next to Mase and put my arm on the table and my head in hand trying desperately to make a small and intimate human partition. And then I stared very intently into Mase's eyes and tried not to blink.

"Mase, I'm not going to shine you. It's urgent and I need your help."

My eyes were getting dry and starting to sting from not blinking. Then they started to tear up a bit, but I thought it was probably a good thing for me to look sad. However, it didn't seem to move Mase one bit, who kept chewing on his sandwich—which also looked quite sad.

Mase was going to take much more convincing and I knew it. For him, Homecoming, being popular, boyfriend issues held no significance at all. Quickly and desperately, I searched my brain's data bank concerning Mase. If I was going to enlist him in my shenanigans, they'd better be wild, outrageous, and potentially dangerous. Oh yeah, and fun. Forgot about that one.

So then I said, "Here's the deal. I'm doing a science project that will show that the students of Gamma High are just a bunch of sheep and can be influenced by the simplest things. And I need you to be my catalyst."

As Mase looked at me through his long bangs, I realized I had his full-on attention, but I wasn't sure if he was intrigued or just didn't know what the word *catalyst* meant.

Still not blinking, I said, "Let me give you a makeover."

After that statement I could tell instantly that Mason Milam had left the building à la Elvis.

"No, it's not going to be like that," I said as I motioned to the J+L table, where everyone was acting totally sophomoric even though they were all freshmen.

"Trust me. It'll be different. It's like . . . well, you know when you're about to do a big jump and you don't know if you are going to make it or not but you do it anyway? It's just like that. Except this will be a *huge* jump. And I promise that you'll make it. And because I know how much you like to freak people out, this will be the freak-out of the century. Especially when you make it as one of the five Homecoming finalists. No one will forget it, Mase. Do it for the underclassmen and the underdogs."

Because Mase was the unofficial poster boy of both groups, I could tell he was at least hanging out with the idea. But I had to push him across the finish line.

So then I said, "You're not *afraid* of a little stunt like this are you?" I noticed Mase flinch and put down his sandwich when I said the word *afraid*—and that's all the help I needed.

"Are you in?" I asked, moving to close the deal.

Mase quickly confirmed with a nod. I could tell he was a bit disturbed by the notion that I thought he could ever be afraid. And it was funny to see that the boy who didn't talk was now acting like one big ole Macho Taco.

I was so thrilled. I gave him a big hug and a big kiss. He turned beet red. It was cute in a brother kinda way. Really.

Now, I was two thirds of the way to getting my project off the ground. I felt golden—that is, until Bridge had to bring up the last detail.

"Have you asked Jabba?" asked Bridge, fully aware that I hadn't. And I must have made a funny face because Bridge snapped my picture with my Pic Purse.

"Gotcha!"

"Very funny," I said, trying not to start a fight with her right after she had officially relinquished her body to science and me.

Bridge showed Mase my mug shot, and he laughed out loud, revealing a mouth full of half-chewed day-old P-and-B sandwich. Ewww.

"Bridge, come with me so I can ask her," I pleaded.

Bridge carefully wiped her crumbs off the table with her napkin and disposed of them in her paper bag. "Why?" she asked.

"So she won't think I'm doing some hideous prank on her."

"Oh, you mean like the time someone told her there were cute puppies behind the fence and when she tried to check them out it was really a Rottweiler?"

Suddenly, Mase wiped what was left of his sandwich on the table, reminding Bridge of a recent lunchroom prank.

"Oh, yeah," Bridge said, "and remember the time Bellini took all the food out of Jabba's lunch sack and rubbed it on the floor and put it back, and then when she came back, she didn't even notice and ate her lunch while everyone was watching and screaming? Or—"

"*Yes*," I interrupted. "I got it, Bridge. Gracias. But now come with me so she doesn't think I'm just one more person who's on the planet to make sure her life here is an utter hell."

"Alright," Bridge said, rolling her eyes.

Since we had to make a journey to the other side of the cafeteria, we gathered our stuff, said adios to Mase, and began our whirlwind cafeteria tour. As we passed by the various cliques, something clicked in my head.

"Bridge, pretend like we're talking. And when we walk by tables, I'm going to pop a few shots of people's faces as they look at us."

"Okay, but it's kinda dark in here and the pictures may come out a bit fuzzy."

"That's okay; just humor me."

So as we crossed to the other side of the lunchroom table by table, we sashayed and I snapped unnoticed.

It was so much fun playing mini spies. And I could tell that the pictures were going to be hilarious. Sometimes we would go back and pass a table again just to make sure we recorded every priceless look. They were so severe but funny at the same time.

"There she is," Bridge said.

As we stopped in front of Jabba, I secretly snapped her picture. For a moment, I had forgotten we were on a mission.

"Hey, Ssssusan [I was being very, very attentive to her real name], I'm working on a project and wanted to know if you would help us," I said in my most engaging BFF tone. Susan finished licking her orange Cheetos fingers.

"What kinda project?" she croaked.

"Well, I'm doing a science project that proves my theory that I can help people be more successful and more popular by just changing a few things about them."

"What kinda things?" Susan asked with great suspicion as she devoured another Cheeto.

Dang. Now Jabba/Susan was going to make me have to think after I had just ingested a big, greasy chili burger with Tots.

"Well," I said, "it would just be small things like the color of your shirt, maybe your perfume and your voice."

"I don't wanna buy anything."

"You don't have to buy anything. I'll provide it for you," I said. I wanted to slap my cheerful and impulsive self as I remembered my microscopic allowance and tutoring income.

"And I'm allergic to perfumes. They make me break out in hives," said Susan.

Bridge was about to bust out laughing, so I stepped on her foot and then took *her* picture. I decided I needed to sit down to get more on Susan's level. I handed Bridge my Pic Purse.

"Listen, Susan, I'm not going to do anything that would jeopardize your social status or cause you any physical affliction. Just let me doll you up a little and you'll get lots of good attention. You could even make finalist for Homecoming Court." Then, knowing that Susan had her eye on the valedictorian prize, which was *only* three-plus years away, I tried to sweeten the deal by adding, "Oh yeah, and you'll earn *extra credit*."

Okay, here I go again lying about extra credit, but I really didn't know what I could do to make her say yes to the project besides faking being her best friend, and time was ticking and the bell was about to . . .

Rinnggggggggg.

Very quickly I said, "Susan, Bridget and Mason Milam [as I pointed to a lone figure in the distance] are on board to do this once-in-a-lifetime experiment. I think you would add a lot to this project. What can I do to make you feel comfortable about joining us? The project will only last about two weeks."

"Let me sit with you guys at lunch, then, for the next two weeks," Susan replied just as fast.

"Whaaa?" said Bridge and with that proceeded to step on my foot and turn my Pic Purse on me as she snapped a photo.

"Uh, Susan, good to see you again. Hey, Luz, I need to boogie on to Spanish. Adios, y'all!" Bridge tossed back with nervousness.

"I'll see you in Spanish, Bridget," Susan said.

Aye! Bridge didn't even realize that Susan/Jabba was in her class. Susan really *did* need to be in this experiment, I thought. Bridge gave a total fake smile to Susan, who wasn't paying attention, because she was drawing some type of elf on her lunch sack.

Then Bridge looked back at me and made sure I caught her scolding eye. I knew we would have a BFF briefing later about this.

"Jaa . . . Join us. It would be fun. So, you're in, right?" I said, trying to seal the deal of this science freak show.

"Can you make sure nothing bad happens?" asked Susan with a hint of caution in her voice.

Dear God, did she know what she was asking? She might as well have asked if I could make sure no natural disasters ever happened on planet Earth. Or if I could make sure no wars ever broke out or if I could make sure she actually won the crown for Homecoming.

So, I put on my Colgate smile and looked her squarely in her eyes, which were magnified by her nerdy glasses, and patted her little scratchy drawing and said, "Sure I can. I promise." And after I unloaded that big stinking lie, I ran to gym.

Chapter

5

"Stretch and do your one-mile warm-up and then we'll work on relays," commanded Coach Smith. With his short salt-and-pepper crew cut and his clean-shaven, no-nonsense *Leave It to Beaver* good looks, Coach Smith looked like he'd stepped out of the 1950s.

He always dressed in a white pullover, white pants, and black shoes. It was a bit off, but it worked for him. And it wasn't like I was in a position to be pointing the "Fashion Don't" finger.

I had forgotten to bring my running shoes, and my only option was to jog in my now multipurpose Chica Speakas. Having done the installation myself I wasn't too concerned with how the electronic innards would hold up, but the added inches of platform put the test to my stability. And even worse, I looked like a go-go girl gone wrong, and I prayed that no one would pay attention.

"Hey, Fashion Don't!" Adam said, paying attention *out loud*.

"Hey, Run Away! Why did you sit at the J+L table today?" I shot back.

"I decided to show Mase what life would be like on his own," he replied smugly, wiping off an imaginary scuff on his Lacoste sneakers.

"Well, he wouldn't be mad if you hadn't nominated him."

"I didn't."

"What?"

"I was going to nominate him but I tore it up, because I'm not that *impetuous*," Adam said, dropping another word of the day.

"What? Sorry, I didn't get this week's vocab list."

"I'm not that *impulsive*, Luz," Adam said, adjusting into a new stretch position. "Because I thought about it, and if I nominated Mase he would have just taken more of my votes." Adam turned and broke into a slow jog. And of course I followed.

He had a point. Adam was cute but Mase was dirty secret cute. I could see how girls could be swayed by Mr. Milam's silent persuasiveness. Still, I was *muy curioso*.

"If you didn't nominate him, then who did?"

"I don't know. I told him I didn't do it and he didn't buy it, and now he's been blowing me off. So, that's exactly what I'm trying to find out," Adam said, with a steady pace and breath.

"Dig up anything good?" I asked, knowing that Adam's the dog with a nose for the best bones of gossip.

Adam slowed to a walk, and as a loyal fan I happily followed. That was, until I could feel my inappropriate footwear beginning to rub blisters on my toes.

"Well, I've been hanging out and working as a production assistant for the producer, named Rod, who's scouting the school before the whole *High School Rules* video crew comes over. And I overheard him say that he didn't think there was enough drama here for a show. And that they might need to stir up the pot. I was wondering if maybe they nominated Mase."

"That's juicy but too much of a conspiracy theory. The facts are we're all just freshmen and our lives aren't that deep. And how would he know to single out Mase?" I said, trying to clear up this crazy talk.

"I don't know. *Not yet*," Adam replied in his in-the-know voice.

Suddenly, Coach Smith barked for us to form lines for a relay race. Adam and I held back so that we could continue our discussion. I was also trying to delay the inevitability of more running.

"Adam, listen up. *Por favor, ayudame*, I need your help! Dr. Hamrock is forcing me to enter Gamma's science contest. I have three classmates whom I must make popular and get elected as Homecoming Court finalists by giving them scientific makeovers."

"Oooh. *Por favor, ayudame!*" Adam mocked me back in his bad girly voice. "Are you gonna give them Santos's Gamma Glamma treatment?" he asked, with bad jazz hands.

"You know it," I said, pulling down his hands so people wouldn't look at us.

"If you let me cover it for the paper . . ." Adam said extra sweetly.

"Well . . . Swen is already covering it."

"What?! You let *him* instead of me? But I'm your BBF—best boy friend!" Adam gasped.

"I didn't give him permission. Dr. Hamrock did. I didn't even want to do this experiment."

I could tell Adam was not happy about being left out. First, Mase had given him the brush-off and now me.

"Okay, let's not talk about my dumb experiment," I suggested.

"You brought it up," he snapped.

Adam was being such a pain. But I really needed him, so I held my tongue (at least this time).

"Yes, Adam, I *did* bring it up. But I only brought it up because I need your help. I don't have time to actively campaign for the Homecoming Court. I wanted you to help me figure out the best way to score votes," I said, gazing at the relay line, which was growing shorter by the minute.

"What's in it for me?" Adam replied, not skipping a beat.

"I thought you were my BBF," I reminded him.

"You're on probation for not letting me cover your freak-of-nature science experiment," Adam said.

"Okay, what do you want?"

"My stipulation is that I want you to get Venus Hunter to go to the dance with me."

"What?" I said, not believing my ears.

"*Escucheme!* You heard me, sister. Get Venus on board to go to the dance with me," he repeated.

"What about Bridge? I thought she was your love for life?" I tried to remind Adam of his deep obsession with Bridge.

"She is, but she will only fall in love with me when I am rich and famous. And right now I am neither."

"But why do you want to go with the person I can't stand *the most*?"

"Because, my little Scientific Señorita, as vexing as it might sound, if I go to the dance with Venus, my story will get covered by the video crew," Adam said, revealing his scheme.

"How do you figure that?" I asked, lacking the brainpower to add it all up as I moved closer to the front of the line.

"Look, we all know that Venus is going to be one of the five girl finalists to represent the freshman class. And you know she'll probably win because, let's face it, she'll get there by any means possible, including murder. If I'm her date, then by proxy I get the first round of press."

"Uh-huh?" I said, trying to get his drift.

"If she wins, then the video crew will follow her, and of course they'll want my side of things, and thus I'll be the narrator of the dirty little secrets of Gamma High," Adam said with a twisted sense of potential power.

"Very tabloid," I said, grossed out.

"More *20/20*-like." He tried to make it sound legit.

"Very tabloid."

"Okay, you're right, but it's a shot and it could be really hot."

"But will you help Bridge and me become finalists?"

"Yes. But it's gonna take a lot of work," Adam warned as he took off his glasses and put them in the pocket of his shorts.

"Then, I'm in."

"Good. Then we are officially a team in this caper."

"Yes!" I said, beginning to experience some relief. "When do you want to get started?"

"Now! Run!" Adam yelled.

While talking with Adam, I had forgotten I was still in gym class and now at the front of the line. Traci Armstrong came charging to hand me the baton. It took me a second to check back in and finally take off. As I started running, I wondered to myself, *Why does it feel like I'm running straight into disaster?*

Chapter

6

After all my misadventures at school, I took a nap. I really wanted to sleep longer but piles of homework and the planning of my now infamous science project, officially titled "Project Gamma Glamma," kept nudging me awake.

I woke up to the delicious smells of dinner, and followed them straight to the kitchen. Still groggy, I sat on the bar stool at the kitchen counter and stared at the happy colors of the mangoes and limes my mom was preparing for dinner. Tonight, we were having my favorite—fish tacos—and for dessert a mango lime pie that was absolutely to die for.

Unfortunately, I was having a hard time enjoying fully the sights and smells of my mom's *plato del dia*, suffering as I was from two blisters on my big toes, punishment for my lack of gym preparation, not to mention my preoccupation with my now-overextended life. I must have had some strange look on my face or my mom's Latina sixth sense was kicking in, because she suddenly asked with concern, *"Mi hija*, what's wrong with you? Are you constipated?"

"No, Mom! I just always have this constipated look when I'm thinking."

"What are you thinking so hard about?" Mom asked while peeling a mango.

"I have a science experiment that I have to get off the ground. I'm just trying to figure out how to do it."

"What's it about?" I knew this inquisition would be as irritating as my bulging blisters, so I went ahead with the full explanation. Mom just laughed.

"What's so funny?"

"I just can't imagine what you are going to do with Bridget," she teased as she shook her head and went back to slicing and dicing. Somehow this had definitely struck her funny bone. Great.

But Mom was right. I wasn't quite sure what to do with Bridge. I mean, by high school standards, she wore all the right things—*basically*. However, it was true that she was a bit overpreppy and rigid about everything she wore. Even as my best friend, I knew in my heart she was still going to be a challenge.

Bridge always thought her bootie was too big and her chest too small. She hated the fact that she was pigeoned-toed and always made sure to square her stance when she was just hanging out. She thought her eyes were too big and hated how her prescript glasses magnified her eyes even more and made her look crazy.

She always dreamed of beautiful fingernails but due to nervousness and life's general aggravations, she chewed them off. This also caused her to have to reapply her lip gloss hundreds of times a day, especially because she believed her lips were her best feature.

I thought she was gorgeous "as is" and I wondered how I would amp her up even more fantástico than she was. Y'know, like Bridge to the second power. Then all of a sudden the pressure started to build inside me like a small cheesy volcano you see in really bad science fair.

Mason. Jabba. I could feel my stomach churning, so I decided to do the most logical thing and ask the Mominator for assistance. Mom was spinning around *la cocina* like a Texas Tornado and tossing spices as I picked at the bananas that were still too green to eat.

Mom's name is Armida and she works as an art director for an advertising agency. She has impeccable taste, and as a strong-willed Latina woman, she knows *exactly* how to make people take notice.

The only problem I have with her is the fact that she has prob-

lems with the way I dress. She thinks I look like a punk rock ballerina looking to start a fight. This may be somewhat true, but the last
thing I want to do is start a fight, especially with my best friends. So,
I decided to open my inquiry.

"Hey, Mom, when you are doing art for, like, an ad, what's the
first thing you do to attract people's attention?" Mom stopped her
kitchen dance for un momento to think.

"Hmm," she said, "I think the first thing I do is to make sure I
know what their perceptions are, and their expectations."

"Yeah?" I said, waiting for more info.

"And then I do something that will surprise them. Throw them off.
Like if they are expecting black and white, I give them color. And if
they are used to color, I give them black and white."

"And this makes them do what then?" I said, feeling clueless.

"Well, first, it just gets their attention. Luz, you have to remember that most folks are so wrapped up in their heads. In order to get
their attention, you have to shake them and *jolt* them."

"Then what?"

"Then you have to show them how this product is going to make
their life better," she continued, taking a bite out of a juicy mango
bit.

"And that's it?"

"I wish it was. The main thing is making them *believe* that they
can have better and then everything else follows."

"Well, how do you get them to believe?" I asked.

"Therein lies the *magic*. It's about listening to what's most important to each individual. To your target audience." She smiled as she
cleaned off her knife before slicing into a lime.

"Okay, all this is sounding crazy. How do I use this concept to
make Bridge more attractive to the rest of the student body?" All
this new info had only added to my frustration level.

"I guess you'll first want to know her audience, her peers, what
things they value, and apply them to Bridge. And you've also got to
make sure she believes she's attractive, because she's gotta be the
one to carry it off."

"Well, if that's the case, then I think I'm just going to take an F in science," I said, reaching down and daring to touch one of my blisters.

"Over my dead body, baby. Now, *dame los platos*. Your dad should be walking in the door any minute," Mom ordered.

As I started pulling out our vintage Fiestaware from the cabinet, I shook my head and laughed. My mom goes from laid-back artsy mom to becoming the Mominator ready to kick my *nalgas* (that's bootie to y'all) the moment I even mention any type of failure. Nothing like livin' *la vida loca* in this overachiever household.

But my mom did have a point. I had to know my target audience, all the various peer groups I was selling my made-over subjects to. So, I did a quick checklist in my head. Doll up Bridge to swoon the J+L table to take her in. Pour Mase into a Dramatica mold. And Jabba, I'd have to start her off slow. Maybe I would work her up to the band table. I mean, she *was* one of them even if she always sat alone.

Something finally occurred to me. If this works, why not try this on myself for Swen? I would have to sacrifice and tone down my clothes a bit and start reading the school rags, but it would all be worth it for the sake of science and a date to Homecoming, wouldn't it?

Just then, another thought struck me like a bolt of lightning. And I had to act quickly. Dinnertime around my house was pretty sacred, because it was supposed to be about sharing my day with my parents so they could dig around and make sure I wasn't getting into deviant behavior like doing drugs, hanging with thugs, or getting into any other kinds of trouble.

And so when my dad, Leo, walked in, I gave him a big hug and told him that I really needed to get started on my science project immediately and I needed to duck out of dinner.

"Whatcha working on?" Dad asked.

"It's a really long explanation. Mom can fill you in. Right, Mom?"

"Of course," she answered, too busy flipping fish to argue.

"I'll come and grab a plate in a minute," I assured her. And with that I grabbed a Coke and a slightly green banana and took off.

Settling into my room, I dimmed the lights, lit a candle, started playing music, and downloaded my purse pictures of the day. Then I began my analysis.

First, I looked at the pictures of the Jocks and Locks. They were very Abercrombie, very clean—a lot of red, navy, and denim. And white. The girls wore their hair straight and long. The boys were either surfer shaggy or sports buzzed. None of these kids wore glasses, and none of them had their backpacks with them at lunch—as if to say they were too cool for school. In my digital recollection, they were all always laughing—probably because they were making fun of the rest of the poor inhabitants of Gamma High.

As I scanned through the pictures, I came across my nemesis, *Venus.* Her lucky genes had blessed her with long, straight, blond hair with no sign of chemical damage. Just like her cutest and latest Luis Vuitton pochette was the real deal. No fakes would do for Venus, especially since her dad was, in a word, *loaded.*

Her skin glowed with perfection and almost outshined her teeth. *Oh, God, why did my enemy have to be so darn freaking* caliente?

Just for the record, Venus Hunter had also gone to my middle school and to my summer science camp. At one time we were friends—almost best friends—until the summer when I met Bridge and I experienced my first crush with a boy named Lee Wagner as well.

I guess he was Venus's crush, too, because she did everything she could to make me look stupid in front of him. And when he actually sat by me at dinner one time, it was over for us, and Venus and me as friends, as well, when she tossed off one doozy of a snide remark.

"Hey, don't have too much fun, Lee. Santos has a very weak bladder."

I was speechless. And I really did want to pee in my pants and not because I had a weak bladder, but from sheer embarrassment.

Ever since that bladder blab episode there has always been an unspoken cold war between good ole Venus and myself.

I know this is going to sound really like I'm nutters, but sometimes I think she is watching my every move just so she can destroy anything good I have going on. It's just a theory so far, but one day, I know I'll be able to prove it.

As I revisited the digital picture of Venus whooping it up and laughing while digesting nothing for lunch, something caught my eye. *El libro!* Venus had the same book that I had knocked out of Swen's hand when I last saw him in Dr. Hamrock's class.

I knew it was a writing book of some sort but something didn't make sense at all. Venus *hates* English and despises writing. I know this because I could always tell when she had written in those forbidden slam books. She would always misspell words, and when I'd try to correct her she'd get mad at me.

Like the time I told her that there was a *T* in the word that describes a female dog. Yeah, she was *that* bad in English, but I had to admit she was pretty fantastic in science, like myself.

She must be trying to woo Swen, I thought. That had to be it. Suddenly, the stakes were getting higher by the minute and I started to get antsy. And just then the perfect formula appeared to me.

Here is what was going to have to take place. And it had to be like really systematic. First, I was going to revamp Bridge. Shorter skirt. Let her hair down. Straighten it. Take off her glasses. Yes, she would be blind as a bat at lunch, but it wasn't necessary to see at lunch. It was just hand to mouth. Hand to mouth.

Besides, it would probably make her feel more comfortable if she couldn't see everyone else at lunch. I couldn't afford to get her an expensive purse like Venus or the other girls at the J+L table had, but I could borrow some of Mom's Gucci perfume and that definitely smelled like bank.

Next, we would need to practice on her laugh. When Bridge laughed it was like a little cartoon laugh. In order to survive and thrive she would need to have a strong and wicked laugh, just like that *bruja* on a broom Venus's.

The next thing I needed to do was make sure that Adam would be at the table with Bridge. I knew that if she didn't have the guts to go through this alone, then the only way she could get through it was to at least have Adam by her side.

And Adam (I almost forgot), how would I make Venus, the queen of snobs, go out with him? Then, I got it. I decided that I would spend half of my lunch period at my regular table because I promised Jabba that she could eat with me. I also needed to have a home base in case something went wrong with Mase or anything else because of this freak of nature experiment.

Then in the second half of my lunch period I would casually stroll by the J+L table and say, "Hey" to Bridge since everyone has seen us together and figures that we are friends. But while I'm at the J+L table, I'll also be sure to be a superflirt to Adam, who would be the pretend atom of my eye.

This way I would be able to see if Venus would take the bait. If Venus were true to her bad self (which I knew she was) then she would throw herself in front of Adam just so I couldn't have him.

And *boom*! This would serve both Adam and myself. Adam would get his date with Venus and his *20-20*/tabloid press opportunity. And then she'd be so totally distracted that she wouldn't have time to dig her dirty little claws into my Swen.

But in the meantime, I'd need to do a little wooing of my own. I didn't think dressing vanilla for Swen was going to do the trick because he's really smart.

But maybe if I could spend quality time with him and, like, get into his mind or something, I could find out what kind of "target audience" he was.

Boy, all this plotting was time-consuming. And so was eating this unripe banana. As I looked ahead to the next two very big important weeks, something told me that I could do this.

Just then the phone rang. I didn't bother to answer it since it was the house phone and if it were Bridge she'd either text me or call me on my cell.

Then from across the casa, I heard my mama yell, "*Luz*, it's for you!"

I almost didn't want to get it because I thought it would be someone stupid. It was anything but.

"Hello," I said, sounding somewhat firm, ready for my first fight with a telemarketer.

"Hey, Luz, it's Swen."

Suddenly, I felt a lump in my throat and my hands started to get really sweaty.

"Oh, hi, Swen. I thought I gave you my cell phone number."

"Oh, that's okay. Hey, do you have a minute?"

"Yeah. What's up?" (This is totally stupid, but *por un poquito minuto,* I was hoping he would happen to ask me to the dance. As if.)

"Well, I got to thinking about your project and it's a great idea. And I want to be responsible so that, you know, nothing I put out there affects the outcome of your project." He sounded very journalistic and businesslike.

I really tried to listen to him but I just kept thinking about how it would feel if one of his strong hands was sliding through my long brown hair and the other hand was gently touching my cheek. My DNA was screaming.

"*Okay,*" I said, pulling myself back to this universe.

"Do you normally keep some kind of journal on your projects?" Swen inquired.

"I guess so. Sort of. I mean, I just summarize my hypothesis and outline my testing protocols, then organize my observational notations to support a logical conclusion."

The line got quiet and I suddenly realized that I sounded like a total geek.

"Well, any notes you could provide me could really help add a lot of color to our story."

Did he just say our *story? Melting. Melting.*

"It's just that I'm not much of a writer," I confessed.

"Don't sweat it; I'll help you," Swen said sweetly but in a totally professional way. *Dang.* My toes were curling and I wanted to scream, and as I tried to stop myself, I bit my tongue.

"That would be . . . great," I hacked out as my mouth was getting dry.

"Have you ever heard of a book called *Elements of Style?*"

Right at that moment, I had a flashback of knocking Swen's book out of his hand. And I remembered Venus with that exact title in the lunchroom. *Hate her. Mean it.*

"Yeah, I think I have," I said, trying not too hard to play dumb.

"I have an extra copy if you want it," Swen continued.

"Sure. Uh, did you give Venus Hunter a book, too?" I asked, deciding to dig for more info. I know this was really a dorky thing to ask but I was dying to know. *Dying.*

"No," Swen said.

"Oh, I saw her today with the book too. It must be a real page turner," I said, in my hopeless attempt at flirting.

"No, not really. Venus left her copy in Dr. Hamrock's class and I found it and gave it back to her. She's working on a novel, y'know."

"Oh, that's cool. I was just curious," I said as I did a silent victory dance.

"Look, I want to get started on this story. Do you have time on Monday after school so you could walk me through your experiment?"

"Sure. No problema," I said as I wrote "Luz *Swenson*" over and over inside the cover of my spiral.

"Okay, cool. How about we meet in the library after school?"

How romantic, I thought, but then I had to slap myself. "Yeah, okay, sounds good."

"Alright, see ya then."

"Okay, bye. . . . Uh, Swen . . . ?"

"Yeah?"

"What's your favorite color?"

He paused a minute. "On me or in general?"

"What color do you like to wear?" I said, trying to be playful like they tell you to do in *Cosmo Girl.*

"Gray."

Gray? Yikes, I thought. *Good thing he's hot.*

"And what colors do you like to see on girls?" I continued.

"Skin tone."

"*What?*" I squeaked.

And then Swen laughed. "No, I'm just totally kidding. I guess I don't really notice color on other people. I just pay attention to their stories."

"Okay, thanks," I said somewhat relieved that he had a sense of humor and wasn't a perv in disguise or something.

"Was that for your science experiment?" Swen asked.

Now, as an expert liar, I quickly replied, "Absolutely."

After we exchanged our good-byes, I was on fire and wired. So, it appeared that picture-perfect Venus was one big, fat liar, too. A novel—yeah, *right!* And to make everything more fab was the fact that Swen was going to loan me his book. His *personal libro*! It was like we were almost a couple. I could almost taste Homecoming and victory. And it was yummy.

Chapter

7

Journal Entry One

Today is the first day of Project Gamma Glamma, an experiment to examine outward personal factors in social mobility. It's Sunday afternoon and I have spent the weekend clothes shopping for three test subjects to help them adapt to the fashion habits of preselected assimilation groups.

I have also created samples of colognes, perfumes, and oils calculated to specifically stimulate and appeal to the olfactory senses of these same peer groups. And lastly, I have engineered disguised photographic devices for each subject to secretly document their experiences and gather additional and essential data that I would be unable to observe directly.

The first subject to which the transformation will be implemented is B., a freshman at Gamma High. My hypothesis is that if I can alter just three basic elements of B.'s self-presentation, this will initiate a corresponding response in the student body's opinion of her, and begin the process of her acceptance into a new social group.

Tonight I will go to the subject's house and introduce her to a new wardrobe combination along with a new hairstyle and a new fragrance, and I will also coach her in developing a more agreeable tonality of laugh.

I read over my journal entry. It sounded kinda dry but, hey, it was a start. I didn't write that Bridge had a fit when I tried to put her in navy and red because she felt like she looked like a Fourth of July float.

"Now why am I doing this?" she asked.

"Because you're my best friend *and* my science partner in crime. And I really need to go to the dance because up until now this will be the biggest moment of our lives. Now which shirt do you want—the red or the navy?"

"Oh, I guess the red, because it'll bring out the red in my eyes after I'm finished crying because I look like a freak."

"Bridge, please. Oh, before you put that on, try on this bra I got you," I said, holding up a Gap bag.

"What? What's wrong with the bra I have?" She clutched her chest defensively as if it weren't attached.

"It's a sports bra," I reminded her.

"Yeah, but it lets me breathe and it's ergonomically aerodynamic."

"They're boobs, Bridge, not airplanes."

"But, I like how it looks seamless under my oxford."

"Yes, well today you and your chicas are getting a makeover. Don't you want Brad Walker to notice you?"

Bridge made her "duh" face.

"Good. Then let him wrestle with this!" And that's when I pulled out this amazing and sizzling bra from Gap Body. I could tell I embarrassed Bridge, but, hey, we're growing up and it's science. Our bodies are changing every day, so it made sense that our wardrobe should as well. After Bridge put on the gravity-defying and shape-defining fab bra and the little red va-va-voom sweater, I think she was a bit surprised.

"Wow!" she said.

"How do you feel?" I asked, hoping she would like it.

"Well, with all the metal in this bra, like the bionic woman." Bridge laughed her cartoon chipmunk laugh.

Bridge loved that old TV show called *The Bionic Woman*, because, sadly, it was the only thing that she and her mom had in common. Mrs. Joiner ran a high-end clothes shop that was really frilly and, by contrast, Bridge was a bit more of a sporty prep type. So, when Bridge first started to take an interest in the wonderful world of science, her mom didn't know how to connect anymore, so she made Bridge watch countless reruns of *The Bionic Woman*.

I laughed out loud with her. "You look fabulosa!"

"Yeah, but I think I need to balance out the proportion of my new boobs to my curvy hair."

"Duh, I'm a scientist and I already thought of that." I handed her my mom's heavy-duty flatiron. "But first check out this scent." And then I reached down in my bag of tricks and pulled out a small bottle of perfume and I took Bridge's wrist and squirted a wee bit of Gucci's Envy. It was just enough to smell, but I was careful not to go crazy, so my mom wouldn't notice the volume disappearing.

"Can you smell it?" I asked.

Bridge wrinkled her nose. "No."

"How about now?" I squirted her again.

"No," she said while inhaling at least a gallon of air.

"Is your nose working?"

"Yeah. Is your perfume working?" Bridge said defensively.

"I think so." And with that I shook up the bottle really hard, and when I sprayed Bridge, a gusher came out right in *her eyes and mouth*! Her room began to reek.

"Ahhh! I told you I'm glad I picked the red sweater, because now my eyes should really match," Bridge said, literally spitting out Envy.

"Sorry, B. At least it smells expensive."

"Okay, what's next before I chicken out?" Bridge ordered.

"Next let's work on your hair."

Bridge has the longest, thickest, waviest hair. And sometimes when folks look at us from the back and see we have matching dark brown hair, they think we are related. But Bridge's hair is much thicker and wavier than mine. And I knew it was going to take a while to straighten it out.

An hour and a half later, progress was finally being made. But because I was getting tired, I didn't notice that I had already straightened out this one section and proceeded to sorta fry it. I could see and smell the smoke, but thank goodness Bridge couldn't, because she was studying for Dr. Hamrock's next pop quiz and the room still totally reeked of perfume. We were almost done.

"Are you ready to look at yourself?" I teased.

"I guess . . ."

After seeing my BFF all brand new and put together, I was so proud of what we had accomplished together. But I remembered one last thing—Bridge needed to ditch the glasses. She had really cute Polo glasses, but if she was going to stand a chance at the J+L table, she needed to amp it up all the way. And with that, I helped her put in her contacts.

She had a box full of them in her dresser drawer but never wore them because she got squeamish about touching her eyeballs. And this is the same girl who can dissect any dead creature laid before her in the science lab and not flinch, can play with molds, fungus, and gooey invertebrates, but if she touches her own eyeball, get out the smelling salts, because the child's gonna hit the floor.

"Hey, Bionic Woman, are they in?"

"Yesss," Bridge said with uncertainty as she was still barely poking her eye.

"Can you see now?" I asked as I waved my fingers in front of her.

"I think so," she said as she tried to bite one of my fingers.

Bridge squinted her eyes like a ground hog coming out of its hole or like the Hollywood starlets who are so tragically loaded when they spill out of their limos.

"C'mon. Are you ready to see your final transformation?" I couldn't stand to wait another second.

"Yes, Dr. Frankenstein," Bridge said, rolling her eyes.

As I turned Bridge to the mirror in her hot chili pepper red sweater, her really straight, long locks, her modified mini, and her bionic bra, I even shocked myself. Bridge took a long look at herself. I couldn't make out if she was sad, happy, or mad at me for burning some of her hair, but then I realized she was in pure shock.

"What do you think?" I whispered.

"I'm kinda *hot*," she gasped.

"Yeah, you are," I confirmed. "Okay, do you think you can go through with the experiment now?"

"I think so," Bridge said, still not believing in her own reflection.

After our long look-see in the mirror, we practiced Bridge's laugh for hours, and it was so funny to hear her go from a little baby laugh to a hot mama laugh that she had me cracking up, too.

I reassured her that Adam would be at her side at lunch. And if she forgot to laugh properly or couldn't come up with any good lunch table convo, she should just listen and mimic Venus. I told her to remember to continually flip her hair, and not to worry, because I would make my daily sweep at the J+L table to say hello to my faux loverboy, Adam. But even with all this instruction, I could tell Bridge was still a bit nervous.

So, we decided to take our minds off tomorrow by testing out Bridge's nail-growing serum. While Bridge was working on her hands, I decided to try out some of my hair harnesser shampoo. When I got some shampoo in my eye, I panicked, but Bridge, being my BFF, helped me wash out my eyes so I wouldn't become blind or something worse.

Later when I went home, I tried to calm myself. The more I thought about Bridge being nervous, the more nervous I became, too. I just had to deal.

Bridge, Mase, and Jabba had already trusted me with their social lives; Dr. Hamrock was expecting a win at Regionals; and Swen was ready to make a date at the library. Retreating wasn't an option.

Since sleep wasn't an option either with my brain operating in overdrive, I decided to be productive and finish the disco version Pic Purse for Bridge that I had been promising her for weeks, and she would now be needing in order to document the experiment. When I was finally done, I looked at my alarm clock—it was already six in the morning and I hadn't slept all night. This was officially day two of Project Gamma Glamma.

When my mom dropped me off at school, I immediately spied Bridge hiding by the buses because her little red sweater outfit popped out against the yellow background. I knew that her Pic Purse would be the perfect accessory, and the extra bling would help get her mind off her nervousness. I quickly ran up to meet her, and as we started going up the stairs at the front of the school, I said, "You know, you really, really look cute."

"Really really?" she said, still surprised.

"Yeah. But before you go, let me give you one more squirt." I took out my mom's perfume and doused Bridge. She smiled.

"At least it smells good." She wrinkled her nose as if she was about to sneeze.

"At least. And Bridge, I just want you to know I really appreciate you doing this for me and I want you to know I have your back. . . ." I looked her straight in the eyes so she'd know I meant it.

"I know." She smiled back.

"And this is for you." I handed her the Pic Purse.

"Ooooh, Luz, I *love* it. It's so tiny. It's a Pic Pouchette!" Bridge gushed, ready to take her first picture.

Suddenly, Bart Marquez came roaring up behind us like a freight train. He ran smack into Bridge, spilling her across the front steps like a rag doll.

"Sorry, sweetheart," said Bart as he scooped her up and brushed her long, straight locks out of her face.

Then three other guys came out of nowhere to Bridge's rescue. Her legs could have been amputated but she wouldn't have cared with the attention she was getting. It was horrible and beautiful at the same time. I wanted to cry, but first I had to take a picture to document this moment. The boys escorted her to class as I trailed behind the small group like a long-lost puppy. When Bridge finally reached the doorway at Mr. Hashem's history class, I said, "Bridge, are you okay?"

Bridge stared at me as if she was looking through me and said, "I'm *fabulous*."

I flipped my hand through her newly straightened hair and said, "Yeah, you are. Now, pay attention and tell me what else happens to you today so I can put some notes in my journal." I winked.

"Got it," Bridge said.

And then the new and improved Miss Joiner floated above the ground and beyond everybody's expectations into class.

As I walked away, I could hear all the students squealing compliments about Bridge's Gamma Glamma makeover.

For a minute, I was feeling like a science fiction fairy godmother and it felt as fabulous as Bridge looked. *With a wave of my manicured magic* mano *would everybody else's dreams come true*, I wondered?

Chapter

8

My classes felt like they were really dragging today. Maybe because I couldn't wait to get to lunch. Not because I was hungry or anything, but because I could finally see Bridge again and check up on her progress.

And I would also see Mase and Susan and could schedule them in for their grand Gamma Glamma makeovers. And then, after lunch, it would only be three more hours until I would have my crush time with Swen. I couldn't contain myself. I was both excited and nervous.

Today I had tried to be subtle with my fashion decisions but still dress cute for Swen. I wore a button-down white dress shirt that I found at Target and tried to roll up the sleeves just like he did. I also made sure to wear it untucked. I was going to wear jeans but decided against it, because I didn't want to look so obviously like Swen's clonerazzi.

So, I purposely wore a gray utility pleated mini with my silver magnetic boots. I love these boots because I had constructed them from faux Ugg boots, which was a good start since I really don't like wearing dead things. Yeah, I know, I eat meat, like taco salad, but I'm working on that.

Anyway, back to my boots. They're silver and I have attached these metal strips to them so I can hang memos, pictures, or whatever on them. The only drawback was that it took me a little longer getting through the metal detector today, but Mr. Sekin, the vice principal, who watches the entrance every day, knows me pretty well by now.

Finally, it was science class and then I was saved by the bell and saved by the fact that Dr. Hamrock was away at some type of workshop. The substitute teacher was nice enough to let us gather our stuff early so we weren't scrambling so much when the bell rang for lunch, like we normally do.

As I bobbed and weaved my way into the cafeteria, I quickly turned to look at the J+L table. The first thing I noticed was that Adam and Bridge were already sitting down. I giggled when I heard Bridge's new and improved laugh. I wanted to go over there really bad but decided to wait.

On the menu today was the school's lame-o version of pizza. And not having any better alternatives, I resigned myself to a slice, added a salad for good measure, and poured myself a purple juice drink that's just called "Purple." I wandered to my usual table and sat down with Mase and Susan, who was already almost done with her lunch.

"Hey, guys," I said.

Mase just nodded and Susan glanced up at me and then kept eating.

"Mase, I have your stuff for you to wear for the week. Do you have time to meet with me tonight?"

Mase shook his head no.

"What about tomorrow night?"

Mase still shook his head no. I wasn't sure if he was playing with me or not.

"Well, what time are you free today?"

Mase showed me four fingers and then switched modes from chewing to drinking, or in his case, gulping.

"Cool. So, you *do* have time after school?"

Mase nodded yes.

"Then could we make it at four-thirty?" I asked, almost forgetting my library date with Swen.

Mase shook his head no.

"*Por que?*" I asked, getting tired of these mime games.

He pulled out his ragged skateboard from under the table and put it on the table. Ew.

"Oh," I said, realizing he wasn't about to cut into his skateboard time in the name of science. "Okay, can you meet me outside the library at four o'clock sharp?"

Mase nodded yes and, relieved, I turned to my next victim.

"And Susan, when can we get together? I'm available anytime. How about tonight? Can I come over?" I squeezed in a bite of cold pizza.

"Yeah, I guess so. But I live far away," she groaned in her usual unwelcoming voice.

"No problema. I can have my mom drop me off."

"Well, okay. I'll still need to make you a map, but it won't be that great."

Susan scribbled her address along with her map and then went back to eating her lunch, or I should say crumbs, at this point. God, lunch was going to be a total drag with these two. I could already tell it was going to be a long two weeks.

I glanced at my "Watchame"—another of my favorite creations. It's a watch that I've programmed to read out daily encouragements, my social schedule, homework assignments, even a reminder to breathe. Mase had come up with the design—it was me with a tiny body and giant head, kind of a Japanese cartoon character like Hello Kitty, with the display screen in my forehead.

Right now it was showing the time, and I noticed I only had enough of that to boogie past the J+L table to say hi to Bridge and Adam.

As I grabbed my lunch tray and backpack, I said, "Okay, guys, I'll check you out later. I need to find Bridge and Adam." Mase shot me a disapproving look at the mention of Adam's name.

"He swears he didn't nominate you," I said. Mase then gave me a small "whatever" face as he went back to adjusting the wheel bearings of his skateboard with a lunchroom fork.

"Hey, Mase, will you take my tray for me?"

Mase nodded quickly, then focused on his skateboard. I set my tray and gathered my bags.

"Susan, I'll see you tonight."

"Alright." Engrossed in her elf drawing, she didn't look up.

As I started walking to the J+L table and looking at the long rows of beautiful people, I took a deep breath. I could hear my boots clanking around like I had on cowboy spurs or something.

Venus was already holding court and, amazingly, Bridge just fit right in like the perfect puzzle piece. She was so perfecto in her new surroundings that she didn't even notice her best friend walking and jingling up behind her.

"Hey, Bridge, how's it going?" I slapped her on the back.

"Shiny," Bridge chirped back, already nailing the stuck-up tone typical to the J+L tribe.

So then I went, "Oh, *shiny* is it?" noticing that *shiny* was such a Venus word. "I'm going to the snack bar. Do you wanna *come with*?" I asked, hoping she was hearing my undertones of "Girl, we need to talk *now*!"

Still quite hypnotized in the J+L mode, Bridge cooed, "Nooo, I think I'm good."

So, I stepped on her foot immediately to remind her that she wasn't *that* good. Her eyes widened and the pain brought her back to her senses.

"Well, maybe I'll just window-shop," Bridge coughed up. "Hey, Venus, Adam, do y'all want anything?" Bridge flashed a nervous smile.

"Yeah. I'll take two Choco Drumsticks," commanded Venus to Bridge as if she were her personal slave.

"Are both of those for you?" Adam asked with great curiosity.

"You know it!" bragged Venus as she flicked back her hair and showed off her Colgate smile.

"Oh, my God, V, how do you stay so skinny?" Tammy Shellhorn, who was sitting next to Venus, and desperate to maintain her welcome in the group, showed off her major suck-up abilities.

"Oh, you know, I just do Luz's 'Hollywood trick.' " Then Venus pretended to shove her finger down her throat, and suddenly, I felt a stab of anger.

"Oh, you're just *precious*," I hissed back with fake sweetness.

"I'm just kidding, Santos," Venus said, with wide doe eyes. "I'm just blessed with a *very fast* metabolism."

I looked at the worn ceiling tiles. *Worn enough to fall,* I thought. . . .

"Yeah, Venus, I know. Ever since Jr. High, you've been *really fast.*" I hoped that the last word of my sentence would rip like an arrow into Venus's self-inflated balloon.

"Ow and meow," said Adam under his breath, looking a bit uneasy.

With that I leaned over to Adam and said, "Let me know if you need anything, *mi vida.*" Then I kissed him on the cheek (and caught him off guard) and grabbed Bridge's arm to join me as I walked away. The showdown was over.

Not only could I feel Venus's hot stare and glare, but I could also hear the gears in her head spin out sinister plans as she turned to Adam and smiled cutely to begin her sabotage of my fake relationship with him. Now away from the J+L table, I could finally breathe.

"So, how has your day *really* been, Bridge?" I asked, hoping now that the distance from the J+L table would allow a safe haven for Bridge to freely speak her mind and *la verdad*—the truth. As we got back in the lunch line, I moved in front of Bridge and grabbed another tray as I checked out the desserts.

"I don't know where to start! I'm just so excited. I mean, it feels *amazing.* My day has really been unbelievable. I can't really explain it. I'm feeling it—the popularity, y'know? Everyone's been super nice. People say I look really great, even some of the girls. Can you believe it? I want this to last forever."

I reached in the ice bin and began weighing my options of grabbing a frozen treat now or holding out for the chocolate pudding that was farther down the line.

"You know I'm glad that it's working out for you and all, but you really have to remember this is just a science experiment, *not* real life, chica," I warned.

"I know."

"Well then do your part and start taking pictures or at least start jotting some notes. You gotta help me out, Bridge, and not fall for the BS—bad science."

Bridge's posture sank back to normal. "I know. I'm sorry, Luz. But everything has been happening really, really fast."

I kind of felt bad for being so stern. So, I turned back to give a re-assuring BFF smile, but I noticed something unusual happening. Bridge started doing something that she's never done before. *Twirling her hair.* We both despised this behavior in girls so much that we in fact classified it as "dumb girl gymnastics."

"Bridge, you're twirling your hair! Cut it out!"

"Was I?" Bridge said in total disbelief as she tried to pull her hand out of her hair, but it got caught. I was still moving down the line.

"Luz, my finger is caught in my hair," Bridge said.

"Okay, now you're being a superfreak and it's really not cute." I went back to my mean voice, knowing her tendency to overreact, re-fusing to turn around.

"Luz, look at my hand! Look at both of them!"

Because I couldn't resist, I flipped back around again and peered down at Miss Joiner's hands and saw the most amazing thing ever—a set of really long shiny fingernails.

"Oh, wow! Bridge, you did it! Your nail gelatin formula worked! I can't believe your nails grew in less than twenty-four hours. That's quicker than our calculations!"

"This is amazing!" She was awestruck by her magical manicure. "Luz, do you know what this means? If this works out, we could sell this at school and become famous."

"Not just at school but *everywhere*. And what better coverage than to have a TV documentary note your new discovery!" I was already worrying about what we should wear for our debut on TV.

I grabbed my tray and loaded it up with more Purple and two small cups of chocolate pudding. Bridge, who was too busy admiring her nails, passed on the sweets but made good on her promise to feed a "fast" Venus with two Choco Drumsticks. We were almost about ready to pay the cafeteria woman when from behind me Bridge said, "And, by the way, I can't believe you kissed Adam. What was that all about?"

And as I turned to her to explain my impulsive actions, Bridge screamed, "Ahhhh! Luz! Your hair is in the pudding! It's *growing*!"

And sure enough, as I looked down my hair had indeed grown *over a foot* since the morning. The strange thing was, I hadn't really noticed it, but my scalp did feel kind of itchy—like when you put way too much product in your hair.

Bridge was still looking at me with her mouth wide open while the cafeteria lady was looking at me with her lips firmly shut. We were, apparently, backing up the lunch line.

After we paid and left with hair and pudding and all, we ran back to our ole home base, the sci-fi section. Mase and Susan had left, so we sat by ourselves. Bridge, true to her best friend self, scored some napkins and water to help me clean my new locks.

"This is sooo great, isn't it, Luz?" She stretched out her hands in front of her.

For the first time in our best-friend relationship, Bridge was the certain one and I was feeling a bit like Miss Insecure.

"I'm so glad I didn't use any of your hair harnesser. Could you see me if I used it? I would be Miss Curls-Gone-Wild by now. How much did you use?"

"I don't remember," I said, feeling stupid.

"What! You didn't calculate how much you used? That's *very* sloppy of you, Luz."

"I know, but I was caught up in trying to figure out what kind of experiment I should propose to Dr. Hamrock when I was creating my special formula, remember? And then when I was trying to get you ready for today, I didn't go back and double-check. I had a total brain freeze." I could feel my face getting hot from embarrassment.

"I'm sorry. I know this experiment has been stressing you out. When do you start everyone else's magical makeover?"

"Well, I start with Mase after school and Jabba tonight."

Bridge's eyes grew big. "Girl, you're gonna be exhausted."

"I know."

"Well, you managed to look really cute today, if that helps."

"Thanks. I'm meeting Swen today after school to talk about this project. So, please do me a favor and take some notes and take some pictures so I don't come off as a total liar."

"You got it. I can't believe you're actually going to see Swen. I'm so happy for you. But don't worry; he won't notice you're a liar."

"Oh, really? Why is that?"

"Because of the pudding stains on your boobies," Bridge said while offering a weak smile.

I closed my eyes and took a deep breath—and prayed to every god in the universe that I wasn't parading a pair of chocolate chichis. Obviously they didn't hear me—probably because they were laughing so hard. As I looked down, the stains were definitely there and my new locks still had a bit of the pudding on them that had tainted me.

"This is why I don't wear white," I said, done with it all.

"You have about five minutes before the bell. Go to the bathroom and see if you can blot it out."

I gazed down at the table for a moment. I think I was still in shock when I observed another small disaster. This one, however, put a smile on my face.

"Hey, Bridge, your precious drumsticks are melting," I said, finding a bit of justice in the universe.

"Oh, crap. I need to run these to Venus before she uninvites me to her party." Bridge was back to her social worrywart self.

"Did she invite Adam?" I asked.

"I don't know," she said, walking away.

"Find out for me."

"Okay. I'll talk with you later." She waved her hand and new nails in the air and scurried away, and I did the same to the girls' *baño*. As I was running off, my growing hair was getting heavier and starting to give me a headache.

The door closed slowly with the sound of a quiet swoosh and I took a deep breath. The girls' bathroom was definitely a nice escape from the roar of the cafeteria.

This area of the school hadn't changed in decades. Still decorated with 1950s pink girly tile, the powder room sparkled softly as the afternoon sun came in and warmed up the color. I always imagined that if I had my own laboratory, I would want it to be bright and kitschy like this. I loved the hardware on all the sinks and light fixtures. It was kind of a Marilyn Monroe meets, well, I guess, Dr. Frankenstein, but not his monster.

But thinking of monsters made me look at the two big chocolate stains on my boobs. As I gazed into the mirror, I started blotting gently with a couple of paper towels and water. Then feeling tense because I knew the lunch bell was about to ring any minute, I scrubbed faster.

"Oh my gawd!" someone yelled.

"I know. It's bad, right?" Without looking up I continued the damage control of my fashion disaster.

"Not as bad as not letting me in on your melodramatic plan to salivate on me!" bellowed Adam and his vocabulary.

"Adam! What are you doing in here?" I asked, my irritation not directed at him but at my stains, which had only smeared and gotten bigger.

"Saving my rep," Adam admitted.

I must have looked confused because Adam continued, "It's not that big of a deal. I usually come in here to the vanity area to get the scoop. In fact, there have been times when I said I was going to the clinic, but instead, I hung out in the handi-able stall and did all my math homework and found out all the goings-on from freshies to the seniors."

"Adam, you're unbelievable," I said as I blotted with the paper towels.

"Not as unbelievable as your hair. Is that *a weave?*"

"No." Like I could scrape up weave money on my allowance.

"Those aren't extensions?" Adam asked, waggling his eyebrows.

"No! I invented a hair growth accelerator potion and I'm the first guinea pig."

"Well, Miss Piggy, you really caught me off guard with those lips! You know I *hate* surprises," Adam said, circling around to the reason why he was here in the girls' bathroom in the first place.

"Sorry. But Venus was riding my last nerve with her bulimic digs. I just needed to create a diversion or something."

"*Diversion?* Excellent word choice!"

I had used up all the paper towels and had to rustle up some TP from one of the stalls. "Thank you," I said, coming back to the vanity area. "So, what happened after I left?"

"Y'know, it's really funny, but she *actually* invited me to her party this Saturday," Adam said, a little surprised.

"Aha! I knew it! She's sooo predictable," I said, feeling proud of my psychic but unscientific prediction.

"Did you predict that she asked Swen to Homecoming?"

And with that, I could feel my lovely acid reflux starting to gush and I really wanted to spew vomit.

"What did he *say*?" I asked with dread.

"Don't have that info . . . yet," Adam said, ready to dive into his investigations.

The bell rang. A gaggle of girls ran in while Adam ran out and said he would try to figure out what we should do next. My angry scalp started to itch again.

Chapter

9

I can honestly say I have no recollection of what happened in any of my classes after lunch, not because of my lack of sleep but because of the shock of hearing that Venus had asked Swen to Homecoming. I must have looked "not quite right" because one of my teachers even asked me if I needed to go to the clinic.

I almost thought about it. But I didn't want to go to the clinic and hang with folks who actually might *be* sick. I had too much to do. I did think about pulling an "Adam" and going to the girls' bathroom and hiding in the handi-able stall, but, then again, I didn't want to run into Adam either.

So, I just stuck it out. My English teacher, Mrs. Franks, told me I could lay my head on my desk and finish my essay on *Pygmalion* and character transformation at home. Wanting to sleep, I put my big ole *cabeza* on the desk. But I couldn't sleep, because my mind kept racing with endless thoughts of science makeovers and romantic mayhem.

Did Venus really ask out Swen? Maybe Adam misunderstood. No, Adam's ear for the dirt is as sure as the earth's gravity.

Okay, if Venus did ask Swen, what if he said yes? Would I still want to go to the dance? And would I still have to go through with this project? Unfortunately, I already knew that ugly answer—yes. I mean, I was already too far along in this project and I couldn't just use *mis amigos* as yo-yos for my own personal reasons (no matter how good they might be). After all, I was a scientist and scientists have to have ethical standards, don't they?

And would it be super bad if I backed out on Swen and his story? I mean, I *love* him. At least I think I could. Would I totally disintegrate my chances with him if I didn't do the story because he went to Homecoming with Venus? And then there was Dr. Hamrock. After the famous fish massacre, I don't think he would easily let me off the hook (so to speak). What to do. What to do. My first reaction was to cry, but that seemed so lame.

Instead, I rested my head on my arm and I watched my silver magnetic *botas* kick back and forth underneath my desk for a few minutes.

And then it came to me like a bolt of lightning. I'm a strong Latina chica and scientific fashionista, right? All I had to do was pull myself up by my silver bootstraps and face the facts.

Fact one: Venus may have asked Swen out but it doesn't mean he said yes.

Fact two: Venus loved yanking my chain and maybe she was. It was obvious how she invited Adam to her party (and not me) after I kissed him. So, maybe she wasn't into Swen after all. I could at least hope.

And perhaps I could make my science experiment work and spend more time with Swen so that he could do thorough research for his article. I could also use that time with him to really get to know him (in a slow-burn kinda way), and then I could tell him the truth about Venus.

Then, finally, with a successful experiment, coverage in the paper, and Adam's help, maybe I would make finalist for the Homecoming Court after all. And end up in Swen's embrace. I could make this work out. I *must* make this work out.

The last bell of the day rang, and with a renewed sense of courage, I gathered up my stuff.

"I hope you start feeling better, Luz," said Mrs. Franks in a motherly tone.

"I already do. Thanks, Mrs. Franks."

Walking to the library to meet Mase, I received a text from Adam: "venus+swen=falz alrm . . ." That made me feel lighter than helium until I got his lead balloon follow-up a second later—an ominous ". . . 4now." It was true I couldn't control the future, but right now I felt I had a new lease on life. Now things wouldn't be weird when I met Swen and I could let my hair down, figuratively speaking.

Literally speaking, due to its rapid growth rate, my hair was becoming an obstacle course. I finally tied it up into a big, sloppy ponytail on top of my head.

As I waited for Mase, I leaned up against the brick wall in front of the library and watched the parade of kids go home for the day. And looked down at my boobs, or more specifically, the stains on my boobs. From my point of view (which was upside down), one stain looked like a little pony. As I stared at the second pudding stain trying to discover what magical shape might emerge, Mase skated up to me and started staring at my stains too.

"Oh, I don't want to even go into it," I said, a bit embarrassed. Mase just shrugged and waited for me to pull out my bag of tricks. I bent down and unzipped my large purple duffel bag, which weighed at least a ton.

For starters, I pulled out a simple-looking black shirt. It was really, really black, unlike the ones that Mase generally sported. Mase's black shirts had all turned charcoal gray from his extreme living. Mase looked carefully at the shirt, then sniffed at it (for whatever reason), and finally nodded in agreement. *Bueno*, I thought.

Next on the fashion train express was a big black hoodie that looked spectacular. Never mind that it was Texas and ninety-five degrees, this hoodie reeked of mystery and coolness. In a word, it rocked.

"It's cool, right?"

Mase nodded again and didn't appear to mind playing along with me.

The next shirt I had for him was my favorite—kinda pirate-ish. When I shook it out of its crumpled state, I saw Mase's face instantly wince.

"No, man, it's really cool. You just need to accessorize it a bit. Here, let me show you what really cool chains I have for you."

My head started itching again. I just figured it was because I was getting hot. I grabbed a few silver chains, and one that even had skulls on it.

As I pulled the necklace with all the skulls on it to display it by my neck, I could feel my hair growing again, and then my elastic scrunchie snapped. My hair spilled out, and as I reached to pull it back from my face it got caught and tangled in the necklace.

"Ahhh! Mase, help me!" I screamed.

Mase lunged to save me, but it didn't help that he was on his skateboard at the time. He fell on me. Hard. His fist not only yanked a wad of my hair but also managed to yank the necklace, which broke, sending a million little skulls rolling on the floor. It was all happening in slow motion and it was just awful.

The quicker we tried to stand up, the quicker we slipped on the rolling skulls. Mase was being so sweet by trying to hold me up and at the same time not grope me.

However, now that my hair had grown another twelve inches, it was blocking my view and causing me to lose my balance. This time I was the one to fall flat on Mase.

"Hey, Luz, do you want to get together another time?" I heard a voice say.

I pushed myself up with my arms and stared into Mase's eyes, because I thought maybe he had said something, but then I noticed him gazing past me in shock. Suddenly, I recognized the voice.

Miraculously, I jumped to my feet, even though Mase's skateboard wheel was tangled in my hair. Mase also managed to stand up and tried to set his skateboard free by yanking my hair. I shoved him off and just held on to his skateboard as if it were a really big hair accessory.

"Uh, no. I mean yes," I said as I gave a corny little wave with my only free hand.

"I just didn't want to interrupt, uh, you guys," said a confused Swen, who was looking at the clothes, the mess on the floor, and a beet-red Mase.

"You didn't interrupt anything. I just fell and Mase was kind enough to help me out. I haven't been feeling well," I explained or, rather, lied. No, actually this *was* the truth. I'd been feeling sick ever since I was summoned to do this stupid science project.

Swen kept looking at my stains. He was probably wondering if they were from throwing up or something. *Omigod, he thinks I vomited on myself.*

"It's pudding! *Really!* You know . . ."

"Hey, Luz, it's no big deal. Just call me and let me know when you want to reschedule, okay?" Swen said.

"Okay," my voice cracked, "I'll call you."

Swen gave a nod to Mase and Mase nodded back from the floor as he tried to gather up the tiny skulls that were all laughing at us.

I fell back on the floor with the skateboard still in my hair and cried that "ugly girl" cry. Poor Mase. It's almost a scientific fact that no guy on the planet wants to be in the presence of a girl who is in "ugly girl" cry mode. He raised his hands up as if to say, "What do you need?" So, I told him. Loudly.

"Cannn yooou taaake meee tooo Briiidge's houssse?!"

Mase, being my true friend, put off his post-school session (especially since his board wheels were still well tangled in my new, long, monster locks) and took me to Bridge's as I heaved and boo-hooed the whole way there.

When we arrived at Bridge's house, Mrs. Joiner, who preferred that we call her Betty, answered the door. Betty, in her typical fashion, was dressed in dark, pressed jeans and a white dress shirt, with tons of silver jewelry and kitten heels. Which she almost tripped backward on as she caught sight of Mase, the maniac skateboarder, standing beside her daughter's best friend with his skateboard attached to her head.

"Luz! Honey, what do you have going on *now*?" said Betty, who was all too aware of the not uncommon scientific misadventures that Bridge and I blundered into. She peered over her sexy librarian glasses and allowed us into her overly clean and perfect living room.

"Are you feeling okay? You seem a little red and swollen."

"Oh, it's nothing really. I just got my hair tangled in Mase's skateboard. I'm just trying new sports and things," I said, with my fake there's-nothing-wrong-in-the-world smile.

"Oh, my. Has your hair always been that long?" Betty scrutinized me as she glanced back at her own hair in a nearby mirror in the foyer.

"Well, it's been growing pretty fast lately. And I haven't really seen you."

I didn't see Betty that much because Bridge said I made her mother nervous. I wasn't sure if it was the way I dressed or the fact that she got really mad the time we tried to make a hair color that would look normal during the day and then glow at night.

Bridge and I love things that glow in the dark. We tried it and it actually worked for a day, but then our hair fell completely out. Betty (who is exactly like Bridge in that she cares what the country club set thinks of her family) had a Texas-size cow over that one.

"Umm. Can, I mean, *may* I borrow some scissors?" I asked in my innocent voice.

"Honey, I think you're going to need a hedge trimmer for all that."

As Mase nodded in agreement, I realized I'd forgotten my manners.

"Betty, this is our friend Mason. He's helping me with my science project. Is Bridge in her room?" I said, hoping Mase and I could make a clean escape.

"Yes, she is." Betty paused for a moment and said, "Mason, would you do me a favor and go to the kitchen? In the top drawer next to the refrigerator you should find some big scissors. I was kidding about the hedge trimmer."

I wouldn't have been surprised if that was actually what it would have taken to set me free. When Mase took off to the kitchen, Betty leaned in very close to me. I knew this was coming.

"He's not a *runaway*, is he?" asked Betty, looking suspiciously toward the kitchen.

"No, he's a skateboarder and an . . . artist."

Betty didn't really understand extreme sports but she did understand artists. She was a big part of the Dallas Art Society, and she and Mr. Joiner were always throwing parties and openings for eccentric artists who were way stranger than Mase.

"Oh, okay, that's such a relief. And you're just going to cut your hair loose with my scissors?" quizzed Betty.

"Yes."

"And that's it?"

"Yep, that's it," I said. I didn't want to give her any more information because she would interrogate me further and Mase's skateboard was wearing me down, literally.

"You're not going to give Bridget any science trims are you?" Betty asked, with her quotation mark fingers.

"No, I promise," I answered and was glad to see Mase trotting back to my rescue. He handed the scissors to Betty, who handed them to me.

"Well, there you go. And if you make a mess, you know where the Swiffer is, right?" said Betty, revealing her type A tendencies.

"Absolutely."

The phone rang and Betty ran off to grab it while Mase shot me a look that said, "What was that?" I smiled to keep from crying anymore today, and we headed to Bridge's room.

With the stereo blaring, candles burning, and pictures of Einstein, Madame Curie, and Calvin Klein hotties staring at me from Bridge's neatly done cream linen bulletin board, I felt myself calm down.

It didn't matter that my face was still puffy or that I was all stopped up from crying so hard. I finally felt like I could breathe for a moment. And it also helped that I had cut my hair and finally set Mase's skateboard free.

Mase also enjoyed a sigh of relief as he pulled out the last stray strands of my hair from his wheels.

Bridge was still in the bathroom so I sat on the floor combing my new locks and loudly told her through the door the story of my latest disaster.

"I can't believe my hair is still growing! I hope it'll slow down tonight 'cause I don't want to wake up like Rapunzel tomorrow."

"But what if you did?" Bridge asked.

I started pulling a stray hair out of my brush. "Then I'll just give myself a quick chop."

"What happens if it keeps growing at school?"

"Well, I guess I'll just borrow your mom's scissors again," I said as I looked at the closed bathroom door.

"You can't take them to school, Luz. It's considered a weapon. You won't be able to get past The Sekinator and his metal detector." Like I hadn't been through that metal detector a million times.

At this point, I was getting a bit peeved with Bridge's negative 'tude. But she was right. Our vice principal (aka The Sekinator) lived for confiscating anything that didn't pass quietly through the metal detector. Rumor had it that he sold all the stuff on eBay.

"Mase, do you have a large paper cutter in your art class?" I inquired.

Mase nodded but didn't look up, because he was totally tranced out drawing on his skateboard with a marker.

"*Él dijo sí.* He said 'yes.' I've got it totally under control. Thanks, Miss Joiner," I said to the bathroom door.

"That's great, Luz. But what about this?" Bridge said as she slowly pushed open the door.

"What about wha . . . ?" And then I witnessed a scientific horror. Bridge stepped out and walked into the middle of her room holding up her unbelievable twelve-inch claw fingernails.

Mase and I dropped our jaws in unison.

"Wow!" I exclaimed. Then I had to say it again. I looked at Mase and he even mouthed, "Wow!"

"Shut up and stop saying, 'Wow'!" Bridge quickly snapped, trying to fight the cracking of her voice so she wouldn't cry. I jumped up and made sure Bridge's bedroom door was locked. Betty would *kill* us.

"Okay. Well, did you try to cut them?" I asked, trying to keep my eyes from growing wider from shock.

"Yes, I did, but they grew back."

"What do you think happened? You measured everything. I watched your every move," I said, trying to remember our formulation.

"I know. I even double-checked my notes. I even bought brand-name gelatin. Remember? I was so careful, Luz. What could have gone wrong?" Tears were filling Bridge's eyes.

"First, I don't think you did anything wrong. You let your fingers soak in the gelatin compound for twenty minutes and then you rinsed, remember? When I was rinsing my hair."

"*Omigod*," Bridge said as a five-hundred-watt lightbulb popped on in her head and then exploded.

"What?" I asked.

"Luz, remember how you were in a hurry when you got your hair harnesser shampoo in your eyes?" Bridge said, pacing around the room as she waved her manicured weapons of mass destruction in the air.

"Yeah?"

"Well, when you were rinsing out your eyes remember that I helped you rinse your hair?" Bridge spun around to me and almost poked me in the eye as she grabbed my hair.

"You're *right*, Bridge. You're totally right! Your nails were still soaking up your solution when you put your hands in my formula. It was a Reese's moment. You got your chocolate in my peanut butter and I got my peanut butter in your chocolate," I said as I gently lowered her talons.

"Yeah, and you didn't measure your peanut butter formula and now we have no idea when this freakish growing phase is going to stop. And I can't return to school like this!" Bridge said with her nails wildly waving around shredding the air molecules.

Mase quickly looked out Bridge's window. Not two "ugly girl" cries in one day. He was ready to jump out the window at this point.

"You have to go to school. We just got started on this experiment," I said, as a wave of panic overtook me.

"I'm not going to school with these platypus nails even if you are my best friend."

Bridge was starting to spin herself out of control. And I had to calm her down. I made her sit on the floor with Mase as I now started to pace around the room like an army general.

"Okay, I'll figure out how we can keep them trimmed throughout the day."

Bridge's mouth started to quiver. "With *what*?"

"With anything I can get my hands on."

"What happens if you can't get past The Sekinator?" Bridge said as she started to visit Doomsville again.

"Bridge, get hold of yourself," I said, now standing over her with my metal boots and all.

"But what happens if . . ." Bridge started to hyperventilate.

"Bridge!!" I yelled. "If I can't get my hands on industrial-size clippers or any other sharp objects to cut your platypus nails, I'll personally bite them off with *my teeth*. Okay, are you happy? Now, sit down and put your head between your knees and start breathing before you pass out."

I had to sit down for a spell myself. I hadn't seen Bridge this freaked out since science camp when she tried to make her own glow-in-the-dark lip gloss and she burned her lips into giant blisters and then had to make a speech the next day in front of some really hot geeks.

Mase inched away from us crazy girls and migrated to a little rocking chair far in the corner. I sat next to my nutcase BFF and grabbed one of her claws to examine how thick her nails were growing. Bridge held her head carefully in her other hand. The room was still for a moment.

"*Omigod*," clamored Bridge as she jumped to her feet, leaving scratch marks on my boots. "What happens if my toenails start growing?"

"Well, are they now?"

"No."

"Well don't worry about it and we'll just make sure you wear flip-flops or open-toed shoes."

Then I started wondering about my hair. If it was growing on my head, wouldn't it also grow *other* places as well? I stepped into Bridge's bathroom and checked my legs and arms and underarms and, yeah, I checked my britches. And thank my lucky stars, no hair was growing wildly out of control anywhere else. Could you imagine the horror if it did while wearing a skirt? Just to be safe, I think I'll wear pants and long-sleeve shirts for a few days.

As I stepped back into Bridge's room, she gave a small whimper. "What is it now?"

"What am I going to *wear* tomorrow?"

"Whew. Now that one I can handle for sure without any disasters."

I reached into my magic duffel and pulled out a very cute plaid mini to pair with a librarian sweater and a cute camie underneath.

"Where did you get those?" Bridge smiled while still fighting back the tears and sniffles.

"The thrift store," I said honestly.

"You're kidding."

"No, I'm not."

"Is it sanitary?" Bridge wrinkled her nose as she covered her mouth with her talons.

"Yes, Miss Germania. I washed it three times for you. It's hot, right Mase?"

I gave Mase a quick hint with my eyes. He nodded yes without any hesitation. He had seen enough crazy emotional girls today. Bridge began to stroke the librarian sweater with her claws.

I put my hand on Bridge's shoulder. "Now, are we cool?"

"I guess so." Bridge took the sweater and held it up to her chest and walked to her closet mirror. She grinned through her tears with approval. I inhaled more oxygen for my poor brain.

"Now, can you please help me get Mister Mason ready to go for his debut mañana?" I was hoping to keep her mind focused on something other than our scientific blunders.

After going through the motions of what shirts Mase would wear, we decided to keep him lean, mean, clean, and James Dean. In other words, the pirate shirt had to walk the plank.

We also decided no jewelry—at least no necklaces after our bad after-school-special moment. However, Mase would wear a big silver belt buckle à la Johnny Cash.

For him, I had also brewed up a special cologne that smelled of cedar and paint. It's the paint smell that all the theatre productions smell like after the scenic artists finish the backdrops. It was faint, but I reasoned that this familiar smell would reignite the same feelings of excitement generated by opening night of a school play. It was a stretch for sure.

But what other smell could I have given him? Musty stage curtains? Buttered popcorn from the student concession stands?

So, in the looks and smell department Mase was good to go, but we still needed to work on one more aspect. If I needed to improve his aural appeal, I first needed to get him to make a sound.

"Okay, Mase, you've gone this far. And you've seen how hard we've been working to make this science experiment successful. I need just a bit more of your assistance."

Mase cocked one eyebrow at me. I pulled out a small package of innocent-looking rainbow-colored gumballs.

"Chew on these. I invented them."

Mase cocked his other eyebrow, not sure of what was to come next, especially after witnessing two of our science mishaps.

"I call them Gabber Gum. It's gum that will help you spit the words out. It's harmless."

Mase immediately grabbed and held up Bridge's hand to illustrate his lack of faith in my scientific process.

"Look, Mase, I hear you loud and clear but that and my hair were just simple miscalculations. I worked hard on these little babies. They're one of my coolest formulas. It's kinda like Willie Wonka. Don't you want to see how they work? Aren't you just a wee bit curious?" I said, hoping to entice him.

Mase scratched his head with Bridge's claws and nodded.

"Bridge, will you help a sister out?" I stretched out my hand with a pink shiny gumball as an offering.

Bridge reluctantly took the gumball and popped it into her mouth making sure not to scratch her face with her nails. And I popped a gumball in mine. And we began chewing. And chewing. Mase waited with great anticipation.

And then we began to talk nonstop.

"It's yummy," I said.

"Yeah," Bridge said.

"I have watermelon."

"I have cherry."

"It's so delish," I added.

"Totally," Bridge said between chews.

"It's like it's energizing my brain."

"Mine too."

"In a good way," I said in my rah-rah voice.

"Totally."

"So, Mase, you gotta try this." I smiled.

"You soo do," Bridge said as she grabbed another gumball.

"We're going to start talking faster than we normally talk," I said.

"But *you* won't come off like a spaz," Bridge said.

"Like we probably sound," I joked. "And it only lasts a little while."

"How little, Luz?" Bridge asked.

"Twenty minutes max, I think."

"You think? Don't you *know*?" Bridge shot a wide-eyed look at me.

"Okay, *I know*," I said, not wanting to get Bridge started again.

"Because Mase doesn't want to experience the horror . . ."

"That we just went through?" I finished.

"Exactly," said Bridge, not skipping a beat.

"Okay, Bridge, you don't have to be so . . ."

"Fierce? Okay, sorry."

Then out of nowhere, like from the sky, we heard a booming voice say, "Shut up!"

"*Omigod*. Bridge?" I said.

"Yes, I can't believe it!"

"Mase, did you try a gumball?" I asked.

"Luz's Gabber Gum?" Bridge added.

"Yeah," said Mase with his ocean-deep voice.

"Mase, you have a hot voice."

"Say something again," begged Bridge.

"Shut up, Bridge."

"That's *dreamy*."

"I didn't know you could sound so sultry," I said.

"And mysterious, too," Bridge added, using her talons as a veil.

"Shut up!" Mase said.

"That's simply amazing," I said, paying no attention to Mase's orders.

"The Dramaticas . . ." Bridge started.

"Are going to freak," I finished.

"If you girls don't stop . . ."

"Talking?" I finished.

"Yeah," Mase said. "I'm going to . . ."

"What?" I asked.

"Punch you."

"Which one of us?" I asked.

"Both of you!" Mase yelled.

"Where?" I asked, pushing his envelope so that he'd talk more.

"Where it hurts."

"Oh, Mase, you are . . ." I started.

"A riot," Bridge finished.

"I can't wait . . ."

"Until tomorrow?" Bridge added.

"Yeah!" I confirmed.

Mase just shook his head in defeat. And we all busted out laughing, and then I realized it was time to leave and continue my work with Jabba. Somehow, I got the feeling I wouldn't be laughing as much on my next makeover.

Chapter

10

Mom honked outside of Bridge's house. As I ran out, I could still smell the pudding on my shirt even though it was now hidden by my neatly trimmed hair. Mom smiled in her purple workout outfit and messy ponytail. She looked cute today.

"How was your day?" Mom asked as I jumped in.

"Let's just say that it's been a really, really long day," I replied as we headed down the street.

By this time the Gabber Gum had worn off and I didn't feel like talking, much less going into a giant explanation about my day. And after my sleepless night, I was just plain pooped.

Come to think of it, the day had actually started off well with Bridge's amazing makeover. She had been accepted at the J+L table and even invited to Venus's party which, of course, I had not. (Me bitter? Maybe a skosh.)

And by me smooching Adam, Venus had now also extended an invitation to Adam. *Good for him.* Maybe he'd make it as a finalist for the Homecoming Court after all and then get to star in that TV documentary.

Where the day had started turning ugly was with the clinical and oh so personal trials of our hair and nail growth accelerators. But luckily, things weren't as disastrous as we had thought and would eventually be super fab (with some minor tweaking, of course).

And finding out about Venus asking Swen to the dance had thrown a big wrench into the mechanics of my master plan, but I wouldn't consider that a done deal yet. I had managed to shake off the psychic ravages of that news by the time classes had let out.

But then the true horrorfest had taken place after school with the extreme gymnastic act that Mase and I had done for Swen. My face still burns from embarrassment when I think of it. *Ugh.* But let's move on to more positive things! There would be tomorrow when Mase debuted his new transformation. I couldn't wait. He was definitely going to be Mr. Dramarama.

"Luz. Hey, Luz!" Mom said, turning her head to me.

"Yes?" I said, trying to pay attention.

"Now, where am I supposed to take you?" Mom said as she slowed down the car a bit.

"Oh, it's easy. Just take seventy-five to University Park and turn right on Mt. Vernon."

"Mt. Vernon Estates?"

"Yeah," I replied.

"Ohhh, that's *muy rico*," Mom said, looking quite impressed.

"Yeah, I know. It's supposed to be really nice," I said, not wanting to get into much more convo.

I wondered how nice Susan was going to be especially when I asked her to test out my latest creation, called "White Away Right Away." They were self-tanner jelly beans to give your skin a slight bronzing from a formula I had developed by extracting beta-carotene from carrots. I just hoped Susan wasn't allergic to carrots.

As we turned right on Mt. Vernon into Susan's neighborhood, I had to do a double-take because the houses were so big I almost mistook them for apartment complexes. They were beyond huge.

Once we checked the address again, Mom turned into a spacious driveway. All the cars were either gone or tucked out of sight. Mom pulled our Tahoe right up to the door. And then, Mom, totally in "Mom mode" said, "Do you want me to come with you?"

"Por favor, no!"

"Okay, well then at least give me a wave so I know everything is alright."

"Fine . . ." I said as I stepped out of the car with my duffel bag. It was so much lighter now that I wasn't lugging around everyone's clothes for the week.

As I walked toward the front door, I felt like I was shrinking and the door was growing larger. I reached for one of the creepy-looking lion-head doorknockers but was relieved when I noticed the doorbell. I took a deep breath to calm my nerves. *Didn't help.* It wasn't because this was a Richie-rich house, because I've been to all kinds of parties and houses before because of my mom's job. I think I was just starting to doubt myself. Was my Cinderella-Frankenstein magic going to work on Ja . . . Susan?

Just do it, I commanded myself.

I rang the bell. And waited. No answer. I looked at the side windows where I could see a very formal dining room with that French furniture that's all swirly and painted gold. You know that kind that looks cheap but is anything but? The lights appeared to be on. I looked back at my mom and shrugged my shoulders.

Maybe it takes a really long time to answer the door when you have a house that big, but then you'd think you'd have a butler or something. Suddenly, the door opened slowly and, lo and behold, standing there was a man, *the butler.* This casa was bank.

"Hi, I'm Luz. Susan and I are working on a science project together," I said in my most appropriate schoolgirl tone.

Before the mysterious butler spoke, Susan appeared from behind him.

"Hey, Luz," Susan greeted dryly.

"Hey, Susan," I said, relieved to finally see someone I knew and know I wasn't going to be murdered (or worse).

I waved off Mom so she could get to her workout class and motioned that I would call her.

"C'mon in. This is Mr. De la Cruz," Susan said as she stepped back to let me in her grand foyer. I quickly looked up at the gigantic chandelier that hung over us. It made me feel a bit squirrelly.

"How are you doing tonight?" Mr. De la Cruz asked, adding some warmness to the big, otherwise cold house.

"Fine, thank you," I answered, trying to take all this fanciness in while making sure my big chunky boots weren't tracking in mud or dirt.

"Can I get you two ladies anything?"

"How about a couple of pizzas?" Susan said as she wiped her eyes as if she had been napping.

"How about *your diet*?"

"*Bueno. Por favor tráigame dos personal pizzas y dos ensaladas*," Susan replied, as if placing her order in Spanish and adding two salads magically made it less damaging in the calorie department.

"You like pizza, Luz?"

"Yeah, that's fine," I said (never mind that I had had it for lunch earlier).

"Okay, then, I'll order up. I'll call you when they're ready unless you want them in your room."

"Yeah, my room is better," Susan said, walking toward the staircase.

As Mr. De la Cruz disappeared into a long, dark hallway, Susan motioned to me to start climbing her monster of a staircase. I secretly snapped a picture of the staircase with my purse. I wanted Bridge to see this joint.

"You don't have to eat your salad," Susan added, without fear that Mr. De la Cruz might still be within earshot.

"That's okay. I like salad," I said.

"Well, *I don't*. I'm just going to feed it to my pet alpaca."

"Aren't they kinda like llamas?" I asked, trying to envision what these creatures looked like. I think I had seen a commercial on TV about them once.

"No, Luz, they are *quite* different."

"Oh, okay . . . well, does your alpaca have a name?"

"Yeah. I first wanted to call him Frodo."

The stairs were steep. I was running out of breath. "You mean like from *The Lord of the Rings* movies?"

"From *the books*, Luz." Susan looked at me with disgust, like I didn't read. "Anyway, I also wanted to call him Fantastic. So, I decided to make a hybrid and call him Frotastic," Susan continued, sounding pleased with her own vast creativity.

"Oh. *That's cute*," I said, trying to sound convincing.

As we finished hauling ourselves up the stairs I wondered what I had gotten myself into. How can I turn this alpaca-loving, salad-hating girl "shiny" (if I may borrow Venus's word of the day). And if I'm successful, then shouldn't I win the regional science competition, a date with Swen, my fifteen seconds of fame on TV, *and* a Nobel Prize in Physics for engineering a miracle?

I shook my head and returned to my harsh reality. I followed Susan down a hallway and into a dark room. She turned on a light.

"Here's my room," Susan announced from halfway across her palace of a crib.

"Oh, *wow!*" I said.

What struck me about Susan's room was the size. It was colossal. I felt so little. I mean, I'm only five feet but, dang, I definitely felt like elfin magic.

And being surrounded by gallons and gallons of dark purple paint, I decided this place wasn't just about elves; this place screamed of wizards and everything else that goes with those folks. There were silver painted stars on Susan's ceiling and crystal balls and other types of unicorny-themed accessories on her shelves and dresser.

Her bed was halfway covered with a very lush velvety black comforter and was housed in a loft area with her desk thoughtfully placed underneath.

And then there were at least a hundred posters and drawings strewn about covering most of her floor. At first glance, I could tell it was all her artwork. She was like this out-of-control maniac artist.

I tried very hard not to crush any drawings with my big ole silver boots as I walked around the edges. I decided to take a picture of Susan in her room as a "before" picture with my camera purse. I had her lean by her wall as I took her picture. Then I began to warm up the ole conversation.

"So, you're, like, into wizards and fairies?"

Susan picked up a stray drawing and set it on her bed. "I prefer *hobbits.*"

"Aren't they all kinda like the same thing?" I said, not really down with political correctness when it came to mythical creatures and freakish beings.

"Absolutely *not*," Susan said with the same condescending tone I knew we would have to work on. As I was trying to figure out what to say next, Susan continued with my education on the magical freaked-out kingdom.

"Hobbits are very similar to you and I but they are smaller and have hairy feet. Elves and fairies are smaller than hobbits and have a humanistic form. And even though they possess magical powers, they are *very mischievous*."

I looked at all the pictures on the floor. One hobbit had some nasty-looking hairy feet. "So, then why are you into the guys with the hairy feet but can't do any magic?" I asked, feeling a bit perplexed.

"Because hobbits are *truthful* and *sincere*, Luz."

I almost wanted to bust out screaming, so to keep myself from totally losing it, I bit my lip and turned away to discover Susan's ginormous bookshelf that I must have missed due to unicorn overload. Her bookshelf had a ladder. *A ladder.*

Must take a picture of this. As I gazed at Susan's books, I noticed there was a rather interesting drawing of a girl who resembled Susan and who, well, kinda, looked like a hobbit. I couldn't be sure if she was a hobbit since I couldn't see the feet in the drawing.

"Did you draw that?" I asked, pointing to the drawing that was hanging a bit on the crooked side.

"Yeah."

"Who is that?" I asked, trying to straighten the picture.

"It's J-girl," Susan said, like I knew *exactly* whom she was talking about.

"Oh, okay," I said lightly, not really having a clue.

"Don't you wanna know who J-girl is?" Since she was fully aware that she had a *captive* (read: imprisoned) audience, she let me give a courtesy nod.

"Well, I'll start from the beginning. There was this beautiful dark elf named Kimus. At first, Kimus wanted to save the hobbits from destruction from this mysterious creature called the Coo Coo Na Na who loved to eat hobbits. And so Kimus thought she could trick the creature by transforming all the hobbits into beautiful elves. She transformed all of them except one."

"Except for J-girl," I anticipated.

"Right!" Susan said excitedly.

"J-girl knew something was up and didn't trust Kimus. She didn't have any desire whatsoever to be one of Kimus's little Kim-A-Long new elves. And so one day, when J-girl was riding Frotastic, her magical alpaca . . ."

I snapped a picture of J-girl. "Like yours?"

"Yes, *like mine*. Anyway," Susan continued, annoyed that I had interrupted her story, "when J-girl was riding Frotastic, her magical alpaca, she overheard some elves from the kingdom of Blisteria. And they were talking about how Kimus was only transforming the hobbits because she wanted to run the elf kingdom. And it was only a matter of time before she would use her new tribe of transformed hobbits to start a war in Blisteria. It was J-girl who saved the day."

"How did she save them?" I asked, knowing I wouldn't believe the answer.

"She made sweaters from the wool of the alpaca and that magically morphed the elves back to hobbits," revealed Susan.

So now at this point, I'm trying to figure out if Susan is talking code to me and doesn't want me to change her or her hairy feet.

"Hey, Susan, I'm sorry I can't stay too long. You know, homework? Can I show you what I have brought for you to wear for the next few days for this science experiment?" I was hoping to muster up some more enthusiasm.

Susan knocked off the picture she had put on her bed and sat down like a bump on a log. "Yeah, I guess so."

I pulled out a few green shirts to show Susan. Thank God she liked them. And then I found out she liked green because it reminded her of leprechauns. Imagine that. We finally found a button-down green shirt that actually was a little more formfitting than the sweatshirt she normally wore and it looked decent.

"I have some green jeans that could go with this shirt," Susan added, as if that color combo was going to wash with me.

I quickly told her that we should go for a dark pair of pants so that the focus traveled from her shirt to her face and then that would complement her red hair.

Next, I had her test a scent that, like Mase's, was formulated to appeal to a specific target audience. For Susan I had the band kids in mind. I figured she liked it because when I sprayed the air so she could take a sniff, she grabbed the bottle and sprayed some in her mouth.

"That's really not to be digested. You should only wear it on your skin, you know, like perfume," I hinted strongly.

"Then why does it smell like brownies?"

"Well, one of my theories that I'm testing is that when people get a whiff of you, they will associate you with that yummy smell. And this, therefore, will make you yummy. How's that sound to you, Suz?" I was trying to get her to jump on the ole freak-of-science bandwagon.

"Don't call me *Suz*. My stepmom calls me that and *I hate her*," Susan snapped abruptly.

"Got it. *Lo siento*. But you gotta admit, it smells great," I said as I sprayed some more eau de brownie in the air to try to quickly change her focus from wicked stepmother to wicked brownies.

"Yeah . . ." Susan wrinkled her nose in search of more brownie smell.

"I have just a few more things that are really small but I think we will get huge results."

"Like what?" asked Susan, now actually sounding curious.

"Your *hair*."

Susan had kept the same horrible hairstyle she had had in elementary school. She wore it in French braids, which would be cool if she was on the drill team or on the cheer squad. But she wasn't. Furthermore, Susan's braids were tired looking and sad.

After I untangled one of her braids, I was surprised how long and thick her hair was. For a moment, I wondered if she had borrowed some of my hair harnesser. I parted her hair on the side and let it hang down, and with a little help from some mousse, it was perfect. Susan actually looked cute!

With a gentle knock on the open door, Mr. De la Cruz finally brought our personal pan pizzas with a small salad for each of us. It totally looked like it was delivered from a restaurant. I was starving. Susan and I took a break and cleared a space on the floor among her sketches and markers and munched down.

After eating, I suggested to Susan that this would be a good time to try some self-tanner jelly beans.

"Don't eat these on an empty stomach. Because the carrots and sugar can give you a frothy feeling like when you take vitamins," I warned.

"I don't like carrots or any vegetables," Susan said, rubbing her nose.

"I promise they don't taste like carrots—that's only one of the components. They actually taste like jelly beans. You like jelly beans, don't you?"

Susan looked up at the ceiling trying to recall any preferences. "I guess," she said.

For starters, I gave Susan five jelly beans and then we waited to see how tan she would go.

"Aren't you going to have any?" Susan asked suspiciously.

I kept my gaze on her arms to see if her skin started to change color. "No, because I'm already tan enough," I said, as if she didn't realize that I was *Latina* and naturally brown.

"Oh," Susan said as she tried to pick out a piece of stuck jelly bean in her teeth with her finger.

We waited for about ten minutes and nothing happened. I wondered if I had given her enough. I mean, she was a big girl, y'know? I was about to hand her a few more jelly beans when I saw her cheeks glow rosy pink.

The hint of color to her face was subtle and I didn't want to give her any more jelly beans because I was afraid she might end up looking like a lobster.

Now with her hair down, her new shirt, new perfume, tan, uh, coloring, I was ready for Susan to check herself out in her mirror.

"So, what do you think?" I asked, very pleased with my new creation.

"Hmmm . . . it's alright," said Susan as she leaned a bit closer to her mirror to see, since I had suggested she not wear her Coke-bottle glasses.

"Alright? You look fabulous! Really. And tomorrow, you're going to have the most amazing day. Now, stand against your shelf as I take an 'after' shot." I had the utmost confidence.

After our photo session I gently talked with Susan about her voice. The girl had a sky-high GPA, but when she opened her mouth, she pretty much sounded like a cross between a zombie and a bull-frog.

Then boom! I had an Einstein moment. When I asked how she spoke to Frotastic, Susan immediately baby talked to me. It was kinda icky at first, but it was definitely a huge improvement over her regular voice.

I told her when she's at school she had to pretend like she was talking to Frotastic all day long, especially when sitting and eating lunch with the band kids. I also mentioned that she couldn't do this experiment partially; she had to go all the way to ensure scientific accuracy and her personal success. And that would include docu-menting her new experiences.

I had made her a very lo-tech Pic Purse—a disposable camera camouflaged by a brown lunch bag. I was sure she'd be scrawling freakish beings all over it before long. She just gave me a blank stare.

"Now, why do I have to eat with the band kids? They're dumb."

"Susan, *you're* in band *with them*."

"Yeah, that's how I know they're dumb," Susan said, having no problem dissin' her peeps.

"Well, I'm having different people mix in different groups. I thought this would be a great challenge for you since you're a differ-ent type of person in, well, the same group. And especially after hearing your J-girl story, I think this is totally you."

"Are you kidding?" Susan asked while eating a stray jelly bean she'd found on the floor.

"You're like J-girl in that you're going to help this band tribe not get labeled as dumb. You can find out what makes this group cool and protect them from all the evil Kimuses at school. You could do that, couldn't you?" Then I shut my mouth tight and waited.

Susan started thinking about what I had said. I felt like I had struck a chord with her, which was amazing in itself, since I had had such a turbulent day and all the neurons in my brain were pretty much fried. In a word, I was desperate.

"Okay, Luz, I'm going to do this for the extra credit and that's it. But if something bad happens to me, just remember, something bad will happen to *you*," she agreed, with the kiss of a threat.

"Oh, Susan, nothing bad is going to happen to you because we are in this *together*," I said in my best Gamma High cheerleading voice, which really fell flat, because I am so not a rah-rah, because I am a scientist for God's sake.

I tried to give Susan a sisterly hug, but it was like hugging a dead person (or dead hobbit, for that matter). So, I decided to start gathering up my stuff because it was late and I still had a pile of homework to do.

And when I reminded Susan not to eat more than five of those jelly beans a day, I could feel her little beady eyes just following me around the room as I double-checked to make sure I had all my stuff together. It was spooky. Her staring was freaking me out so much that I decided to jump into one last attempt at *la conversación*.

"Hey, Susan, you didn't finish your story. What happened to the beautiful elf named Kimus?"

"She was *murdered*."

"Oh, well, that's fascinating. I think you definitely need to illustrate that story," I said, disguising the freaked-outness in my voice.

"I have. Do you want to see the part where Kimus is destroyed?" Susan said, now totally sounding like a freak as she kneeled down and looked through the hundreds of drawings on the floor.

"You know what, maybe some other time. I've really got to go. If you have any questions about this experiment, then call me or text me, okay? Don't worry, I'll let myself out. See ya tomorrow. Oh, *y gracias por la pizza y ensalada*," I said quickly as I left Susan alone standing in the middle of her room with her drawings and J-girl.

I ran, or really I flew, down the stairs like that ill-fated fairy. I called my mom, who was already on her way. I was going to talk in Spanish and tell her I was being kidnapped except I know Susan makes straight A's in Spanish and if she heard me it would destroy everything I had created in the last two hours.

She was the last Gamma Glamma transformation on the books. And now I could finally get some sleep, I thought. But I began to wonder if I could with this itchy scalp.

Chapter

11

My hair was now growing at a freakish speed and I looked like a mini Bigfoot. The sprawling strands were so long, in fact, that they'd started to collect all kinds of debris, like dead frogs, stray schoolbooks, and even a slam book. Walking was like trying to navigate an obstacle course. I tripped on my new locks and fell on the dirty school floor helpless and called out to Bridge.

When she answered my 911 call, she tried to speak, but because her nails were so long and were actually dragging and scratching the floor, they made a horrible scraping sound that drowned out her voice and pierced my ears.

As I peered through the veil of my Rapunzel locks, I saw Adam skip by oblivious to me and wearing my favorite silver magnetic boots. He was using my camera purse to take pictures of Venus and Swen, who were in total make-out mode.

I tried to scream in horror but my mouth was muffled by hair. Then out of the girls' bathroom came a giant hobbit carrying a sky-high stack of pizzas. As he passed me, his huge hairy feet tangled in my locks, causing him to fall *on me.* The hot cheese and pepperoni oozed from his boxes and burned my face.

I struggled toward the water fountain to cool the blisters that had formed on my forehead and nose. And at that moment, Mase came screaming around the corner running from a giant fairy who was on a skateboard wielding an axe.

"This can't be real!" I screamed.

And at three o'clock in the morning, it wasn't. But what was real was the fact that I hadn't slept in days and it wasn't getting any better. So, I did something I hadn't done in a really long time. I found my dog, Señor Shortie, a rat terrier with a huge belly, and took my pillow and just laid down with him. As I started to pet him, he farted in his sleep. It wasn't that bad. I mean my life, not Shortie's gas attack. My real life couldn't be as bad as my nightmares, right? And after a few more moments, I finally fell asleep.

At school in the morning, I saw the world through half-closed eyes. I could barely take two steps without yawning. But it wasn't like anyone could see me anyway because I was hiding behind the large prickly bushes by the side of the school. I did, however, wake up for just a sec when I leaned in too close and snagged the crap out of my pink sweater, which, ironically I'd accessorized with hundreds of safety pins.

On this bright and sunny morning, I played science spy and watched Bridge and Adam, who were hanging out with some of the J+L crew. B-Dawg actually came up and talked to Bridge! Even though she flipped her hair (like we had practiced) and gave a big smile of confidence, I could tell that she was still very nervous. She kept checking the length of her nails every so often to make sure they hadn't started growing again.

I could also hear Bridge's new and improved laugh. It made me laugh too, because from this distance I could tell that Adam was getting a wee bit jealous from all the attention that Bridge was receiving. He was pretending like he wasn't noticing by scrolling through his phone for some important info. Or maybe Adam was upset because Bridge and B-Dawg had almost matching nerd-alert librarian sweaters.

I jotted these little observations in my special journal I had decorated to show Swen how professionally I kept my "scientific notations."

"Is spying part of your scientific method?" said a voice from behind me.

Startled, I scribbled my purple gel pen all over my journal page. Dang. As I turned around to stare down my latest stalker, I froze. There was Swen standing with his hands in his pockets.

"Yeah, you could say that. Is spying part of your investigative reporting?" I tried to flirt back.

"Without a doubt," Swen said, moving closer to me.

"Hey, I'm sorry I haven't called you back yet. This experiment has been taking over my life."

Swen inched in even closer and I panicked. I still had a science project to tend to, but secretly, I wanted to pass out.

"It's okay. So, how's it going?" Swen said, looking in the direction of the J+L crowd.

"It's going really well." I put on my science voice. "You see that girl in the red sweater?" As I pointed to Bridge in the distance, Swen leaned in next to me to peer through a branch. My heart started beating so loud I was almost afraid he would hear it. So, in my most professional, scientific manner, I continued, "That's my best friend, Bridget. She was the first to undergo the experimental protocols and her transition into the J+L clique has been pretty seamless."

"That's interesting. But do you have a more dramatic case than her? I mean, she does seem pretty cute to start with." Swen was sounding totally like a serious journalist.

My stomach was about to drop when, as if on cue, Mase rolled up on his skateboard and popped off of it. Nearing the front of the school, he was joined by four other black-clad kids roaring on skateboards.

"When did he have time to meet *those* guys?" I thought out loud.

"Isn't that your boyfriend?" asked Swen.

"*Omigod*, no! That's Mason Milam. He's kind of a loner, so that's why I've been experimenting with him to gel with the Dramaticas." I wanted to make absolutely sure I cleared up any confusion as to my status with Mase.

"What have you done to change him?" asked Swen, pulling out a small pad of paper to jot some notes.

"For starters, I put him in a wardrobe appropriate to his selected social group, threw in some tricks to help him vocalize, and added some special cologne as a mood enhancer." It sounded more scientific than it was.

"How's it going so far?" Swen looked up from his pad, ready to make more notations.

I was even more curious than he was. "This is his first day."

Swen laughed. "Wow, that's exciting."

"I just hope it's not too exciting for him," I said under my breath, looking at my Watchame. The bell was about to go off at any second.

"Look, I know you're just getting started but I'd like to do a teaser to this story. I think the science cluster will get a lot of mileage from your project. That's why I wanted to meet with you."

The bell sounded and terror struck my gut. "No, we can't. It's too soon! From a *scientific* standpoint, that is. If this were in the paper too early, it would blow their covers and mine. And the consequences would be *nuclear*. I can't risk it. I'm sorry."

"Okay, then let me know when you think a good time would be," he suggested, putting away his notes in his back pocket and adjusting his backpack.

"Okay," I said, feeling a huge wave of relief.

"Are you just documenting everyone's experience on campus or are you doing it off campus as well?"

"To be completely honest, I'm just working on the school aspect of it. But you're right. I guess I should observe these cliques outside school. I'll just have to find the time to schedule it all in," I said, pondering where I was going to magically find more time. We both started to walk away from the bushes to the front of the building.

I must have looked really tired because Swen took a moment and just stared at me. I figured that I probably should have applied more concealer under *mis ojos* to cover up my dark zombie circles so I wouldn't be scaring him and the rest of the student body.

"Let me know if I can help you, Luz. I'm really good at research." He smiled and I swooned.

"Thanks," I said as he disappeared. Then, before I left, I snapped a picture of Bridge twirling her hair, a now completely natural gesture for her, and wondered to myself what dark forces I had unleashed on my friends.

I have no idea how I made it through the first four classes. In science, Dr. Hamrock wanted to know how everything was going. I told him things were fine and on schedule. He left me alone only because we had Vice Principal Sekin auditing our class. At least during study hall I was able to sleep. Kinda.

My mind was at lunch. I just wanted to know what was going to happen or not happen with my scientific specimens. It's funny how I came to this school so I could be a science goddess *and* be fabulous and now all I do is live for lunch period.

As I walked into the cafeteria, my nose informed me that today was lasagna day. I hoped that the overpowering smell wouldn't smother Susan's eau de brownies.

I looked at the J+L table. It looked like everyone was there. I decided to make my rounds past the other cliques.

I strolled by the band table and saw that Susan was sitting in the middle of everyone. So far so good, I thought. She wasn't talking, but at least no one was showing her any dislike or disgust (I mean this *was* high school and it's hard-core). I made really quick eye contact with her. She gave me a weak smile, but that was better than the scowl she usually doled out. I didn't say anything and just let her bask in all her hobbit gloriousness.

Next, I looked for Mase at the Dramaticas table, but there wasn't anyone in that section. I wondered if there was some type of drama assembly I didn't know about.

Just then, like in the movies, Mase entered straight down the middle of the cafeteria, which was a pretty bold move for anyone to do, especially a freshman. And he was walking between two black-clad girls with the rest of the Dramatica army marching behind him in slow motion. It was like a freaking parade. This sea of blackness definitely drew an audience.

As Mase passed the J+L table, a piece of Choco Chip ice cream fell out of Venus's mouth. I wished I could have documented that because then I could have died with a big smile on my face. It's severe, I know, but true. I also saw Adam kicking Bridge's leg under the table. Bridge made a scrunchy face and checked to be sure that Adam hadn't left a bruise.

Today Mase's hip-o-meter had just started kicking into overdrive. As he passed the band table, the band girls started to squeal. Trying to follow their cue, Susan was a bit delayed in her awkward squealing.

When Mase passed the sci-fi table, I sensed a strange admiration from my geek brothers. I stared deliberately at Mase, and then he turned and gave me a quick nod of acknowledgment. He was so cool that I took a secret photo. But since Mase knows about all my gadgets and my Pic Purse, he just raised his eyebrow in disapproval.

When the black sea of Dramaticas finally came to their row of tables, they all seemed very smug with their new Dramatica prince. It was almost too good to be true.

At this point in my oh-so-short lunch period, I went to my very own table, which, without Mase, Bridge, Adam, and even Susan, was really kind of lonely. Normally, with adequate sleep I would have wallowed in self-pity for a while, but today sleep was at the top of the menu. I put my head down on the sticky wood laminate. And after twenty minutes of solid sleep, I had "sleeve face." And when my scalp started to itch again I knew it was time for this Rapunzel to give herself a trim in the girls' bathroom.

When I entered the bathroom, to my surprise, I found Bridge already there giving her T-Rex nails a trim.

"Do you have an appointment at the Clip and Snip?" chirped Bridge.

"Like clockwork," I said, with a yawn.

"I think the serum is slowing down, because I am not having to cut my nails every hour. What about you?" she asked, hoping to get a good confirmation on our freakish growth.

"Yeah, I think my scalp is getting less itchy. That or I'm just numb to the feeling because I haven't slept."

"You should take something for that," Bridge suggested.

"I think I'll wait on that. I don't need any more drama."

"Or *Dramaticas*." Bridge laughed.

"*Omigod!* Did you see that?"

"His entrance? It was hypnotizing." Bridge beamed proudly, knowing she had a hand in the successful transformation.

I used my hand to comb through my hair. "Did you hear him talk?"

"No, how about you?" Bridge asked, plucking a fingernail out of the sink and preserving it in a plastic receptacle for further scientific observation.

I shook my head. "Has he used his gum?"

"I don't know," Bridge said as she was comparing the new length of her nails.

"How did he get the hookup with all those people?" I said as I pulled out a small laser pen. As I put up my hair in a ponytail on the top of my head, I held the excess and sliced through with the laser like butter. Singed butter. I was proud of my in-school grooming solution. Much better than an art class paper cutter.

"I'll definitely need to find out the specifics," I said, holding a wad of hair in my hand and waving away the small cloud of smoke. Bridge nodded in approval.

"And I'll need your help finding something teamo supremo to wear to V's party," Bridge said, sounding more and more J+L each day.

"Bridge, you're calling her 'V' now. That's kinda freaking me out." My voice whined more than I would have liked.

"Hey, now. *You* wanted me to fit in with that group, didn't you?" Bridge said, reminding me that I had started this sci-fi drama.

I held up my ponytail to see if I needed to trim any more. "Yes. Yes. *Tienes razón.*"

Being a true best friend, Bridge tried to cheer me up. "Did you see Venus's face when Mase walked in?" We both made eyes at each other and laughed.

"Oh, you mean when the ice cream made an emergency exit from her mouth?" I said, reliving the whole play-by-play of it all.

"*Exactly*," Bridge said.

"It was priceless." I beamed.

"Yeah. Well, I got a picture of that," Bridge said, standing up straight and tall in the mirror. "For your *research*."

The door swung open and a couple of band girls came in to inspect in the mirror the food that had collected in their braces during lunch.

"I love you, best friend," I said with utter love in my heart as I moved over closer to Bridge so we could continue our private conversation.

"I love you, too! Now here, let me help you. That's not even straight. You're off by at least forty-five degrees." Bridge took my laser pen to my hair as I glanced at my Watchame to see how much time we had left.

"Don't worry, we have plenty of time, Luz." As she sliced through my hair, the door flew open and Adam ran in, causing the band girls to make faces and groans as they fled to the halls.

"Luz, you need to get out of here. You're running out of time," Adam said.

"What is it?" I said, feeling a new wave of panic.

"Venus is going to ask Swen to the dance at her party. You need to bust a move *quick* because I also just found out that the Student Council is having people cast their votes tomorrow and again on Monday for finalists," announced Adam. His forehead was beading with perspiration and it looked like he had run from somewhere far to deliver this information.

"Okay, I'll try to figure out a plan or something," I said, having absolutely no clue what to do next.

"Better let me in on your plan because you know I *hate* surprises," Adam reminded me.

"I know, I know. Me too, Adam."

We all three scattered outside the girls' bathroom. And from nowhere Swen popped up in front of me. I swear, he must be carrying around a whacked-out GPS sensor because he always finds me in the worst places and at the worst times.

"Hey, Luz, do you have a sec?" Swen said, sounding mysterious. Adam (who is always interested in my business) hovered over us a bit too close.

"Bellows, do you always use the girls' bathroom?" asked Swen.

"Only when I'm doing interviews," Adam snapped back.

Thank God Bridge was picking up the telepathic message I was sending her. She grabbed Adam's arm and said, "Adam, it's your lucky day. You get to carry my books to class. Let's go."

Adam knew exactly what we were up to. "How lucky for me."

Now that the coast was clear (and this is speaking relatively, because there were tons of other kids coming and going to class and to the next lunch period), Swen and I got back to our little sweet nothings (I *wish*).

"I'm sorry. Now, what were you saying?" I asked, trying not to get lost in his eyes.

"Remember how we talked this morning about how you need to observe your test subjects outside of school?"

"Yeah," I said, worried about what he was going to say next and about being tardy to my next class.

"Well, Venus Hunter just invited me to her party on Saturday. Do you want to come with me? For your research, I mean."

"Sure!" I said, without thinking.

"I can pick you up if you want to give me your address," he added, pulling out his notepad from his back pocket.

"Oh, yeah . . . Can I text you later—if that's cool?" *I* was trying to *be* cool.

"Sure, I'll catch you later." He nodded.

And again he vanished—unlike my problems. No problem? No problem at all. How about a thousand *problemas*?

How about that I'm going to the party of my archenemy? How about that I'm going to a party that I wasn't even invited to?

How about that I'm going with my dream date and my archenemy is going to ask him at the party to go with her to the Homecoming dance?

How am I going to go to a party and be the scientifically neutral observer if I am in the thick of it?

How am I going to convince my parents that this is *not a date* so that Swen can pick me up?

How can I *make* this a date? Am I terrible for wanting to make this a date? I mean, c'mon, this is a chance of a lifetime.

But most importantly, what am I going to wear?

Chapter

12

I ran into Susan when I was scurrying to class. She still looked great but had knocked it down a notch by putting her monster Coke-bottle-sized lenses back on. Chatting away with a guy (of all people), Susan offered him a drawing of a hobbit in a Gamma band uniform.

I was shocked. The guy seemed to genuinely like her drawing. But something struck me as odd, very odd. He seemed to be sporting the *same* tannish complexion that Susan was. I had to intervene immediately.

"Susan, what's up? Who's that?" I asked while putting my hand on her shoulder and steering her away so he couldn't hear us.

"Oh, that's Hector." Susan pushed up her glasses.

"Is he in the band?" I asked, trying to hurry, but be discrete. Susan was having none of that. She turned around and started staring right at him.

"Yeah. He plays the oboe. He said I smelled nice."

I sniffed twice at Susan's neck. She still smelled like brownies. And this was important because I had made the perfume from only all-natural ingredients and didn't use any preservatives, so there was always that off chance that my concoction could go stale and bad. But then again, I couldn't remember if I'd ever smelled bad fudge before.

"Uh, Suz—I mean Susan—I noticed that your friend Hector looked freakishly tan today."

"Yeah. He's from Colombia," Susan said, not getting the sense of my drift. (Obviously, she was going to need a little more prodding.) Yes, it was true that Hector was of Latin descent, but his cheeks and nose were so red it looked like he was on audition for the Ringling Brothers.

"Let me just say . . . *no*, let me just shout it out. Did you give him any of your self-tanning jelly beans?!" Susan didn't stop looking at Hector.

"Yeah. So what?" she said.

I grabbed her broad shoulders and turned her with all my might to look at me. "Well, you can't do that," I said, trying to calm down and override my first instinct of freaking out.

"Why not?" Susan croaked.

At this point, I was pretty much ready to strangle her for challenging me, especially after the bell rang and now I was going to be late *again*. Ever since I started this Gamma Glamma project, my usual punctuality had suffered and I was starting to catch grief about it.

I didn't have the luxury of time to explain to Little Señorita Hobbit in Love that this would blow our cover, ruin our experiment, and possibly make all of us the big butt of high school jokes for the next three years. So, I kept it short and sweet, just like one of my mom's tag lines on one of her campaigns.

"Well, it's strong enough for an hombre but made for a chica," I announced. I think I stumped her.

I continued, "Susan, you didn't happen to mention to Hector what these jelly beans *do*, did you?"

"No. He just saw me eating them at lunch and asked if he could have some of my candy."

"Okay, well, next time tell him he can't have any. And if you can't say that, then tell him they help control your PMS. I promise he won't ask again," I warned.

"You want me to *lie*, Luz?" Susan said, with a hint of disgust.

"Susan, I just don't want anyone else to consume these jelly beans because I only have enough for you."

"Kimus was a liar, Luz. That's why she was murdered," Susan said, to taunt me even more.

"Well, maybe Kimus and I should be locker mates. I gotta go. I'll check in with you later, Susan." I ran as fast as I could to class.

When I got to my algebra class, the students were working on a bunch of word problems. And since I couldn't focus, I decided to do algebra at home later because I needed to solve other problems now. And I needed to come up with a plan. Pronto. The clock was ticking. Not only could I hear the ticking from the loud quartz clock on the wall but I could also definitely feel the time slipping away.

Today was Thursday. I needed to sleep. I needed to figure out how to get people to vote for me. I needed to get my sci-fi friends to get the word out. Maybe I could charm them with my baking, or more specifically, *Bridge's* baking.

I needed to intercept Venus before she asked Swen to the dance and that was going to be as easy as splitting atoms.

And if I showed up at Venus's casa (unofficially not invited), what would she say or do? I started making a list of everything I needed to do. And hypothesized about what would happen to me in every possible situation.

I must have looked like a crazy student because when Mrs. O'Hara came up to me and handed me a note and said someone needed to speak to me, I didn't respond.

"Luz, didn't you hear me? There's someone in the hall who needs to speak with you," Mrs. O'Hara said with her strong Texas drawl. Normally, I would have responded to her, especially because she is one of my favorite teachers. She has the most amazing long red hair, has three kids, looks like a supermodel, and excels in math. She's kinda all perfect and that's how I want to be once Swen and I . . ., well, I'm getting ahead of things here.

I gathered up all my so-called work and hid it under my notebook. I didn't want anybody to know what I was really doing. I grabbed the note and glanced at it as I made my way out the door. The note just read, "Need to speak with Luz Santos." I stepped out and was very surprised to see my visitor.

Lo and behold, there stood Mase, the unofficial newly crowned

prince of the Dramaticas. He just stood there staring at me not saying anything. I wasn't startled by this, since I was used to him starting off the conversation this way.

"Is everything okay?" I asked suspiciously.

Mase shook his head.

"Did you run out of Gabber Gum?" I asked, knowing full well
that I had given him at least fifty gumballs.

He reached into his pocket and pulled out a fistful of colored
gumballs.

"So what's the deal-le-o?" I went on, wondering why he didn't use
any of the gumballs I'd invented. They had a lot of cinnamon in
them, but other than that, they didn't taste *that* bad. Mase grabbed
his throat with a forceful hand.

I didn't know what to make of it. "What? Were you bit by a vam-
pire?"

He shook his head again.

"Dude, you gotta speak. What's going on?"

Mase pulled out a wrinkly piece of paper with a drawing of his
face with a pair of worn-out lips. And around his neck he had drawn
some jail bars with a huge padlock on it. Now, I knew exactly what
he meant.

"You've got to be *kidding* me," I said, shocked.

Mase shook his head no.

"Was it the gum?"

Mase nodded this time with great excitement as he pointed to his
nose to inform me that I indeed had hit it on the nose this time.

"You mean talking nonstop gave you laryngitis?"

Mase tossed his arms up in the air and made a face as if he had
just screamed, "Bingo!"

Suddenly, I had the urge to pick off an old sticker that was on a
locker I was leaning on.

"You know I never thought about that. That's *very* interesting. I
mean Bridge and I are used to talking all the time, so I guess talking
more when we chew the gum doesn't really mess with our vocal
chords. But since you don't speak, I mean out loud, I guess I can see

how that could mess you up. Sorry about that," I apologized, then waited to see his reaction.

He nodded as he accepted my apology and then just gave me a small shrug as to what he should do next.

"I'm not sure, Mase. I need to think about this one. From what I can tell, it seems like you're really rocking with the Dramaticas. It's pretty wild how everyone is drawn to you."

He turned red.

"You have to admit it's pretty cool, right?" I asked, with a smile.

He gave me a quick nod.

"Well, you're still in, right? I still really need you. I know you don't care about being popular or being on the Homecoming Court, but I need you to do this for the greater good of science." I begged him with my eyes as I grabbed one of his rough hands.

Mase rolled his eyes and gave a big sigh. I immediately took that as a yes.

"Is your cologne still working?" I asked as I took a sniff. And, thank goodness, he still smelled good, in a theatrical sort of way.

"Let me talk with Bridge after school about this. We are going to need to figure out how we can get your voice back and the word out so that people will vote for you for the court," I said.

Mase shook his hand loose from mine, which was getting hot and sweaty, because I'd forgotten to let it go. *Yikes.*

"I'll call you later, Mase. *Gracias por todo.*" I grabbed the door handle, ready to get back to my "word" problems.

Mase just shook his head and took off down the hall. As I walked back into class, I gave a little smile to Mrs. O'Hara, who was grading papers at her desk. As I sat back down, I pulled out my personal set of word problems again and just stared at the paper this time wondering how in the world I was going to get out of the mess that I'd invented.

Finally, when school was over, I took a nap. Then I had Bridge come over to talk strategy. I leaned on the kitchen counter for support. Bridge sat on a bar stool with her fingers and nails stretched out across the counter for inspection.

"You look really tired," Bridge said.

"Thanks, Bridge. That's a nice way of saying I look like caca," I grunted as I lifted my head from the counter.

"I wasn't trying to be snarky. I'm just making an observation," she said, beginning to file one of her nails uncontrollably with an emery board.

"Yeah, well my life is a big *ole* observation these days," I said as I poured myself a glass of tea, hoping the caffeine would kick in.

"Hey, how's Susan doing?"

"So far so good. Do you want any tea?"

"Nah," said Bridge, as she continued to file away.

"Well, nobody did anything hideous to her all day. So, I'd call that progress. And if she doesn't give away all her jelly beans, we'll be golden, or at least she'll be rosy. She really doesn't tan that much," I said, then gulped my tea.

"Do you think the band kids will actually vote for her?" Bridge asked.

"You mean for the *Homecoming Court*?"

"Yeah, her name *is* on the list of the freshmen fourteen. Remember?" Bridge said.

"Yeah, I think the first time I heard it, I thought it was a joke."

"I know, me too," Bridge said.

"I mean, the fact that she hasn't been harassed today should be considered a scientific miracle. Anything more, I think I might be pushing it."

"Totally. I know. So, what do you need from me?" Bridge asked as she watched me get up and start pulling out every shiny pot and pan this familia owned.

"Your skills—your baking skills. I need to woo our peeps so they'll vote for us. But it needs to be something really, really amazing and yummy," I said, pulling out a package of chocolate chips. "Maybe with some special ingredients to build up extra enthusiasm."

"Well, vanilla is a good mood enhancer," Bridge suggested.

I opened the bag and enjoyed the aroma. "*Y el chocolate también.*"

Bridge walked over to me since she couldn't resist taking a sample of chocolate. "And you remember that amino acid complex we used in the rat experiment last year to elevate the levels of their empathetic hormones?" Bridge asked.

"Do you still have some?" I recalled the most cooperative rodent habitat I'd ever seen.

Bridge nodded.

"Well, do you remember how that stuff tastes?" I asked, trying to remember if I had tasted any before.

"I can't really remember if I tried any, but, hey, if it tastes funny, then we'll add more sugar and more chocolate."

After several hours of measuring, mixing, and baking, not to mention Bridge running home to get our secret ingredient, we finally decided to test our concoction.

Using extreme caution this time, we started with just one itsy-bitsy bite each, because we didn't want to get too crazy during the first human trial of our new baked goodness.

We waited patiently—being patient is a very important trait for a scientist. As we waited, I pulled out Mase's drawing of his laryngitis to show Bridge.

"Did I tell you that Mase has laryngitis because he was talking so much?"

"Shut up! Was that because of the Gabber Gum?"

"Yeah."

"That's such a cute picture," Bridge gushed.

"Yeah. It is. Just like Mase," I gushed back.

"He's the best. He's such a great artist."

"Yeah, he is."

"Hey, you know what? Since Mase can't talk, we should just get him to draw cute pictures of all of us so that people will vote for us." Bridge now sounded like a totally devoted fan.

"Shut up! That's a great idea," I responded, caught up in the heat of the moment.

"You're my best friend," Bridge said lovingly.

"And you're mine."

"We're sooo lucky."

"And Adam is too," I said, making sure to include Adam in our lovefest.

"He's so lucky to have us as friends," Bridge said kindly.

"I love Adam," I said fondly.

"So do I!" Bridge said, as if she had little hearts for eyes.

I leaned on the counter. "I love Swen, too."

"I love Swen *for* you," Bridge said, giving me a big hug.

I put my arm around my best friend and whispered, "Did I tell you he invited me to Venus's party?"

"How sweet. I love Venus," Bridge said, almost sounding like a robot as she beamed a smile to me.

"So do I," I said, without skipping a beat. Then I felt very, *very* strange. Suddenly something struck me. *The truth.*

"Shut up! What am I saying?" I yanked my arm away from Bridge. "For the love of science, these cookies really *do* sugarcoat things." I waited a minute and looked at my Watchame to see how much time had passed. The cookies should have worn off now, by my calculations. Fifteen minutes had passed since we had taken our small bite, which only meant that a bigger, full-size cookie could promise longer-lasting results.

"Okay, I think I'm myself now. What about you? Are you okay?" I looked very closely at Bridge to see if I could notice any changes.

Bridge looked around the room to see if she felt any differently. "Uh . . . I think so."

"Are you my best friend?" I quizzed Bridge.

"Shut up," Bridge said without a doubt, shooing me off with her hand.

"Okay, maybe that wasn't such a great question. Do you love *Adam*?" I asked, as a trick question.

"Absolutely," Bridge said without a doubt again.

Normal Bridge would never say she "loved" Adam. "Okay, then obviously the cookies still haven't worn off on you."

"But I *love* those cookies. They're the *best*," Bridge said as if she was trying to defend her life.

"Sure, they are," I responded calmly, understanding what I was dealing with.

"Hey, Bridge, do you love it when Shortie farts in my room?"

"Absolutely . . . *not*!" Bridge said, caught in the middle of a love/hate moment.

"Woo, I am so glad you're back," I said, now feeling somewhat relieved.

But I had to be sure so I went, "Do you love Adam?"

"Ewwww," Bridge reacted quickly, like her old self.

"How about Bart?"

"Are you trying to make me vomit on purpose?" That one got Bridge peeved.

"Okay, now I know you're *really* back to normal."

"That's really 'speaking relatively' during your experiment."

"Very funny, Bridge. But at least we know the cookies work and will last through lunchtime. But that's all the time we'll need to get people to fall in love with us and then vote."

"That was *amazing*. I can't believe it was only one bite!" Bridge picked up a cookie and inspected it. "That's so funny."

"They are pretty potent, aren't they? Hey, I did like your idea about getting Mase to create some campaign drawings to help get the vote out. That could be really *potent*, too."

"Just make sure he makes me look pretty, because if he makes me look ugly or fat, I'll just have to make a serum that will cause me to vanish into thin air." Now she was sounding like her usual scaredy-cat self.

"I'm really glad you're back to your old self, Bridge!"

Bridge and I carefully measured the cookies. We figured each cookie's power of persuasion would roughly last between twenty and thirty minutes.

Next, I would tell Mase that he didn't have to worry about talking. We would let his art speak for him. We would still consider it as a communication skill, and I broadly included it as a "vocal variable" under my experimental protocols.

While cleaning up the kitchen, Bridge warned me that arriving with Swen to Venus's party would be certain social suicide. Venus had already announced to the J+L girls that she had been planning on going with Swen to Homecoming since the school year started and was going to "make him an offer he couldn't refuse."

I decided I would tell Swen that I would meet him at the party. This way I could secretly act like Adam's date so that Venus wouldn't suspect anything or razz me about not being invited to her elitist soiree. And when I had my chance, I would ask Swen to go with me to Homecoming (in the name of science and journalism of course).

Then when Swen would tell Venus he couldn't go with her, she would come after Adam just to be a burr in my butt. I would let her steal my faux beau Adam. It could be the most perfect plan I have ever devised.

As Bridge finished loading the last of our baking mess in the dishwasher, I called Mase and asked him to draw illustrations of himself, Bridge, Adam, Susan, and me for our Homecoming campaign. When I hung up the phone, I heard my mom struggling through the front door and went to help her with her armful of groceries.

"Hey, girls, how's it going? I see you've done some serious baking."

"It's some serious *science*, Mom."

"Yeah. It's for our school project tomorrow," Bridge said, carefully laying out a layer of cookies on wax paper. Mom started putting away the groceries but the aroma was too overpowering.

"Gosh, they smell *muy deliciosa*," Mom said as she looked at the display of perfectly packed cookies.

"Thanks. It's our *secret* recipe," Bridge said.

"Ohh, here's a little broken cookie. If you don't mind me eating it, I won't mind about my excess carbs."

"Well, Mrs. . . . ," Bridge stuttered. But before Bridge could catch her, Mom inhaled the cookie.

"Mmm! That's really good," Mom said, licking the chocolate off her fingers.

A pang of panic pinched me. "Thanks . . . ," I said.

"I love them. Luz, what do you call them?" asked Mom, the curious.

"Uh, we haven't made a name for them yet."

"I think you should call them 'Fantastics'!" Mom said, as if *that* was a good idea or something.

"Okay . . . ," I said, slightly annoyed as I decided to pick up a wash-cloth and wipe down the already clean counter.

"Or how about 'Snacktastics'?" Mom continued.

Bridge gave a weak courtesy laugh. At this point, I had to inter-vene—it was way too much for me to witness. My mom was acting crazy. These cookies must work fast, I thought.

"Hey, Mom, do you like my shirt?" I asked, conducting a little test, and shooting a look to Bridge to make sure she was paying attention.

"Now, what is that . . . a kitten dancing with a skeleton and a bulldozer?" (Another Mase masterpiece.)

"Yeah."

"It's adorable. You have fantastic taste, just like these Snacktastics." Mom gave me a courtesy hug.

Bridge shot a look of shock at me from across the kitchen. She, like me, totally knows that my opinionated mother *hates* my clothes.

"Well, I'm going to let you girls finish up and I'm going to get dressed so I can make my favorite *hija* her favorite *comida*," Mom said in a singsongy voice as she made her exit.

"I think the Snacktastics got a hold on your mom."

But by the time we finished cleaning the kitchen and my mom came down, I decided once again to ask her what she thought of my wardrobe choice. This time her answer was definitely different.

"It's a little . . . bizarre, maybe? But you should always remember that it's just my own opinion and you're old enough to make your own choices. *And live with them.*"

She's back, I thought. Bridge and I just rolled our eyes at each other.

After dinner, Bridge went back home and I went back to my room/laboratory. I decided to make sure I had all my equipment in check for school the next day. Tomorrow was going to be a big day for all of us.

I made sure my camera purse was downloaded and ready to shoot. I made sure I had fresh batteries in my pen microphone. I loaded new tapes in my shoes just in case I had to document tons of convo. I bagged extra pieces of Gabber Gum. I thought I'd give some to Susan if she didn't start making more chitchat. I also made sure to have backup supplies of everyone's cologne and perfume.

Most importantly, I made sure to put the cookies in Tupperware. Bridge said she would make a few extra batches of Snacktastics. It wasn't that bad of a name now that I thought about it.

In addition to all of my accessories, I would bring an extra pair of nail clippers for Bridge. Come to think of it, though, my head hadn't itched for hours and Bridge's nails hadn't needed a trim. Woo-hoo. Maybe the activator serums were finally wearing off.

Oh, what to wear?! Tomorrow, I would again brave wearing a white button-down shirt. But this time I would be ready for any stain disasters. I pretreated this shirt so that nothing embarrassing would stick on it.

I tried to write down in my journal what was planned to take place next, but I just kept imagining what it would be like if Swen did pick me up and what would I wear to Venus's party.

I'd like to look a bit more flirty, so that maybe he would see me as more than just a kooky science experiment. As I sat on my bed, I imagined that he would pick me up in his cool-looking Scion. It's so cute. It looks like a little bread box with wheels. I could totally see him opening my door when we got to Venus's house and holding my hand as we strolled up to her door. At this thought, I could feel all my DNA strands tingling with happiness.

We would walk in and all our friends from school would tell us how perfect we looked together. Swen would then offer to get me something to drink and ask me if I wanted something to eat. I would tell him, no, not right now because I was watching my figure. And then he would say he was watching it for me!

Okay, maybe that was a bit too much *queso*, but in my imagination it sounded pretty good. I thought about sending an e-mail to Swen to let him know that I would just meet him at Venus's, but it was getting late, so I decided it would be better if I told him in person. That way, I could have another chance just to *look* at him.

And I also needed to spend some quality time with Adam to figure out how we planned to orchestrate this date with danger at Venus's house. I just hoped she would take the bait.

But right now, I wasn't going to start worrying about what I'd do if she didn't, because all I wanted to concentrate on was how my friends and I could become finalists. And even more importantly, how I would ask Swen to the dance.

I started feeling extremely sleepy and it was such a great feeling. I wasn't worried about nightmares because I knew I would totally pass out tonight. And as far as mañana went, I would be prepared. Without any evidence or scientific fact, I just knew in my gut that something amazing was going to transpire tomorrow, and I could hardly wait.

Chapter

13

I hit the school steps an hour before the bell and ran up to Mase so fast that we almost had our second megacollision of the year. I could tell from the smirk on his face that he'd held to his agreement and was extremely proud of the drawings he'd made. Popping off his skateboard like a pro, Mase got on his knees to unzip his backpack. Slowly and methodically, he began pulling out his postcard-sized masterpieces. Time was a tickin' and Mase was stickin'. I couldn't wait any longer. He was *killing* me.

"Por favor, let me see. Let me see!"

Mase handed me the first picture. It was of Bridge. She looked very pouty, and she was twirling her hair. The scene looked like it was pulled straight out of an Abercrombie & Fitch catalog. It was beyond cute. Mase had her sitting on the beach looking at the sun in a red tank that popped from the black-and-white landscape. It was fabu.

Standing over him, I messed up Mase's bed head even more. "Mase, you're brilliant," I said.

Mase, who now sensed my urgency, decided not to waste time acknowledging my compliment as he yanked out the next drawing. Again, it was a black-and-white portrait, this time featuring Susan on a half shell just like that famous painting *The Birth of Venus*, which I've only seen in art books and on fridge magnets.

In this rendering of Susan, Mase had made her hair much longer, like the hair those girls in the Pantene ads have, and he had her in what looked like a band shirt except it was a tad longer, kinda like a cute polo shirtdress.

As Susan was gloriously standing in her half shell, she was also holding her French horn like a shield. The only thing that was in color was Susan's green band shirt. I was totally tripping, because, well, she looked *amazing*.

"What else?" I asked, feeling like a kid at Christmas, totally bratty and impatient.

The next postcard portrait was of Adam. Adam was whispering, and in the word bubble that normally contains words, Mase had created fantastic images of Hollywood lights, Hummers, and money. Visually it totally represented excitement and scandal. And at the bottom of the drawing there were chicas of all sorts (one looked very similar to Venus) grasping at Adam as if he were some type of teen idol!

"Adam is soo going to love that. Don't be surprised if he tattoos that on his body," I teased.

Mase smirked.

"You and Adam should clear up your misunderstanding," I pleaded. "I *know* he didn't nominate you."

It killed me that these two weren't putting their differences behind them. If Adam had actually nominated him, so what? I mean, with these postcards, Mase was now helping all of us become finalists (himself included).

Mase just rolled his eyes as he pulled out the next drawing. And it was for me and it was to die for. It had clusters of geeks who were creating this science experiment with test tubes. In the picture, the tubes had exploded, and in the middle of the explosion, Mase had drawn the cutest picture of me, or rather my Watchame chica avatar.

I know that sounds totally like a me lovefest, but it was really sweet. He had drawn my little cartoon character wearing his test tube T-shirt and boots that he'd made for me (in my real life). And then he had given her a punk girl tutu with like fiberoptic lights on it so it glowed like a Christmas tree. (That was a rockin' idea, and I thought, *I* must *make one of those skirts for real*.)

And in this rendition, instead of the buns that are on my little mini-me chica, he had drawn long, flowing hair tied up in a high ponytail on top of her head secured with steel chains. It was super cute and awesome, to say the least.

So then I said, "Mase, I love you. I mean it." And then I gave him a big ole brotherly bear hug. He turned red. I get such a kick when he blushes. *Es adorable!*

Then something hit me. "Mase, you did make one for you, didn't you? I mean, a drawing of you to get votes, right?" I asked firmly, with an arched eyebrow.

Mase grimaced.

"You did, *didn't you?*" I said, now sounding like a total science control freak.

Mase nodded and I can't tell you how relieved I was. Then he reluctantly pulled out his drawing of himself.

"*Wow!*" That's all I could say. Mase had drawn such a profound picture that there were no words to do it justice.

At first glance, it looked like hundreds of Dramatica kids in the picture looking out. But when you looked at it from a distance it was a self-portrait of Mase made up from tons of Dramatica kids. It was *dramatic.*

"Boy, you *are* good," I declared with complete conviction.

As I looked at all these pictures again, I couldn't believe how realistic and fabulous they were. We all looked so good—like we should be in a band or have our own TV series. But I also thought they needed something more. A bit more *Gamma Glamma* action perhaps? Well, for starters, we at least needed our names on these postcards, because even after three months at this school, we were still newbies to this establishment.

Next, I wanted to add some kind of ad slogan (like my mom does) so that people would remember us. But before I'd even consider taking out a Sharpie and scrawling random verbiage, I'd have to ask for Mase's blessing. Otherwise, I'd feel like I'd be destroying his art or something.

"Mase, can I put our names on these drawings? Just so folks know who we are?" I asked extra sweetly.

He nodded.

"What about if I added like a teeny little slogan so that people would remember us. Is that okay?" I asked, trying to push the envelope a bit more.

Again Mase nodded. He really didn't seem to mind. But he seemed tired, like I'd been. Then it hit me. Had he lost sleep over these drawings?

"Mase, you stayed up all night, didn't you?"

He just fiddled with his bag and didn't look up.

I kneeled down to get on his level. "You stayed up all night for me?"

Mase nodded.

"Man, Mase, I really owe you. I'm sorry, but I have to ask you to do one more thing. Don't hate me, but I need you to help me document your experience."

Mase stood up and started to walk off, and I had to jump up and follow full steam if I was going to close this sale.

"I know you don't like to write, but you can journal. I mean, you can draw what goes on in a day in the life of a Dramatica. Or, if it's easier, you can take pictures."

Mase shot me a crazy look as he glanced down at my Pic Purse like I was going to give him that. I'm a bit crazy but I'm not that big of a freak.

"No, no purse for you. You get *this*," I said as I pulled out a little black box. I quickly opened it and pulled out a big, shiny ring.

He stopped in his tracks. It was a little skull ring. And all he had to do was push on the skull's head and the eyes would take a picture. It could only take ten pictures at a time but it would still serve its purpose. I could tell that Mase thought it was cool by the way he cracked a smile. His smile cracked even wider when I gave him the lunch that I'd actually brought from home. It was the least I could do.

Next, I zipped off to find Adam, but not before I took a picture of Mase with all his drawings.

Alone in the school's media center, I found Adam purposely highlighting people, places, and things in the *Gamma Gazette* newspaper—anything that was important or trendy. Today, Adam was carefully decked out in a yellow polo with a pair of long denim shorts and a *Gilligan's Island* bucket hat. He looked hot, for, like, my friend.

"Hey, Gilligan, I thought they only made pedal pushers for girls," I teased.

"Well, then I guess you'll never get to experience this sweet sensation, Skipper."

Ow and meow. Adam could cut deep. After we kissed and made up (I mean figuratively), I told him that I thought he really did look good.

After showing him Mase's postcard portraits of all of us, Adam was totally pumped to be a part of the campaign. And he agreed with me that they needed some kind of zippy, smart slogans and he would be more than happy to help me write them.

To Bridge's beach portrait we decided to add the tagline "Want to Sea Fresh? Vote for Bridget Joiner." It was a play on the word *sea*, and I thought that was really cute.

And for Adam's drawing we wrote, "Want to Be in the Know? Vote for Adam Bellows." For Susan's drawing we came up with "Want Music to Your Ears? Vote for Susan Seamus." It was a bit of a stretch, we knew, but it worked.

And for my picture we were going to put "Want to Experience Scientific Elegantz?" but then I reminded Adam that most of the kids in the science cluster were boys and the last thing they want to do is be elegant. So we changed it to "Want Scientific Intelligence? Vote for Luz Santos."

And then when we came to Mase's portrait, it was easy. We wrote, "Want Drama? Vote for Mason Milam." But then we crossed out the word *Vote* and wrote *SCREAM*. We knew this would definitely help get those Dramaticas' attention.

Our next project was to make copies of our campaign postcards. We made so many copies that we had to replace one of the ink cartridges in one of the copiers. I stuffed as many postcards in my backpack as I could. As Adam was stuffing his messenger bag, we talked about how we should get these cards out. "How about the library?" I began.

"No, Luz. No one ever really goes in there," Adam said, making his "you're so dumb" face.

"How about the study hall?" There wasn't much to do in there but sleep and eat and, yeah, maybe study.

"People can't walk around in there, plus Miss Dooley throws away any left-behind scrap of paper in her room."

"Then where do you suggest, Mister know-it-all?" I asked, feeling a bit irritated.

Then Adam said, "First, I think you should put me and Mase in the girls' bathrooms. Girls don't graffiti and tear up stuff like us men folk. Then I'll put you and Bridge in the boys' bathrooms and locker rooms. Y'all are cute enough not to be defamed."

"Gracias," I deadpanned.

"Then, for Susan, the band room and the vending machine by the band hall. It's a *must*," Adam ordered.

"Why?" I asked, as if it were a silly idea.

"Because the band kids here either hang out in the band room before school to practice or hide. And if they aren't there, then they are loitering by the snack machine. And we don't have to worry about them doing something dastardly to Susan's drawing," he added with brutal honesty, but I knew he was really right.

"How about the lunchroom?"

"No, we need to keep the lunchroom neutral. Otherwise you risk us being overexposed, which is way worse than being unpopular."

"*What?* You're kidding me. You love to be overexposed, Adam."

"Let me break it down for you. You know how we feel about stars that are on magazine covers every freaking day? We love them for a few weeks and then the next thing you know we have an insatiable desire to start blackening their teeth at bus stops."

"You are *so* right."

Adam handed me another stack of cards to stuff in my already full backpack. "We need to keep this *viral*."

"Huh?"

"I mean that we can't look like we're trying too hard, or for the next three years Gamma's gonna be our house of pain."

"So where's this line we don't want to cross?" I said, trying to zip up my bag and not crush the postcards that were bulging out.

"Just be random, like we didn't think as much about it as we are now. Scatter these babies in the hall, by the trash, in desks. Wherever and whatever, and keep a close eye on where they land and travel."

"What about doing a news story and a blog about the postcards?"

"What, are you kidding me? I can't write a story about me. I mean, I'm a press junkie but not a narcissistic junkie." And then Adam kissed his own postcard.

"What about Swen?" I asked, in desperation.

"Oooh. She lives, she breathes, she thinks!" Adam squealed, going off the deep end and starting to get on my nerves.

"Adam, shut up."

"Alright. Just leave it alone and maybe your Super Swen will come up with the idea."

"Adam, we don't have time."

"Okay, then ask him and tell him you'll make out with him or something."

"That's *so* trashy."

"Nothing wrong with trashy, if it's biodegradable," Adam noted as he started to pick up the trash and put away all of the supplies that we'd used.

"Oh, did I mention that I was invited to Venus's party by *Swen*."

"Ahhh, disaster!" Adam said, as he was beginning to power down the copy machines.

"Yes, I know, but I'm gonna tell him I'll just meet him there and then I'll ride with Bridge."

"Clever," said Adam, relieved that I was putting thought into the matter.

"And then I'll snatch Swen as my date for Homecoming before Venus does."

"Nice."

"And just to make sure Venus doesn't suspect anything or kick me out when I get there, I'll pretend you're my little boo," I said as I leaned my head on his arm as he bent back up.

"And you'll be my little burrito," razzed Adam as he patted my head and scrunched his nose like a little bunny.

I rolled my eyes. Playtime was over. I grabbed my backpack, which was so full it looked like it had spiraled to obesity or something.

"*Gracias mi vida.* Now, let's kick it, shall we?" I said, ready to roll on my new mission.

So, off we went to send Adam's viral advertising on its way to benchmark my experiment and boost my little gang's social status. With Mase's fresh, new voice emerging through his artwork, people from all over were going to hear what we had to say loud and clear.

But before I departed Adam, I threw him a chubby, purple lipstick. "Hey, Adam, take this."

"What is it?" Adam quizzed.

"I call it the 'Licky Sticky.' It's a walkie-talkie I made out of a lipstick tube," I announced proudly, as I hung mine around my neck.

Adam furrowed his brow. "And I want it because . . . ?"

"You want it because Bridge and I used to use these before we had cell phones. And since we can't talk on our phones at school, you can still give me the four-one-one as it happens, *comprendes?*" I said, with a knowing grin and a wink.

"*Si, Señorita, me gusta mi walkie-talkie,*" Adam smirked back.

"*Bueno,*" I said, pleased that he was pleased.

But then Adam said, "Do you have a better color than this? I mean, it's the exact color of that horrible purple drink we imbibe at lunch."

Looking very serious, I spoke into my hot-pink Licky Sticky, "Adam, can you hear me?"

"Yes. Good. Check."

"Adam?" I asked, like I couldn't hear him even though he was only about five inches away.

"Yes?"

"Shut up!" I screamed.

We both rolled our eyes lovingly at each other and parted. Next, I went to find Bridge to make sure she had brought her cookies so that they could be divided for all the groups at lunch.

When I finally caught up to Bridge, I saw she looked extremely cute today. She had on a fuzzy, happy, yellow tank with denim pedal pushers and she wore a bucket hat with her hair in a braid. She looked like the grooviest little fisherman. Just like Adam. No, strike that. *Exactly* like Adam.

She cautiously asked, "Do you think it's a bit too much?"

"No, I think it's the right amount of cuteness. Plus, by now the J+L kids know you. And they'll probably think you're just acting out and being wild and crazy—like Adam." I didn't reveal what Adam's wardrobe of the day was. I mean, she would find out soon enough, anyway. I didn't want to spoil a good thing so early in the day. And right now she had work to do.

"You think it's cute?" Bridge asked, needing her fix of my assurance.

"Yeah. And if they don't get your fabulous self, just tell them it's Friday and you got a little crazy. They're slow like that."

Bridge gave a big sigh. "Yeah, I guess you're right."

"No, I'm *totally* right. Now, did you bring in your home-baked goodness?" I asked, knowing that we had to stay focused on our mission today.

"Yes, I did," Bridge chirped as she pulled out a container from her Gamma High duffel bag.

"Did you stick to the formula we created?" I asked, now sounding like a science freak; no, totally sounding like *mi máma*.

"Well . . . ," she said sheepishly.

"Well what?" I asked, feeling a twinge of panic.

"Well, I deviated just a *smidge*," Bridge said, with a devilish little smile.

"What does that mean, Bridge? You're scaring me now." I grabbed her container and opened the lid, not sure as to what I'd see.

"All I did was add a bit more chocolate chips," Bridge said while waggling her eyebrows. "It's not going to hurt anything. Everyone *loves* chocolate."

"I don't know, Bridge. I have a weird feeling about this," I said. Not like the way that chick felt in that old *Alien* movie when that baby alien popped out, but something kinda like it.

"Maybe it's because your Licky Sticky is stuck," Bridge observed.

"What?"

I looked down, and sure enough, my walkie-talkie had its red light on and I had been broadcasting our convo. I felt superdumb.

"It keeps getting stuck," I said while I handed the cookies back to Bridge so I could jimmy around with my walkie-talkie. I shouldn't have used such cheap components, but on my allowance, the Dollar Store was good enough.

"Anyway, I don't think it's a big deal to have more chocolate," Bridge commented, completely ignoring me as she made sure to carefully secure the lid on her cookies.

"I don't know, Bridge," I said, still unsure as we walked down the hall toward one of the girls' bathrooms.

"Listen, Luz, you're the one who got us into this mess in the first place, remember? And I don't think my extra little chocolate chips are going to do anything to ruin your precious experiment." She shot me a look straight in the eye, trying to act tough and all. I let her win.

"I'm sorry, Bridge. You're right. It's just that I've been trying to control things for days. I guess I'm just stuck like my Licky Sticky." I offered her a smile.

"That's okay," Bridge said, feeling all proud of herself since she thought she showed me who was boss or whatever.

"Okay, could you now help me put up these postcards so people will vote for us?"

"You're controlling again!" Bridge said loud enough that her voice echoed in the still-empty hallways.

"Hey, it's going to help you win a spot on the Homecoming Court and there's a really hot drawing of you."

"Shut up! Really?" Bridge said, wanting to hear more.

"Yes, totally. I wouldn't lie about that."

After we looked at Mase's drawings, Bridge calmed down and we began our campaign to get the word out to Gamma's student body.

We started in the girls' bathrooms by scattering them in the "vanity area." And at every stop, I made sure to take pictures of the displays we made, documenting for the sake of Project Gamma Glamma, and for our scrapbook as well.

Next stop was the band hall. And since it was still *muy temprano* in the morning, not many of the kids were there yet. So, I just placed Susan's postcards on the various shelves where the band members kept their musical instruments. I even put some postcards on their music stands. Then I got supercrafty and I put one on their giant metronome so that when the band members start warming up they can see a picture of Susan swaying and moving to the beat.

Bridge definitely showed me a thing or two when she borrowed my laser pen and made a key out of a paper clip and opened up the snack machine. I took a picture of Bridge smiling proudly. We taped Susan's postcards on all the snacks in the machine so that when the band members would buy a snack they'd also buy a bit of sponsorship. Priceless, I thought. My mom would be so proud.

After that, we went to the auditorium and scattered Mase's postcards on the stage. We even went back to the construction shop and placed more of Mase's postcards on a large papier-mâché dragon's head.

We only had about five more minutes before the bell, so we started scattering postcards of all of us in lockers, between lunch trays, in the trophy cases. Adam walkied to inform us that not only had he been able to place our arty images in the boys' locker room but he'd also managed to have his fellow colleagues on the newspaper staff insert them into Friday's paper as it was being folded up. Sheer brilliance.

"Do you have any cards left to put out?" I asked Bridge.

"Nope. This is my last one," Bridge said as she shoved it into the slit of someone's locker.

"Yeah, I'm out too. Look at my hands! I need to wash this ink off my fingers."

"Don't touch your white shirt," Bridge warned, making her famous scrunchy face.

"Got it," I said.

I lifted up my Licky Sticky. "Adam, what's your twenty?" I waited for my response.

"What does that mean?" Bridge whispered.

"It means what's his location."

"He's right behind you, doof." Bridge laughed in her new laugh.

"Oh," I said, feeling a bit stupid as I let go of my walkie-talkie.

"My twenty is by the two most popular Homecoming finalists representin'. . . the freshman class. Ladies and grunts, let me introduce Gamma Glamma's finest," declared Adam to an audience of no one—well, except for us.

"We *are* Gamma Glamma," Bridge gushed and then noticed Adam's outfit exactly matched hers. "Gawd, Adam Bellows, you *didn't*!" she yelled.

Suddenly the bell rang and the previously deserted halls were packed with students, sounds, and commotion. I took a deep breath and looked at Bridge and Adam. My stomach was trying to get ready like you do when you're about to go down a roller coaster.

"I think I'm freaking," said Bridge, doing a double-take at Adam's attire.

"Don't be too timid and squeamish about your actions. All life is an experiment," Adam said in a crazy old man's accent.

"Who said that?" I asked, not really wanting to know.

"Emerson."

I looked at Adam. "Did he make it as a finalist for the Homecoming Court?"

"No."

"I didn't think so," hissed Bridge, taking off her matching fisherman's hat.

"But that's because he was a writer and not a scientist and he didn't have secret scientific 'Snacktastics,'" I reminded Bridge, who wanted to stay mad but couldn't given the impending excitement set to transpire this day.

"You're so right," said Bridge, looking down at the scientific breakthrough she was carrying in her Tupperware.

"See you 'finalists' at lunch!" Adam yelled as he darted up the stairs.

For a brief moment, I did make the observation (and this would make Dr. Hamrock proud) that when the social pressure started to kick in, it was really cool to see how people reacted. But even more so, it was amazing to see what a force of energy we could be when we stuck together. I just hoped the Snacktastic surprise we would serve at lunch would be sweet enough to keep us together.

Chapter

14

As the day unfolded, I could hardly contain myself, I was so excited. Walking through the swarming crowds between classes, I saw countless kids curious about our postcards.

Some were actually looking around for us in the hallways like we were Hollywood stars or something. Others were commenting on how cool they thought the artwork was. And one boy even walked up to me and said I looked good in ink. I didn't know how to respond so I just said, "Thank you." It felt weird but it was really cool.

When I walked outside to the courtyard to get to my next class and take in some fresh air, I witnessed the strangest sight. A few Dramatica girls were trying to see how many postcards of Mase they could collect. Some of these newborn groupies even started stapling them to their leather jackets.

As I walked back inside and back into the stale school air, I passed the band hall. The band members were warming up and playing their scales, but not quite in harmony yet. A tall, cute-looking Asian boy who was exiting the room had actually taped Susan's postcard to the side of his trombone case. *That's so amazing*, I thought.

I saw one teacher pick up the postcard of Adam that fell out when she opened the daily school paper. She smiled broadly and looked around as if she knew this was Adam's doing all along.

I decided to walkie-talkie Mr. Bellows to check on his status.

"How's it going?"

"It's pretty crazy here," Adam replied. "Has anybody said anything to you?"

"They ask me if I know what's going on," I said.

"And what do you say?"

"I just say I just found out about the pictures this morning. Which is partially true," I confessed.

"*Partially*," Adam emphasized. "But it's definitely the buzz around here today."

"Do you think people will vote for us?"

"Too soon to tell. At least we're all on the radar . . . and Mase's doubtlessly upped his art cred."

"Yeah, he's pretty *fabuloso*," I whispered back. Just then Bridge appeared down the hall and started walking up to me with big eyes.

"Hey, Adam, Bridge's here. I'll talk with you later, okay?"

"Ten-four, good buddy," Adam grunted in his Elvis trucking voice.

"Ten-four," I signed off.

Bridge was simply beaming as she finally reached me. I could tell she was about to burst with some really important info.

"Guess what?" Bridge whispered quickly as she grabbed my arm.

"What?"

"Guess?" she asked again, wanting to play games.

"Girl, I'm a scientist, not a psychic."

"I just saw Bart Marquez making out with you." Bridge laughed, holding her mouth.

"*What?* Have you been touching our Snacktastics?"

"No. When I was hanging out with V and Tammy Shellhorn by the boys' locker room, I saw Bart kissing your postcard and mine. He was acting all stupid like he normally does, and then B-Dawg came up and snatched my postcard from him. And gave it to me! Can you believe it? I wanted to die," Bridge said deliriously.

"In his arms?" I added, with a knowing smile. "Hey, what happened to mine?"

"Well, Bart just laughed and licked your face." Bridge grimaced as she revealed the ugly truth.

"Ew," I said, totally visualizing the whole horrible event.

"Hey, at least it was just the postcard and not real life." Her attempt to provide comfort didn't work.

"Ew again."

"He got ink on his tongue, if that helps. But anyway, I'm just very, very excited," she kept gushing.

"Why?"

"About the fact that B-Dawg saved *me* instead of you. That means he must think *I'm special.*"

"You *are* special, Bridge."

"But you know what I mean, Luz. This might mean I have a chance with him." Then, jumping on a new train of thought, Bridge added, "Oh, I just remembered. You know what? I also saw Venus looking at our postcards."

"Really? Did she say anything?"

"Yeah, she wondered if you did this."

"Why would she think that?"

"She said that this had the desperate smell of you. Like the fish you killed in Dr. Hamrock's class."

"She's such a liar. Did you confront her?"

"Are you kidding me, Luz. I can't say something to her in front of B-Dawg. She would have twisted it to make me look stupid in front of him. You know she would have slaughtered me."

"Yeah, I know, but I can't let her win and ruin my rep, Bridge."

"But remember, Luz, this is for the experiment and *Homecoming,* right?"

"Yeah, I know, but it still totally sucks—unless we win. So now we have to do whatever it takes." I was feeling ruthless.

"What about science with a conscience?"

"What about being a big fat sheep who's dateless for Homecoming and unpopular for the next three years?"

"Okay, so what's the game plan now?" Bridge asked as she climbed on board the vengeance train.

I instructed Bridge that she and Adam would hang back during lunch and that I would place the first tin of cookies on the Dramaticas' table. Next, Susan would bring her batch to the band table. And after that, Bridge and Adam would bring their sweet treats to the J+L table. And when they were done, I would take my batch to the sci-fi table.

Pacing was going to be an important factor here. We didn't know how people were going to respond, so it was necessary to stagger the consumption of the cookies.

Once the cookies were eaten, it would then be important for us to encourage our constituencies to exercise their rights as Americans—or at least as students of Gamma High—and make their votes count for the Homecoming Court. Now that Bridge was briefed with the final lunch instructions, I dropped her off at her class and went on my way.

I was still a bit nervous about everything but tried to think positive thoughts. If we ran out of cookies, Bridge and I could still make some more on Sunday. And in case Susan decided to dive into the cookies, I had made sure to tell Bridge to make Susan her own batch without the secret recipe ingredient. Every contingency was planned for.

But I couldn't shake the knowledge that Venus was spreading the evil rumor that I killed Dr. Hamrock's fish. How was that going to affect our outcome or my reputation?

And something else was also bothering me about Bridge adding extra chocolate chips to the batch. I couldn't pinpoint it right away, and my brain was trying to review the molecular structure of chocolate and how it could affect the other ingredients. What could possibly happen that would be bad? I decided there was nothing else we could do about it now. We just had to go forward.

After science class, I made sure to give Susan very specific instructions about giving the cookies to the band kids.

"So, will you just repeat to me my instructions, so I know we are on the same page?" I asked as sweetly as I could.

"I'm not a baby, Luz. And if you weren't aware, my GPA's higher than yours," Susan grunted.

"Yes, it is, Susan, but, whatever, okay? What did you get from this convo?"

"You want me to bring the cookies to the band table."

"And what else?" I prompted.

"And wait about three to five minutes and then encourage them to vote for the Homecoming Court to exercise our rights as Americans," Susan said, now sounding like a total android.

"Okay, you can skip the Americans part. I was just on my soapbox. And then what?"

"And then talk to them in my baby voice, like I do to Frotastic."

"Okay, well, that's partially correct. But really, I need you to be absolutely sure that you don't partake of any of the cookies from the tin. If you absolutely must have some cookies, then eat the cookies from this baggie," I stressed.

"Alright. Hey, what do you call these cookies, anyway?"

"They're called Snacktastics," I announced, thinking of my mom.

"Can I give a Snacktastic to Frotastic?" dreamed Susan.

"No! Absolutely not," I ordered.

"What about from the plastic bag?" Susan pressed.

"Let's say no," I said, trying to stop the madness before Susan continued to argue with me (which she loves to do). I changed the subject (which is something I love to do).

"Susan, did you see the postcard that Mase made for you to help you get nominated for the Homecoming Court?" I asked with faked renewed enthusiasm.

"Yeah," Susan said.

"What did you think?" I was trying to stir up some passion.

"It was alright," Susan said with no passion whatsoever, which totally irked me.

"Didn't you think it was the spitting image of you?"

Susan stroked her hair with her fingers. "Yeah, except my hair isn't that long."

"It was a fantasy-type rendition of you. You know, like your fairy kingdoms and unicorns," I said, still working her into the zone.

"I'm not *that* into unicorns, Luz," Susan said, revealing some kind of hidden prejudice against unicorns.

"Well, have people been treating you *special* today?"

"I guess."

Dang, girl. She was killing me. My blood was coagulating. So I decided to kick it to her with my spurs on.

"Let me be more specific, Susan. Has anything *muy malo* happened to you today because of the postcards?"

Susan took off her glasses and rubbed her eyes as she tried to focus on something in the distance.

"Well, there was one person and they drew a sombrero on my head in one picture."

"Okay, well, there's nothing wrong with a little sombrero action. It's the hat of my people," I said.

Susan looked at me as if she had just run out of gas. And I was running out of time. So I told her I would be around if she needed me. And I also reminded her not to pass out any of her jelly beans as I scampered off to the cafeteria.

"Luz, where are you?" chirped my Licky Sticky.

"I'm outside the caf," I said as I rushed to open the cafeteria door.

"You took too long, so Bridge and I are heading to our table. Over and out," Adam said, sounding rushed.

"Okay, Adam. Sorry about the delay and good luck."

I raced to the Dramatica table and, of course, there was no one there because this group likes to make an entrance. So, I just left the tin around where Mase usually sits. Working my way to my home base, I passed the band table and saw Susan sit down and open her tin. She took a big whiff, and for a moment, I thought she was going to dive in and I would have to dive in after her. But my fears calmed down when she carefully put the lid back on.

Finally, I arrived at my beloved sci-fi table and sat down closer to my fellow geeks than I normally do. Then I offered up my treat of the day.

I was all girly-like and said, "Hey, guys, would you like some homemade goodness?" And with my biggest smile ever, I opened the tin for them and let them get a good, strong whiff. Normally, these giant, happy sugar cookies with chunks of chocolate chips would attract people like a magnet to a fridge. But not these people.

My sci-fi pal Jimbo scratched his curly brown hair as he peered above his overly rose-tinted giant spectacles. "I'm not sure how I feel about eating refined sugars so late in the day."

"You know you shouldn't really keep those things housed in aluminum," informed my other sci-fi classmate Todd. "Didn't you review the research on the connection between aluminum and Alzheimer's disease? You know, the disease that makes you forget things?"

"I know what Alzheimer's is, Todd. I'm in the science cluster. Remember?" I was slightly annoyed at their collective air of superiority.

"I'll eat one if *you* do, Luz," said Jimbo as he squinted his eyes suspiciously at me.

"What? Do you think I'd put something in the cookies?" I asked, trying to fake my innocence.

Jimbo started, "No, we're just giving you a hard time because you are transparent as a . . ."

"Beaker glass?" finished Todd.

"Or a protozoan?" snickered Neal, who sat at the end of the table and never really spoke.

"Or as transparent as the human body is to low-frequency radio emission," continued Jimbo, attempting a proof of his amazing grasp of scientific trivia.

"Alright, already!" I said, having enough of being the scientific butt to their lame humor. "I just wanted you to vote for me for the Homecoming Court," I added, coming clean.

"Okay, then, why didn't you just ask us?" asked Jimbo.

"I just did. Will you do it?"

"Yeah, we will," Jimbo said as he nodded at all of his sci-fi colleagues as he took a bite of his bologna sandwich.

"Well, do you still want any of these cookies?"

"No, we know you're cool in science, Luz. But based on research, we know that scientific intelligence doesn't always carry over to the domestic sciences," Jimbo joked, nonetheless still totally serious.

"Okay, that's fair. Then I'm off to feed my toxic cookies to other unsuspecting students," I said, totally not kidding either.

The sci-fi guys all just laughed as if they had won the battle of the minds. One thing was for sure: those guys were all smart *and* tough cookies themselves.

About ten minutes later, I walked back by the band table. I was about to ask Susan, who was sitting by herself, where her fellow bandmates were when I discovered the sea of green at the voting table. It looked like the cookies had worked magic. I asked Susan if everything went okay and she shrugged and nodded and then went back to drawing on her lunch sack.

I did notice that she had taken a postcard of Mase and was trying to draw him and transform him into what looked like a hobbit. I didn't stick around to find out for sure.

I pretended I was going back into the lunch line, so I could observe the J+L table at a closer distance. I noticed the empty tin and knew the cookies were at least good enough to be devoured.

Now, from the edge of earshot I could hear the complete lovefest that was going on at the table. Everyone was talking about how fabulous the next person was. Come to think of it, if you excluded the hostility directed toward those on the outside, that kind of conversation was pretty much the norm at the J+L table. But with the cookies it became much more amplified, and at least temporarily, maybe more sincere. I just winked at Adam and Bridge as I made a U-turn and walked toward the cafeteria exit.

When I reached the Student Council voting table, it was hard to squeeze past because it was crowded with the band posse and the Dramaticas. I gathered that the Dramaticas had also polished off their Snacktastics—they were all emoting in an enthused and happy sort of way instead of being dark and mysterious.

I did note something unusual when I was near the voting table: there was a heavy gas aroma. And I'm not talking about cooking gas here. I'm talking about Señor Shortie gas. I didn't pay too much attention to it, though, because (1) who would want to pay attention to a thing like that and (2) it was Frito pie with chili day.

I decided this would be a great time to step outside and record my observations since the audio level was definitely on the rise in there. Speaking into my Chica Speaka wireless pen mic, I described the cookies, Mase's postcards, and how Bridge taped Susan's pictures to the snacks after she broke open the snack machine.

I thought I might need to erase that last comment, but Bridge wasn't really stealing anything when she broke into the vending machine. If anything, she was *adding to*.

Then I continued on with a progress analysis of my experiment, how everybody's transformation had been carried out as planned and that so far my hypothesis had proved accurate. I mentioned that the voting process had started and that I expected all my subjects to be freshman finalists.

I also said that I couldn't wait to see Swen and that he had asked me to Venus's party. I wished that I could go with him but for now I had to act like I was with Adam so Venus would take the bait and ask Adam. Then Adam would shoot into the popular hemisphere and I could have a chance with Swen.

Although this bit of reportage didn't apply to the official Project Gamma Glamma notations, it did make me excited just to say it for the record. And if all worked out, then this *would* be the science experiment of a lifetime.

As I was thinking about what else I needed to include, I saw Swen outside the cafeteria heading back to the media center. I walked quickly to catch up with him.

"Hey, Swen," I said, catching my breath.

"Hey, Luz."

"I just wanted to tell you that I might just meet you at Venus's tomorrow. Is that okay?"

"Sure. Is everything alright?"

"Yeah, I've just been really, really busy with this project and I don't know when I'll be ready for the party tomorrow," I said.

Just then Swen pulled out a postcard of me. "Yeah, I can see you've been putting in a lot of time . . . *on this*."

"It's kind of funny, isn't it?" I said, now feeling kinda hot and uncomfortable.

"It's the talk of the day," he replied. "So is this a part of your experiment?"

"Well, yes, actually it is. I mean, if I can get all my subjects voted in as finalists by their peers, then my experiment will be a success. That would be the most indisputable proof that my theory was correct."

"But what about you? Why do *you* have a postcard campaigning for the Homecoming Court? Are you putting yourself through the process?" Swen asked, inquiring into my intentions.

"Well, uh . . . because in order to better observe my test subjects, I just thought I would participate in the process as well. Strictly in the interest of science, you know. You can never collect too much data, right?"

Just as Swen's questions were making me more and more uncomfortable, Bridge and Adam ran toward us and pulled me aside.

"Something awful has happened," Adam said urgently.

"It was completely foul."

By the look on both their faces I knew it had to be really bad. "What is it?"

"Now I know why I shouldn't have put so much chocolate in the Snacktastics," Bridge revealed.

"*Omigòd*, why?" I asked, not really wanting to hear the answer to this. Bridge leaned in close making sure that no one heard her. "People started having gas attacks."

"What?!" I screamed. Swen turned his head in our direction and I just waved him off that everything was okay.

"Yes, Luz." Bridge grabbed my face and looked directly in my eyes. "People started expelling large quantities of gas," she said very slowly, to make sure I knew exactly what she was saying.

Knowing that Swen was waiting on me, I signaled for him to give me one more minute with Adam and Bridge.

Adam spelled it out all the way. "What she is trying to say is that people were having a fartfest, Luz, and it got really bad. Not just the smell, either. When people started voting, they started passing gas, and then they started passing blame."

"Yeah, and fights started breaking out between some of the band kids and the Dramaticas. Then the jocks started jumping in. It was a bloodbath, Luz," said Bridge.

"No, it was a fartfest *with* a bloodbath. It was all around disgusting," Adam remarked, still a bit shaken from the whole event.

"*Omigod*," is all I could say.

"It took the principal, vice principal, *and* Coach Smith to break it all up. And they closed voting down for today," Bridge reported sadly.

"You're kidding," I said, still in shock that this had happened.

"I wish I was. I also wish I hadn't added all the chocolate."

I waved at Swen begging for one more minute. He just nodded.

"What do you think happened, I mean scientifically speaking?"

"I think the combo of the metabolic stimulants in the chocolate and the fiber from the beans in today's lunch sent people over the gastric edge," Bridge replied.

"Hmmm," I said, needing a moment to digest this whole gas thing.

"Luz, are we going to be in a bunch of trouble? My parents will kill me. And then what about my reputation?"

I could tell Bridge was building up into her ritual freak-out. "I'm not so sure they will be able to trace it back to the cookies," I reassured her.

Adam jumped in, "No, of course not. Everyone will always blame the lunch food. Don't give yourselves too much credit, girls."

"Well that's optimistic," I said, desperate to find some silver lining. "I think our next step is to not do anything more today. It's been a big day of postcards and Snacktastics. Let's just try to get through the day," I declared, trying to sound strong and sure—like the captain of the *Titanic*.

Bridge, who finally realized that I had been talking with my dream date, quickly excused herself and dragged Adam with her. I rushed back to Swen, who was waiting patiently the entire time.

"Swen, I'm sooo sorry I made you wait."

"You're a hard subject to investigate. Are you always this busy?"

"No, really. I promise to give you the inside scoop on Saturday night, okay?" I offered.

"Let's shake on it, then." Swen reached his hand out and held mine. My dumb hand started shaking. His *mano* was nice, warm, and strong. I just wanted to melt like the extra chocolate that Bridge had melted into our terribly tragic fartmakers.

After we said our sweet good-bye and Swen left, I wondered if I could just stop this entire experiment from blowing up in my face. Was I trying too hard? Why did everything seem so difficult? I mean, science was about observing the ways of the world and putting the facts together to discover the truth. So what did all this commotion, chaos, and lies have to do with *my* path to the truth?

Chapter

15

Saturday I spent the entire day in my closet. Even though I had 1,958 combinations to wear, I still couldn't find anything that was perfect for tonight. I called Bridge and she came over immediately so she could help me get ready for Venus's party.

On a positive note, my hair looked great and finally had stopped growing. The final length I kept was midway down my back. Bridge's nails also had stopped growing and she kept them just a little longer than she normally does, which isn't that big of a woo since she normally chews them down to the quick.

Bridge had actually gone shopping earlier today (without me—*wahhh*) and purchased some new things that were perfect J+L material. She'd matched up a dark denim mini with a cute little red bolero top and a pair of fantastic beige suede boots. She looked really pulled together and I was starting to feel a bit inadequate.

Bridge flipped her hair back and stood strong with her French-manicured hands on her hips. "So, what do you think?"

"You're really getting the hang of this. I'm surprised you haven't gone into withdrawal not wearing any of your Polo shirts," I said, sitting on the floor next to my pile of clothes.

"I know, right? But at least Adam can't try to play mini-me in this outfit."

"You underestimate Adam."

"No, not really. I've got my backups," Bridge said, with a twinkle in her eye, as she pulled out a little flirty tunic dress in pale blue.

"Dang, Bridge, this experiment is really turning you into a fashionista fiend," I teased.

"I think you need to sort through this"—she picked up a silver scarf and a black leather mini from my pile—"and classify yourself before you make that conclusion."

"Shut up and help me pick something."

I put on a purple metallic skirt with my black boots and a white Swen shirt, and I looked in my dresser mirror. From behind me Bridge gave me a hard stare with very wide eyes that were frozen à la Bambi. Okay, she hated it.

"Luz, I think you're trying *way* too hard with that white shirt."

"Really?"

"Yes, plus I know how stain happy you get with food or condiments. And aren't you supposed to be going as Adam's date?"

"Yes, that's the game plan so far," I said.

"Then why don't you let me help you tone it down a bit, my friend," Bridge said condescendingly sweet as she moved me away from my mirror.

"What do you mean by that?"

"I don't mean *anything* by that," Bridge said, switching on her old defensive mode.

"Don't be such a *coward*, Bridge; just say it," I called her out.

Bridge crossed her arms in front of her new ample chest (thanks to the Gap Body), took a deep breath, and then exhaled quickly.

"Okay, are you ready? Then fasten your safety straps. You dress like a total cartoon, Luz. Can I just say it's hard enough that we are science geeks but you really make us stand out in a bad way."

Without my permission, my mouth just dropped.

"And one thing I have learned being in the city of J+L is that it isn't so bad to be in with the 'in' group. But you wouldn't know this because you're *not in*."

Pow and ow. I wasn't ready for *that* explosion. And boy, did it burn. I got mad at first, and I wanted to fight back but then there was a part of me that knew she was right. I mean, not about the cartoon thing, because I did love how I dressed. But I *was* out of the "in" group.

I had fashioned this perfect creation to fit into this new group based on my scientific observations. However, Bridge was now more schooled in this group than I was. And now that I was about to visit the inner sanctum of the J+L universe, I knew I needed to listen to whatever advice she had to give me.

So, I surrendered. "Alright, Bridge. Unfortunately, there is one thing you've always been consistent with and that is the truth. So, what do you suggest I wear?"

"For starters, nothing sci-fi or punk," she said without hesitation.

"Okay," I said, hoping to recapture some dignity as I gazed at the floor.

"Next, you have to let Venus be the shiny one. I know she's spreading rumors about you being the fish killer and God knows what else. But it's still her party and you gotta remember, you *weren't invited.* I know that's really harsh, but if you're going to crash it, you really need to blend." Bridge was really pouring salt into the old wound there.

"Got it, Bridge. I'll keep my mouth shut. What do you want me to wear?"

"Nothing here, that's for sure. Let me pick up something from my house and bring it back." Bridge was now my official commander in chief for fashion.

In a flash, Bridge ran home and returned with new threads. We didn't have time to play dress up, so I just put on her chosen outfit without a discussion.

My outfit for the evening was anything but spectacular. I had a pink Polo pullover shirt with no mods (geekspeak for modifications) at all. It was a bit tight because I'm bigger in the boob department. And Bridge's khaki mini was a bit roomy in the trunk, since Bridge trumps me in the bootie department. We are totally each other's yin and yang when it comes to our curvaceous (read: not fat) figures.

And lastly, my pair of Cinderella shoes came in the form of some thin, black, nondescript flip-flops. At least I got to equip with my reliable Pic Purse and my Licky Sticky.

Bridge pulled my extralong hair into a low ponytail with a severe part on the side. She gave me a pair of stud earrings to wear. You know, the kind they give you when you first get your ears pierced at the mall. Yeah, I know. *Preteen*.

But I did it. I had to trust her. She had been there for me when she put herself on the line for this experiment. And now it was my turn to give her props. I still was a little mad about *la verdad*—the truth—but didn't have much time at this point to dwell on it. So, I just put on my big-girl panties (so to speak) and just dealt.

Twenty minutes later, Bridge's mom dropped us in front of Venus's house and we were kinda grossly early. Mrs. Joiner said to call her especially if we found out there weren't any adult chaperones. Bridge and I just looked at each other blankly. *As if*.

As we walked toward the door, Bridge pulled me by the side of the house behind some bushes and said, "We should make separate entrances, since Venus hates you."

"Okay." I was feeling like a whipped puppy.

"Adam should be here any minute. Wait for him here," ordered Bridge again, my new J+L commander.

I didn't like being taken out of charge of my own experiment, but I did what I was told by my fellow scientist and waited by the side of the house where no one could see me. Five minutes passed. Ten minutes passed and it felt like hours.

The usual suspects of the J+L crowd showed up looking glossed up and magazine ready. They all smelled really sweet and clean with their various colognes and perfumes wafting past in the breeze. Some J+L girls had gone and fake baked today and were wearing shimmering lotion on their newly tanned skin.

Then a group of hotties walked in. I didn't recognize them and I suspected that they were upperclassmen since they didn't show any outward signs of weakness. I continued to wait behind the bushes for the next parade of pretty party people.

Then something unexpected happened. I heard a thunder of skateboards. I looked up and it was Mase with a group of about six guys rolling to the party. I couldn't believe it. Was *he* invited? How did that happen? After a few more minutes, more Dramatica kids popped in. I didn't know what to think. I was in complete shock. I wanted to run up to Mase, but something told me to stay behind the bushes.

But nothing could have prepared me for what happened next. Two large "soccer mom" vans pulled up and stopped. Then the next thing I knew the entire Gamma band squad piled out. Surely, there had to be some mistake. The musical herd moseyed up to Venus's door and didn't even knock. They just strolled into the party like it was an everyday occurrence or something.

How can the band be invited to Venus's party and not me? This was heinous. I immediately called Adam on his cell.

"Where are you?!!"

Adam replied, "I'm coming. I had to take care of some family matters."

"Quit lying! You don't have any family. The only family you care about is yourself."

"Control yourself, Attitude. I'm on my way," Adam snapped.

"Sorry. I'll see you in a minute," I said, realizing I was losing my cool.

Obviously, this wardrobe makeover and the witnessing of my entire freshman class showing up to this party (to which I wasn't invited) was getting the better of me.

Finally, relief had arrived—I saw Adam's little shiny Altima. He could drive at age fifteen because of a so-called hardship. Yeah, right! What kind of hardship could Adam have? Wearing the wrong mega-expensive name brand to the party? I think not.

Adam parked way down the street and then started jogging toward me. I was so glad to see him. What I wasn't glad to see was that he was wearing the *same exact* color combo as me!

In unison, we both yelled, "Why are you wearing *that*?!"

"Bridge made me tone down my outfit so I would blend," I said. "Now, why are you wearing this outfit?" I demanded.

And then the Bellowsstalkerazzi said, "I thought Bridge was going to wear that outfit. I saw her leave her house with it."

"Yeah, but obviously you didn't stalk her long enough to see that she came to my house and gave it to me," I quipped.

"That's just the topper to *my* day," Adam said, like he was looking for pity. I wasn't feeling so charitable at the moment.

So, totally feeling slighted, I barked, "Well, why did you want to dress as her dude at this party anyway? You're supposed to be *my* dream lover, *remember*?"

"I thought if I dressed like Bridge then the guys would stay away from her. And if Venus noticed that Bridge and I dressed alike and then I had you on my arm, I would look like I have it going on," Adam revealed shamelessly.

"Boy, Adam, that's pretty convoluted and calculated even for you," I said, not believing what was happening to me.

"Yeah? And what about you and your little faux preppy threads you're shamelessly working, punk?"

"Okay, let's not go there now. We have a mission here, right?" I was trying to keep our slowly crumbling plan going forward no matter what.

As Adam and I walked—okay, *stomped*—up to the door, someone threw open the door and, to our surprise, it was Susan. I don't know if Adam and I were more shocked that she might actually be invited to the party or that she actually came.

But the straw that broke this camel's back (no, let's make that this alpaca's back) was that Susan was wearing the *same* pink shirt and beige bottom combo as both Adam and myself. We all looked like we were in a choir or trying to be the world's freakiest geeks.

So, in my most surprised voice, I said, "Susan! What are *you* doing here?"

"I was invited."

"Really?" I looked at Adam speechless.

"Yeah, I even brought the invitation to prove it." She pulled out a crumpled piece of paper from her pocket.

She wasn't kidding. Susan had an e-vite that had been mass-mailed on Friday right after school.

"That's impressive, Seamus," Adam said, with a smirk.

"Yeah, that's cool. Did you just get here?" I asked, now trying to be cool, too, as I tried to draw more valuable information out of her.

"Yeah," Susan said.

It was just such an awkward and horrible situation, so I did what any other "normal" and boring person would do. I suggested we find the food.

We walked through Venus's house, and it was gorgeous, as expected. It was all, like, midcentury modern, you know, all that furniture that looked like it came from the cartoon *The Jetsons*. The house was all white and stark and totally bank. And it was such a crazy backdrop for all the variety of kids from Gamma.

The party definitely segregated itself just like at school, with the band kids congregating together on one side and the Dramaticas on the other. The J+L crowd, like always, took over the middle of the room and made its presence known. Adam said he was going to hang back with the J+L crowd and catch up with us in a minute. I knew he needed a moment apart from our matching fashion spread.

Susan and I wandered on to the backyard, where the food was being served. The pool was lit up with tons of little Christmas-type lights and I felt like I was at one of those parties you only see in the movies.

On one table, there was the typical party food, chips and salsa and such. However, across the way, the Hunters had hired a person whose job it was to grill burgers or fajitas to order for their guests. Now, that was impressive, I hated to admit. I decided to start off slow with the chip-and-dip table. Susan decided to be my Klingon.

From here, I was able to take in a wider view of la fiesta, which grew to be filled with all the guest stars of my daily life. From my sci-fi tribe, there was Jimbo, content to munch on the wide variety of snacks at the end of the table.

"Hey, Jimbo, how's it going?" I asked.

Still chewing a mouthful of chips, he spit out a "Pretty good."

"Have you been here long?"

"For a while. The boys and I got here early. We'd calculated that since Venus had invited the entire freshman class to her house, the food supply would either be gone or highly contaminated with parasites after about forty-five minutes to an hour," Jimbo said in his brainiac, all-knowing voice.

"Right. That's really true," I agreed, hoping to scuttle away before I was kidnapped and tied up for a whole night of geekspeak.

So, I made my break. "Well, I'm going to find some more 'para-sites' to munch on. Susan, why don't you hang out with Jimbo. I'm going to tell Adam where we are," I said, praying that she wouldn't want to come with. Fortunately, she didn't seem to be paying much attention to me. She was too busy taste testing all the dips on the table.

From across the other side of the pool, I spotted Bridge, and she sent a text for me to come quick. Pushing through the sea of Drama-ticas, I accidentally stepped on this Dramatica Goth-looking girl's extremely long skirt. My flip-flop made a dusty imprint. I hoped she wouldn't notice. This was no time to get into a culture clash espe-cially since I was flying J+L colors. Finally, I reached Bridge.

I tried to catch my breath. "What's up?"

"I don't know. I thought you'd know or at least Adam."

"You mean what's with all these *odd* people here?" I asked.

"Exactly," Bridge said, reapplying her lip gloss.

"I'm sure I'll find out soon enough. Is *this* why you called me?" I asked.

"No. I wanted to let you know that Swen is in the building," Bridge whispered, looking around making sure no one was listening to us.

"Really? Where is he?" I asked, scanning the backyard.

"I don't know but I do know that V's looking for him as we speak."

Then from out of nowhere, Bart Marquez grabbed me from be-hind. "Hey, *chica mas fina*, want to take a dip?" He swung me near the pool.

Totally taken off guard, I let loose. "Bart. Don't. I swear *I'll kill you*," I said in the meanest voice I could muster.

He said sarcastically, "*Relajaté*, Luz, I was just kidding. I thought you *liked* the water. Especially after you dove into that aquarium after that frog fell in."

"You mean after you tossed it in there. *Es verdad*, Bart?" I dared him to tell the truth.

"Yeah. So, who cares?" Bart said flippantly.

"The dead fish, that's who," I said matter-of-factly.

Puffing out his chest and flashing me his grill, he said, "*So?*" wait-ing for me to take his bait.

Bridge quickly jumped in and grabbed Bart by the arm and said, "Hey, Mr. Marquez, why don't we get out of here and quit hanging with nerd alerts. I'm dying of thirst. How do you say Gatorade en español?"

For a moment I was shell-shocked. I thought I was just dumped by my BFF. As she walked away, I overheard her tell Bart she needed to grab her lip gloss. Quickly, she ran back to me and said, "Hurry and get outta here and find Swen!"

Yeah! My BFF had my back! I grabbed my Licky Sticky as I ran to find Adam.

"Bellows, what's your twenty?!" I yelled breathlessly.

"I'm in the garden!" Adam said.

"Where?" I asked, having trouble hearing him with all the music and the crowd noise.

"Just look for the fire pit!" he hollered back.

I could see at the far end of the backyard a large outdoor fireplace. People were sitting on the lounge chairs with a few others dancing and grooving to the blaring music by the fire.

I instantly spotted Adam, who wasn't hard to miss since tonight we were a pair of Twinkies (triplets if we counted our third-wheel wonder, Susan). And then that's when I saw her. *Venus.*

She was wearing all white with a still-steaming fake bake and a salon-fresh do. Her hair was pretty much platinum at this point. Add in her silver flip-flop heels and she was totally popping out now that it was getting dark. She was "shiny." I suddenly felt like a dork in *my* outfit, but we still had a mission to do.

I ran to Adam and I gave him a big smack on the cheek. This time he wasn't surprised.

"Hey, Luz," Venus said, visibly surprised that I had actually dared to show up at her house.

"Hey, Venus, some party," I remarked, giving her props.

Flipping her hair back with both hands Venus said, "Well, it's not as impressive as your postcard campaign for Homecoming Court. That was pretty 'precious.'"

"Well, you gotta do what you gotta do, right, sweetie?" I said as I put my arms around Adam's neck.

Adam nodded with a stupid, nervous grin.

"You know you're *so* right, Luz. I decided to open my party to *all* the kids at Gamma because I thought it was important that they get to know their freshman Homecoming Queen," Venus hissed with more than a hint of venom. I knew she was dead serious.

And then right in the middle of our little convo, Tammy Shellhorn brought Swen over to Venus while I was still clinging to Adam like a monkey to a giant tree.

"Hey, V, here's your *special* friend," Tammy purred as she released Swen to Venus.

Then she turned to us. "Hey, guys. Did y'all plan your outfits? It's sort of cultish but cute." Then she ran off to do more of Venus's secret evil bidding.

"How's it going, Bellows?" said Swen politely.

"Good," replied Adam, who could tell that I was at a loss for words at this particular moment.

Swen stared at us as if he was trying to figure out just what the heck was going on. I started to feel dizzy and nauseous.

Venus didn't waste any time and was right on her schedule when she grabbed Swen by the arm and said, "Hey, Mr. Swenson, I need to talk with you in private. Let's let these matching mates mate. Did you like my use of *alliteration*?" Venus gushed. Swen gave a courtesy smile. Then he looked straight at me and said, "It was good to see you, Luz," and walked off with Venus. Just like that.

I looked at Adam with dread. I wanted to start crying, but I couldn't remember if Bridge had put waterproof mascara on me after I'd taken off my purple liner. So I decided to postpone the boo-hoos.

"Adam, you gotta tell me what just happened. That was totally not part of the plan," I stammered out, stunned.

"I don't know. But you did lay it on kinda thick, chica."

"Me? I'm not the one who showed up with a matching outfit," I said, hearing my voice start to crack.

"Look, if your gonna start, let me get Jabba, so you can yell at her too," Adam said sarcastically.

"This is going to mess up my whole experiment!"

"Luz, what are you talking about? The only people you were trying to elevate into the higher gene pool were Bridge, Mase, and Susan. You weren't part of your own science experiment. *Or were you?*" Adam said, injecting me with a dose of reality.

"No. I wasn't. I just didn't want Venus to get to Swen. She's totally *evil*. She doesn't care about any of these guys at the party. She just wants their votes," I whined, dwelling on the unfairness of it all.

"Oh, but you weren't doing that with your 'Snacktastics,' were you?" Adam said, not holding back any punches tonight.

"That was science," I said, knowing full well that I was still lying to myself.

"Yeah, whatever, Luz. Fess up. Just admit it—you're just jealous of Venus. She hasn't done anything to you except be hot, popular, and smart," Adam punched again.

"Not *that* smart. She bites in English. I'll prove that she'll eat anyone for lunch so that she can get her way." I knew I was grasping at straws.

"Maybe so, but I think you give her way too much credit."

He started to look above my head to see who else was around. I could tell he was done with this conversation.

"I can't believe it! Since when are you suddenly Venus's shiniest fan?" I asked, still seething and hoping to drag Adam back to argue with me some more.

"Shut up, Luz! V's coming back!"

Venus had a strange look on her face. I wasn't sure what it was all about.

And without skipping a beat, Venus got between us and taking Adam's arm said to him, "Hey, sweetie, you'll take me to Homecoming, won't you? It's all right with you, Luz, right? I know you're going to be at Regionals during Homecoming and stuff, right?"

I wondered how she knew that.

"That's only if I win the school's competition," I reminded her.

And then Venus dropped her bomb. "Oh, right. Well, you *will* win and be qualified for Regionals because there isn't going to be any freshman competition at the school level. I told Dr. Hamrock that the rest of the freshman science cluster and I thought you would make the ideal candidate for Regionals."

"What?"

"I knew you wouldn't resist, Luz, because you're kinda soft and funny that way. I thought this would be great for your self-esteem after that tragedy with the fish tank and all."

I was at a loss for words, but obviously, Venus was not. And what had she done to convince the rest of my fellow geeks to resist their natural competitive urges to show off their smarts? Did popularity carry that much power? She was more calculating than I was, and that was saying a lot.

"Thanks for being such a sport, Luz. I couldn't go to Homecoming and be forever immortalized on TV without a date, you know. Adam, hurry and come to my room. I want to show you what I might wear since I know you are such a stickler with your wardrobe," Venus said pointedly, glancing to our hideously matching outfits. A confused Adam looked to me for guidance.

"That's okay, Adam. Go ahead and go. I need to get home anyway. It's getting late."

"Are you sure?" he said, still not sure what had taken place.

"Yeah," I said, with a strained smile. "*Go!*" I ordered.

"Okay, well, I'll talk with you later." His eyes motioned to his closed fist, which held his Licky Sticky.

My head was still spinning. Did she ask Swen? Did he say yes? If he said yes, then why did she just steal my fake boyfriend? I was so confused with all the possible awfulness. The music was still blaring and my feet felt like they weighed a hundred pounds each.

As I walked back toward the house, I found Bridge and told her I needed to leave. I didn't want to give her details because I would have totally lost it at the party. Bridge informed me that she didn't want to leave just yet because V had a special surprise for her that had to do with B-Dawg.

I told her I couldn't wait. So, I started to walk away when I saw Mase. I would have tried to talk with him but he and his new group were having so much fun catching air over various pieces of pool furniture that I didn't want to spoil it.

I walked past the snack table again, and there were Susan and Jimbo standing there as if time had stood still for the last thirty minutes. Maybe Susan would leave with me, I hoped. I just felt weird leaving a party by myself. I walked over to Susan, who was licking guacamole off her fingers.

"Susan, are you leaving anytime soon?" I inquired.

"No," grunted Susan.

I walked closer to Jimbo and flipped my ponytail and batted my eyes sweetly. "What about you, Jimbo?" I asked in my higher girly voice.

"Only if I'm kicked out," laughed Jimbo, now admitting that he loved the "in" crowd, or at least the "in" parties.

Okay, so my cute girly powers were off circuit tonight. "Well, y'all have fun. I'll talk with you guys later," I said in my regular lower and *plain* voice.

It took forever but I finally made my way to the front door. Once outside I looked down the street and estimated that my house was approximately two miles away. I could have called home, but I didn't want to wait on the porch outside this party for my *mom* to pick me up.

It was a pretty humiliating night already. And I figured if I walked at least I could clear my head. As I started to make my way down the darkened street, I felt a car pull up behind me and I didn't want to turn around.

But I did reach into my purse for my phone and pepper spray (thanks to my mom and all those safety episodes on *Oprah*). And I was also prepared to run back to the party if the car didn't stop trailing me. It didn't. Suddenly from the car in the darkness I heard, "*Luz*, it's late. You shouldn't be walking home. Do you want a ride?"

Chapter

16

I turned around slowly so as not to be too obvious. It was hard to see the car at first because of the headlights. Once I recognized the little bread box of a car, I went in a few brief moments from total rejection to terror to gushing ecstasy.

The familiar voice said, "Luz, get in the car. I'll take you home."

My ears must have still been ringing from all the music blaring at the party because I swear I thought I heard Swen say, "I'll take you to the prom." And that was another three years away! The car stopped with the passenger's side window rolled down. As I peeked in, I caught a whiff of that inviting new-car smell.

"Hey, I didn't realize this was *your* car," I said, trying to sound all casual-like. This was a big lie, because every day when my parents drop me off at school in the morning, I always run back and check the student parking lot to see if Swen and his cute little *coche* are there.

Before I opened the door, I slid my phone and pepper spray back safely in my purse. I had a quick flash of my pepper spray going off in the car. I double-checked and made sure the lid was on. Tight.

"You're dangerous," Swen joked.

"Oh, you don't even know the half of it," I said, not even wanting to go there this late in the evening. I stepped into the car and it was really low to the ground, unlike our Tahoe, but it was definitely cute. And speaking of cute, I checked out Swen for a moment. He hadn't dressed up for the party or anything. He was just wearing a plain white T-shirt and jeans. And he still looked *mucho caliente*.

But something was funny. I thought I faintly smelled cologne. I was about to take a deeper whiff when Swen asked, "So, where to?"

"Just go down Lake Highlands and then turn left on Tranquilla," I directed with my hands. I started to feel a bit giddy.

Swen stepped on the gas and we made our way down the street. I couldn't get over the fact that I was sitting *so* close to him. It made me nervous. I wondered how my breath was, so I fumbled for a mint in my purse. Finding my package of Gabber Gum, I thought, *Omigod, no way! Not now!* Finally, I found a stray peppermint in the side pocket of my purse. I popped it in ASAP.

"So, why are you walking and why are you leaving the party so early?" Swen asked.

"I was, uh . . . ready to leave," I said. Then I quickly added, "I mean, I did what I needed to do for my *research*." I didn't want to tell him that nobody wanted to leave Venus's fab party with me or that I didn't want to look like a "nerd alert" and call my mom. Knowing that two could play this game, I then said, "So, why are *you* leaving the party so soon?"

"Well, *I* came to the party to help *you* with your research, but it looked like your hands were full and you didn't need my help."

Omigod! He totally thinks you were with Adam! my brain screamed at me.

"No, not really. Oh, make a left *here*!"

Swen yanked on the wheel and made a quick left turn. I fell in his direction and my mint fell out of my mouth and landed somewhere in the car.

"Sorry about that," he apologized, recovering.

"Oh, that's okay," I said, lifting myself back over to my side of the car. Swen *did* smell really nice. I tried to spy my mint on the floorboard without him noticing.

"There's my house, with the red door," I said as I pointed.

Swen stopped in front of my house and kept the car running. Trying to figure out what to say next, I became fixated on the little hula girl on his dashboard, who was shaking her hips, and on my missing mint.

"You know, when it comes to reporting and writing, I can be really patient. Especially when it comes to finding out the truth, because the truth is really exciting. Like with this science department story, I think you have some really cool theories, Luz."

"Thanks . . ." I smiled and gazed helplessly into his eyes.

Swen frowned. "But honestly, I gotta tell you, it seems like either you are avoiding me or you don't want me to help. So, what's the deal?"

I shifted uncomfortably in the car seat and looked down at Bridge's boring flip-flops hoping for the right words to appear. They didn't. So, I decided to try a new experiment—telling the truth.

"Look, I'm so sorry, Swen. I'm totally not trying to avoid you. *I swear*. It's just that my personal life and my scientific life are kinda all tangled up right now. Especially with the science competition, I feel Dr. Hamrock's really putting the pressure on. And if I go to Regionals, I'll totally miss Homecoming," I explained, getting a load off my chest.

"We all have to make sacrifices sometimes," Swen said, sounding unsympathetic.

I was a bit taken aback, but I figured if he was going to ask some tough questions, then I would, too. So I asked, "Aren't you going to Homecoming?"

"Nope."

"Didn't Venus ask you?" I asked, fully aware that I was acting like a total freshman now.

"Yeah," Swen answered without giving any more information. Boy, there's a reason I'm not in the journalism department, because the only questions I seem to ask get a yes or no answer. So much for my investigative reporting career.

"What *are* you doing then?" I finally asked, proud of my question.

"I'm working on an important story on Gamma High's participation in the Regional Science Competition."

"Well, why are you so fascinated with science? You're not really the type. I mean, the *science* type," I said, hoping not to offend. I looked out the window to make sure no one was coming out of my house.

"I'm interested because of the human-aspect story."

"Okay . . ." I'm sure my face showed that I had no idea what he was talking about.

"Look, Luz. I'm going to tell you something and you can't tell anyone and I mean *anyone* about this. The science cluster is not pulling in the students it once did. And the extra outside funds it needs to help cover things like equipment or new programs aren't coming in fast enough. And because of all that, Dr. Hamrock might lose his job if Gamma is forced to downsize." Swen sounded truly concerned.

"So, what does this have to do with me?"

"Well, you're the fresh new face of the science cluster. If you do well in competition, then it helps Gamma and the science department."

"Really?" I said, caught in a mixture of emotions. "I know that kinda sucks for Dr. Hamrock, but why do you care so much about him?" And then I spotted my mint on the floor and picked it up really quick. It was sticky but I just kept it hidden in my closed fist.

Then Swen connected the dots. "He's my uncle."

The classic lightbulb came on in my head just as the front porch light did. And I was terrified that my mom (or worse, my dad) would storm out. And not only would that be totally embarrassing but then there could always be the parental grounding factor because of the boy-bringing-me-home thing. *Aye Dios!*

"Luz, I don't want to put pressure on you too," Swen said, as he patted my hand with the dead mint. "I just think you're smart and talented. And you could really be the shot in the arm that Gamma needs."

"Wow. That's so wild. I don't know what to say to that." I was too freaked out to look at him.

"Just let me help you, Luz."

"Okay . . ." I glanced back up from my Pic Purse at him.

And then that crazy dangerous thing happened. Just like you see in the movies. Just like they tell you in the magazines. We looked into each other's eyes. The streetlight was streaming in the car just enough to see his amazing blue eyes with just a speckle of gold in them.

There was a long pause. It was terribly exciting and uncomfortable. It almost made me want to throw up. But I didn't. Hallelujah! He just smiled at me. But—and this is an important "but"—he didn't *lean in* for the kiss like they tell you he is going to do in those magazines.

And even though everything in my DNA said to give him a big ole smooch, my brain kicked in and told me, *Don't even* think *about it!*

When I thought I heard my front door unlock, I knew I'd better get this brown butt inside.

"Thanks for the ride, Swen, and the offer. I'll have a better idea of where this project is after they announce who makes the five freshman finalists on Monday afternoon." Then I quickly started to make my way around his car to the sidewalk.

"Okay, and Luz . . ."

This was absolutely killing me. I wanted to hang out, like, the whole evening with him but I knew it wasn't possible. I paused for a second and prayed that no one would come running out my door to drag me inside by the hair.

"Call me if you need me." He was being really sweet. Or at least it felt sweet to me, or a little bit more than just being nice. Whatever.

I nodded and ran inside my house and shut the door quietly. I was twittering around as if I had been jolted with electricity. My brain was spitting out all the glorious facts to me: *He's not going to the dance with Venus! Ha-ha. Dr. Hamrock is his uncle! What happened in that gene pool there? He said I was* gifted! I wanted to shout it out, but instead I decided to spy on him through my living room curtains and watch him drive away.

My mom was in her big, fuzzy, white bathrobe and was deep conditioning her hair in a shower cap. I didn't hear her come up behind me until she said, "So . . . that didn't look like Mrs. Joiner unless she's bought a new car. Who was that?"

"Umm, that was my new science partner," I said giddily.

"Well, it's a good thing your father wasn't up to meet him," my mom said suspiciously.

"Nice outfit," I said, moving off topic.

"*Escuchame.* Don't try to change the subject with me, lady," she replied, turning it back around and totally busting my chops.

My mom just shook her head and walked back to her bedroom. I, on the other hand, defied gravity and floated back toward my room but decided to grab a snack first and get rid of the peppermint that was still stuck to my hand and covered with Swen's floorboard carpet.

What a night! I went to the kitchen and tried to figure out what I wanted to eat but I couldn't even think. I texted Bridge to tell her the amazing news. I waited. And I heard no reply. So I did it again. She finally hit me back, "Cnt tlk hre. Wl tlk L8r."

I was flabbergasted. Like, what did she mean she'd call me back? I was her best friend, for crying out loud.

So, I did the next best thing. I called Adam on his cell phone. I received a message that his phone was disconnected.

That was weird, I thought, since I had reached him earlier in the evening. I opened the fridge door looking for a snack and decided to try to reach Adam on his Licky Sticky. I was afraid that because of the distance he wouldn't be able to catch my signal, but thought I'd try anyway. I mean, I believe in miracles and all.

"Adam?" I called softly. "Adam?" I repeated a bit louder, trying not to wake up my mom again. "Hey, it's Luz, I don't know if you can hear me or not, but I have some really juicy news about Venus and . . ." And before I could continue I heard another voice. It was definitely *not* Adam's.

"Hey, Luz, Adam had to leave in a hurry but he did happen to leave your little gizmo behind. Cute invention, but you could totally stand to engineer better reception on this thing. Maybe next time you won't buy your components at the Dollar Store. Oh, well. Now, what was the latest and greatest news you had to share about *me* and *my* life? I'm really anxious to hear," Venus dripped with sarcasm.

"Uh . . ." I took a careful moment to figure out what exactly to say next. Lives depended on it.

So I continued, "Well, V, I was just surprised to find that you sent a mass e-mail invitation and how funny it was that I didn't get one."

"Yes, that was 'funny.' But you know what's even funnier, Luz? It's the fact that you are trying to call people who are no longer your friends. If I were you—and thank God I'm not—I would leave Bridget and Adam alone, especially if you don't want them to blame you for ruining their lives," Venus said bluntly.

"Is that a threat?"

"No, Luzy Lu, it's a promise. *A juicy one.* Over and out," Venus finished with an ominous tone.

Either her walkie-talkie had faded out or the battery had died, neither of which was a good sign. None of this was good. Alone in the kitchen, I started going over the events of the party, the ride home with Swen, and why nobody had called me back. What had happened at the party after I'd left? Suddenly nothing in the kitchen looked appetizing. I shut the fridge door and stood in the darkness.

Why didn't Venus want me to hang with Bridge and Adam? And what would she do to them or me to ruin all our lives? I walked slowly down the dark hallway to my bedroom. My body became very tired, but my mind wasn't about to stop racing trying to figure out what was going to happen to me and Bridge and Adam next.

Chapter

17

Sunday was pretty much a wash since Venus's threat had kept me awake all night. I didn't really get to sleep until the sun came up, and when I finally woke it was already like two in the afternoon. With a bad case of bed head and crusties in my eyes, I crawled out of bed and stumbled to my purse to find my cell phone. I called Adam to find out what had happened after Venus had kidnapped him.

Unfortunately, Adam's cell phone was still out of commission and I didn't even have his home number, because, I mean, who uses landlines anyway?

Obviously, I couldn't call him on my trusty Licky Sticky since you-know-who had it. So, I hopped on my computer and resorted to e-mail. I told him if he got this e-mail to please call me ASAP or, otherwise, I'd see him at school tomorrow. But I really wanted to talk with him today.

I was really surprised and hurt that he hadn't called me at all, since I was accustomed to hearing his daily report of what was going on in his life. Oh, well, I guess I was just going to have to wait until Monday, but I wasn't going to wait until Monday to talk with Bridge.

I phoned Bridge on her cell and I even texted her several times. After ten minutes of nothingness, I sent her an e-mail. And then finally when I couldn't stand it anymore, I resorted to calling her landline. When I called, Bridge's dad actually picked up.

"Hi. This is Luz. Is Bridge home?"

"Oh, hello, Luz. No, she left with a friend about an hour ago."

A friend? I thought. I'm her best friend. Who else would she be hanging out with? My stomach started to feel queasy.

"Was it Venus Hunter?"

"I didn't catch her name."

"Was she blond?" I asked, trying to narrow the field.

"I think so."

"Did she have really straight blond hair and look a bit leathery because she fake bakes too much?" I spit out, desperately wanting to know, with my jealousy in overdrive. "Were there other kids with them?"

"I'm a realtor, not a private eye, honey," Mr. Joiner said, becoming a bit bored with my twenty questions.

Realizing my insanity was taking over, I said, "Oh, I'm sorry."

Mr. Joiner laughed. "Are you and Bridge having a fight or something?"

"Not at all!" I replied, hoping Bridge wasn't really mad at me for something I didn't know about.

"Oh, I was just wondering because you normally know more about my daughter than I do," teased Mr. Joiner.

I laughed. It was so true. Bridge's mom was pretty tuned in to what we were up to as well as who our friends and foes were, but as for her dad, he was definitely clueless.

After hanging up with Bridge's dad, I guessed I would just have to be patient. Dang. I hated being patient and especially hated not knowing if someone was mad at me. But, I did manage to pass the time away by doing all the things that needed to get done after a week of Gamma Glamma madness—like studying. I even cleaned out my science accessories and equipment as well as loaded and unloaded the washer and dryer at least a million times.

I tumbled into Monday morning as quickly as my delicates did in the dryer, and still no contact with Bridge. I even got to school early to check things out, but oddly enough, things were different today and *I* felt different. So, I didn't observe or spy on anyone this morning. And I didn't pass postcards or serve batches of cookies or try to contact my crew. I didn't journal my day in my notebook, take pictures, or even record anything with my shoes, for that matter. Today was just simply school.

On this last day that would control our fates, I did something that is almost scientifically impossible. I didn't meddle. I did absolutely nada. I even walked throughout the halls without my scientific eyes on. And I just blended into the great Gamma melting pot. I went to my classes and was surprised not to see anyone from the gang. I felt like I was in *The Twilight Zone*.

I was really relieved to see Susan, and I'm embarrassed to say it, but I was so relieved and excited to see her that I almost bowled her over. Susan was busy drawing J-girl being chased by two hobbit boys. The hobbit boys looked fairly familiar, but I didn't pay that much attention to them because I couldn't control myself and I started grilling Susan.

"Hey, Susan, did you have a good time at the party Saturday night?" I used my best friendly Monday morning voice.

"Yeah," replied Susan automatically.

"Did anything exciting happen after I left?" I asked, hoping that I didn't miss anything really exciting, especially after having had such a traumatic time.

"Well, they did bring out a very large tray of peeled shrimp. It went pretty fast. And the cocktail sauce was too hot and it gave me an ulcer in my mouth." Susan finally stopped what she was doing so she could peel down her lower lip and show me that she wasn't lying. I just nodded as I inspected the tiny ulcer. Ew.

"What else happened?" I continued to pump.

"Wewl, I wus asthed to the danth," Susan said while still holding her lip.

A bit frustrated, I helped Susan remove her hand from her lip and asked her, "Now, what did you say?"

"I said I was asked to the dance. By two band boys."

"Oh, Susan, that's so cool! Aren't you excited?"

"I guess."

"Who did you say yes to?"

"I didn't say yes to anyone. I told them I didn't know if I felt like going because they're going to have *The Lord of the Rings* trilogy at the Alamo Cinema on that day." Surely, she was joking, but I had to find out for sure.

"But, Susan, you can rent those DVDs anytime," I reminded her.

"Yeah, but this is going to be on the big screen," she said, totally not kidding.

"Susan, your familia can afford to buy you your own cinema," I said with total conviction, knowing that her family not only could afford to buy a cinema for her, but could also buy her her own *country* stocked fully with alpacas and pizza.

"It's not the same, Luz."

"I think you should give this decision some deep thought."

"I guess," Susan said, slightly irritated with my insistence.

I was so caught up in her elfin magic world that I almost forgot to ask her if she saw Bridge, Adam, or Mase.

"Oh, by the way, Susan, did you happen to see Bridge or Adam Bellows at the party?"

"No," Susan said as she went back to her drawing.

"How about Mason Milam?"

Susan started to erase with a vengeance. "Yeah, I saw him."

"What was he doing?"

"He was doing stunts over the pool furniture."

I laughed out loud. "I'm surprised he didn't jump over the pool."

"He did," Susan said as she started to shade the hair on one of her hobbits.

"What?! Shut up!" I said in total disbelief.

"He did."

"How did *that* happen?"

Susan took a deep breath because she knew I wasn't going to let her off the hook easily. "Venus dared some kids to do it. She even dared Claude Klopp. He said no, and so she said he had to leave her party. Mason moved Claude out of the way and jumped, I think on his behalf or something," Susan reported.

"Did he make it?" I asked, hoping that nothing bad had happened to Mase.

"Yeah."

"*Then* what happened?" I said, feeling like I was pulling teeth.

"Nothing. Venus started to hang out with Mason."

"Well, I'm glad he made it and I'm glad he had fun," I commented, trying to wrap up this convo.

"He didn't," Susan said, striking up my interest once again. Dang.

"How do you know?" I asked, trying to have some patience.

"When Venus started to hang with him, Mason just made a face and left. He made the face that Frotastic does when I feed him cucumbers soaked in vinegar," Susan replied.

"You mean pickles?" I said, surprised.

"Yeah. I guess," Susan said, putting away her drawing materials and getting ready for class.

"Thanks for the info, Susan. I'd better get back to my seat."

Today science class was a whole new experience knowing that Dr. Hamrock was Swen's uncle. I tried to see the resemblance, but it was nowhere to be found.

As we reviewed the periodic table and how the movement of electrons from one energy level to another could cause incredible instability on the atomic level, I couldn't focus because I knew I was going to have to talk with Dr. Hamrock at the end of class. I was afraid, to say the least. Class went faster today than I wanted it to, which is funny because I'm usually the first one waiting for the bell to ring.

But, alas, today would be *muy differente*. After class, Dr. Hamrock called me up to his desk.

"Luz, how's your project going?"

"I guess I'll really know at the end of the day, but overall I think it's gone well. I mean, I know that I have enough evidence to substantiate my theory about influencing group opinion and manipulating social hierarchies and all," I reported.

"Well, that's good. But I wanted to let you know that you wouldn't have to sweat about Wednesday evening. Gamma isn't going to have its science competition this year. It's just going to be your project and we are going to give you all the help you need to focus on Regionals."

"Thanks," I said, trying to act all surprised even though Venus had already spilled the frijoles on my fate and Regionals.

"Let me know when you have your project and presentation roughed in so that I can look at it with you," said Dr. Hamrock almost kind of sweetly. Weird.

"Okay, thanks," I replied again.

After I left the science room, I turned back to look at Dr. Hamrock. He was looking intently over his lesson plans, and for the first time ever, he looked like a human being to me. It was really weird.

I boogied down to lunch as fast as I could. I knew I could finally talk to Bridge and Adam at some point even if Venus was lurking around. I stepped into the salad line and I was one spot behind Bridge.

After I grabbed my tray, a plate, and a spork (it's a really bad plastic hybrid of a spoon and fork that should never have happened), I didn't pay attention to what I was putting on my tray, because I was trying to make eye contact with Bridge.

I whispered, "Hey, Bridge, are you mad at me?"

Bridge shook her head.

"You haven't returned any of my calls. What's the deal?" I asked urgently.

"I can't really talk with you, Luz," Bridge said, looking around nervously.

"Then when?" I asked, trying not to cause a scene. My heart started racing because I was being snubbed by my *best friend*.

"*Later*," Bridge said, trying to shake me off.

"How much later?" I asked, trying to hang on.

"Just later, Luz," Bridge said as she looked at me with big eyes as if to say, "leave me alone, freak."

Bridge walked away from me as if I were a leper, or worse, as if I had digested a whole tin of our fartmaker cookies. I was so stunned and hurt. I blinked hard to fight the tears that were forming. And I tried to hold my breath to keep the lump in my throat from coming out.

And finally, when I got to the lunch lady, she asked me if I wanted more than just the large heap of lettuce I had put on my plate. I didn't know if it was scientifically possible, but I felt dumb and mad at the same time. And I didn't care who saw me go back in the salad line again to add more "fixings" to my large serving of iceberg lettuce. I started to feel a bit lightheaded because my low blood sugar and soaring level of adrenaline were shaking up my biochemical balance.

As I walked toward my table, I gazed at the J+L section. Venus was there, but she seemed to be in deep thought today. Next, I noticed Adam *wasn't* there. *Where was he?* Surely, he wouldn't be absent today when we find out who the finalists are going to be at the end of the day. Suddenly, I discovered that he was right in front of me throwing away his trash.

So, I said, "Hey, Missing, what's going on? Why haven't you called? Didn't you have the cash to pay for your cell bill or did you burn it on that vintage Polo you're wearing?" I laughed, trying to act normal and funny and whatnot. But listening to myself, I could totally tell I sounded like a desperate girlfriend.

And then Adam said, "I've had a lot of things going on."

"Me, too," I said proudly, ready to download my news.

Adam seemed impatient or at least distracted. He was looking around like he was looking for someone.

"I can't talk right now," Adam said without any emotion.

"But let me just tell you this one thing about Swen and Venus," I started.

"Luz, here's a news alert for you. There's a world outside high school. And right now I don't have time to deal with you and your little tween affairs, so you're just going to have to *deal*. Later," Adam said loudly enough for people to hear.

I felt a bit embarrassed. No, I felt *really* embarrassed. My face felt hot. I'm sure my cheeks were really red. I didn't know if anyone overheard us or not, so I decided to just brush it off and act like it wasn't a big deal even though *it was*.

"Hey, no problema, Adam. That's cool. I'll just catch you later . . ."

I don't think he even heard me. He was already halfway down the cafeteria at this point. So, here I was with my cold salad getting warm. With my best friends MIA I couldn't tolerate sitting by myself at the sci-fi table, even if they were my people. It was too freaking lonely and my insides were churning frantically over the thought that I may have lost my best friends. In a desperate panic, I decided to sit by Susan.

"Can I sit here?" I asked Susan, praying that she wouldn't be the third person in a row to shun me.

"O . . . kay," mumbled Susan, who was now finished with her meal and digging through her big ole fringed suede bag to locate a pencil. When she at last pulled out her discovery, the pencil's lead was so small that Susan had to peel at the wood with her nonexistent fingernails.

Too upset to eat, I just raked through my salad with my plastic spork. I overheard the band kids discussing such topics as the importance of squads being in sync as well as making sure they have perfect "camel toe." I looked at Susan with a surprised face over the term "camel toe," and she informed me that it's the position of your foot when you are marching. Weird.

As I tried to eat my brand-X crackers, a dark-headed band boy asked Susan to Homecoming. In total Susan style, she mumbled to him and said she didn't know if she was going or not. After he walked away, Susan rolled her eyes at me, which were emphasized by the magnification of her glasses, which she has been refusing to take off.

I can't believe she already has had, like, three offers. No one's asked me yet. I mean, it's not like that's a big deal or anything because I only want Swen, but dang, Susan?

I thanked everyone at the table for letting me sit with them. And then I ran away as fast as I could. After dropping off my trash, I decided to pick up an ice cream sandwich and look for Mase.

Now in the Dramatica zone, I felt like I was sticking out a bit much because I had chosen to wear orange today and now I looked like the great pumpkin among the witches.

Mase was sitting down and he smiled at me. I took that as an invitation and decided to sit down.

"How's your laryngitis?"

Mase gave me a thumbs-up.

"Did you ever catch up on your sleep?"

Mase nodded as he continued to work on a drawing of himself

jumping over what looked, at first glance, like Venus's pool. Upon further inspection, I noticed it was actually her mouth! I hate to say it, but seeing that drawing was the best thing that had happened to me all day.

"You haven't talked with Adam lately, have you?"

Mase just shook his head no and went back to drawing in between bites of his sandwich.

I felt some of the Dramatica girls staring at me, and it made me feel really uncomfortable, because I couldn't tell if they were jealous or if they were going to beat me up. I decided not to wait and find out, and I told Mase that I would catch up with him later.

Finally, at the end of the day in English, the loudspeaker came on. Mr. Sekin said, "I'll announce the freshman finalists first and then continue all the way up to the seniors. If your name is called, then please gather your books and come down to the auditorium. A video crew will be there to talk with you and conduct an informal interview."

As Mr. Sekin started to name the freshman boys, I put my pen down. Bart Marquez, who was first to be announced, wasn't a surprise and neither was Brad Walker, aka B-Dawg. I just kept staring at the loudspeaker and waited. The next name called was Adam Bellows. I wanted to stand up and cheer, but I tried to be cool and just stayed in my seat and smiled really hard—until my face hurt. But I was sure that Adam had to be bouncing around somewhere in the school.

The next name to be called was my science partner, Jimbo Billimek who was actually in class with me. Some of the kids in our class were chanting, "Geek! Geek! Geek!" in a totally supportive grunt fashion.

Jimbo clasped his hands together and shook them from side to side in victory. Mrs. Franks had to tell us to settle down which was good because I almost missed the next important name of the day when Mr. Sekin said, "Mason Milam."

I was ecstatic. I could only imagine what Mase was doing as he heard his name being called out loud across the building. I bit my lip and listened intently for the rest of the names to be announced.

"And now, for our five girl finalists from the freshman class . . ."

Mr. Sekin continued. I could feel my neck muscles tighten and my mouth become dry.

The first name called was Susan Seamus. Everyone in class kinda gasped and laughed. I had to admit I was thrown off a bit, but the excitement was building so much that I couldn't dwell on just one thing. The next name was Traci Armstrong. The class roared in excitement. Traci wasn't totally unexpected, but I thought we would have heard from someone from the J+L camp by now. I also suspected there were a few J+L girls freaking out right now.

The next name was Venus Hunter. No surprise there. *Next!* I thought. The P.A. went silent. Mr. Sekin said to hang on for a moment. During that *very* long moment, Jimbo informed me not to worry because, by his calculations, he was confident that I would make the cut. I tried to be polite, but I was seriously on edge. Then Jimbo informed me that the newspaper article that came out would help as well.

I looked at him as if he were from Mars. That's when he handed me today's edition of the school paper (which, regretfully, I hadn't read). On the front page there was a little article about *moi*! The headline said, "The Fresh Face of Science." It was a small blurb that said I was a freshman and I had an unusual approach to a science experiment and that there would be more to come in the next few weeks. I couldn't read any more because Mr. Sekin came back on the P.A.

Mr. Sekin said sorry for the delay and said the next name was Bridget Joiner. I was so happy for her (even if she wasn't speaking to me right now). We did it! Project Gamma Glamma had totally worked! It was fabulous. I couldn't hold it in any longer. I knew that if I saw Bridge now, things would be different. And so I screamed for her.

And then the last name was called. Mine. I didn't even recognize it because I went back to try to read the article again.

"Luz, I told you! I told you you'd make it!" screamed Jimbo. Again the class roared, "Geek! Geek! Geek!" But this time it was for *me*! It took a while for it to sink in, and I felt, well, *honored*. I couldn't stop smiling. I felt kinda stupid and glorious at the same time.

Mrs. Franks finally spoke up: "Jim and Luz, congratulations. Go on down to the auditorium. But remember, you still have a vocabulary test tomorrow."

I gathered all my stuff and crammed it into my backpack while Jimbo held the door for me. We ran down to the auditorium laughing and yelling.

When we finally arrived at the foyer outside the auditorium, a crowd of finalists from the other grades had emerged. I overheard someone say that the TV crew was starting to do interviews. So, I decided I had better run to the girls' bathroom and do a quick make-over on myself. I pulled out some lip gloss and started to apply it without even looking in a mirror.

The bathroom was only quiet for a second before an elated Bridge bounced in. At first glance, we hugged each other and screamed. And did our little Gamma Glamma victory dance.

"We did it! We did it!" I announced.

"Yeah, I can't believe that Gamma Glamma worked. It's really happening," Bridge said, sounding like her old self.

"Me neither."

Then Bridge said, "Look, Luz, I'm sorry for the silent treatment. I'm not even supposed to be talking to you now. Venus got B-Dawg to ask me to Homecoming!"

"That's great! I'm soo happy for you, Bridge." And I meant it sincerely.

And then Bridge said, "But there's more. At Venus's party, Venus said that if I wanted to keep my date with B-Dawg I needed to campaign for her. And I also needed to stop talking with you. Luz, I'm sorry. I didn't know what to do."

I was a bit surprised, but at least now I knew what Venus had meant by her threats.

"We're BFF, even undercover. It's okay," I said, finally able to put two and two together.

"No, it's not," Bridge jumped in. "I didn't want to mess up your science experiment. And I didn't want Venus to ruin it for you since we all worked so hard. And really, I just wanted to go to this dance with B-Dawg. It might be my only chance at a date like this. You know how I feel about him and . . ."

Bridge started to turn on the waterworks.

"Bridge, don't start now. This isn't the time," I reminded her.

"Junior High was the worst for me, Luz. But now, here, I'm at least skinnier and I'm in the science cluster and people think I'm smart. But all I ever wanted to do was to be pretty or just a little popular. And now, *I am*. And it really feels good. I'm not such an outsider now, Luz."

I just nodded and listened.

"So, please help me out . . . just for a little while . . . until the dance. I can't go through the next three years like I did in Junior High. *I just can't*, Luz . . ."

Bridge started the waterworks again. I knew what she was asking and it kinda burned, but we didn't have time to get into it here. So, with my stern voice I ordered, "No tears! Bridge, you're about to be on camera. Wash your face and get it together."

As Bridge tried to clean up the crying damage, Venus slithered in and walked in front of Bridge to the nearby sink.

"So, what's going on, *finalists?*" she hissed, tossing me a pointed stare. I stared right back at her, but from behind Venus, I saw Bridge's eyes widen with a fear that totally screamed, "Help me!" Bridge was a mess at this point, and no gadget, potion, or serum was going to work for her now. So, I did what needed to be done.

"Fine, Bridge. If you're refusing to talk to me because you're in love with your plastic newfound friends, then that's great! I officially don't know you. Hate you. Mean it. Adios," I huffed.

And then I stormed off as loudly as I could with my boots, which weren't really that loud because they have rubber soles. And it was hard to even slam the bathroom door because it was on those slow-moving hinges. But, I'm pretty sure they got the gist.

Outside the door, I heard Venus in her so sarcastic voice ask, "What was that about?"

Bridge, who was still sniffling, faintly said, "I don't know."

Chapter

18

Our first interview with *High School Rules* was supposed to be the most exciting thing that has happened to us so far at Gamma. But no one had ever mentioned the terror that was also going to go with it.

After my "frienemy" encounter with Bridge and Venus, I bolted back to the auditorium entrance to see what was going on. The only other freshmen I saw in the crowd were Mase and Traci. So, we just stood together as we watched the equipment and lights whiz by, while we wondered who was leading this parade.

A tall man dressed head to toe in black walked up to us and grinned. "Hey, guys, I'm Rodney Stringer, director of *High School Rules*. Are you excited to have your first on-camera interview?"

Mase looked at me and nudged me.

"You mean by ourselves?" I said, feeling a small lump in my throat.

"No worries. You're actually going to be interviewed in small groups. That always seems to help with the on-camera jitters. I'll ask a few questions but I'll make sure you know the answers, because we want you to look *good* on camera," he joked. "You three are freshmen, right?"

We all nodded yes and followed Mr. Stringer inside the auditorium. A crew guy directed us to sit on the edge of the stage and Mase sat down first. I sat down next to him and became the middle person when Traci followed at the end. With a clipboard in hand, Mr. Stringer sat in front of us by the cameraman.

"Like I said, guys, this is going to be very casual. So, just look at me. And don't pay any attention to the camera or the microphone." Rod pointed to the high-tech mic above us.

Mase was first in the firing squad. "So, what's your name?" Rod asked.

Mase shot me a look as he motioned to his throat and widened his eyes like a deer in the headlights as he grabbed my leg hard. Reacting to the pain, I jumped. "Uh, his name is Mason Milam," I said, now looking like his fellow deer in the headlights.

Mase pointed to his mechanic's jacket with his name patch on it to emphasize that the information I had disclosed was indeed true. Rod looked at us a bit puzzled. I jumped back into the ring of fire and said, "Mason has a case of laryngitis. I can speak on his behalf . . . at least for now." Then I shot a look back to Mase to remind him that I couldn't keep doing this forever.

"Okay, well, I wanted to know what Mason thinks about being a freshman finalist," Rod said as he looked at both of us waiting for an answer to appear. I looked at Mase and he just gave me a shrug.

"He says he wasn't expecting this but he thinks it's cool. Right, Mason?" I said, looking for reassurance. Mase rolled his eyes.

Rod flashed his Hollywood smile to me. "And what's *your* name?"

"I'm Luz. Santos. And I'm a freshman," I answered, totally sounding like a robot.

"And what's your take on being a finalist?"

"Oh, I'm just happy to be a part of the process and I'm proud to be a part of the science cluster at Gamma," I said, trying to smile, feeling like I should add a parade-float hand wave and knowing perfectly well that this was so cheesy that all I needed was a couple of meatballs to complete the deal.

"Was science a factor in helping you get to this point?"

Was I that transparent? I was taken aback by Rod's question and I wondered if he was trying to dig up some dirt.

"You mean as a finalist?"

"Yes."

A wave of nervousness came over me in that instant and lingered. "Well, kinda. Uh, if it weren't for my colleagues in the *science* department and my best friend, Bridge, helping get the votes out, then I suppose I wouldn't be here today."

"Okay, that's good," replied Rod as if that answer worked for him at the moment. Next, Rod turned to taut and tanned Traci as he leaned in to ask her what she thought about being a finalist.

"It'll work," said Traci as dry as a cracker with her 2 percent body fat.

"But, in your *heart*," Rod said, trying to bring on the drama, "what things do you believe worked in your favor to become a Homecoming finalist?"

"It was probably because people thought I'd beat them up if they didn't vote for me."

Rod laughed out loud. "Oh, *that's* funny. You're kidding, right?"

"No," said Traci, without blinking.

I felt Mase slide away from me and Traci. There was an uncomfortable silence that lingered between us. Taking charge, Rod cleared the air when he cleared his throat and changed the subject.

"Alright, well, let's talk about dates for the big dance," encouraged Rod. "Mason, have you had a chance to ask that special girl?" Again Mase looked at me like I was his ventriloquist.

"No, he hasn't asked anyone . . . *yet*," I commented. Then I continued, "Oh, I'm not sure yet if my date can go."

"And Traci?" continued Rod.

"I've got some options and I haven't decided either," Traci said as she flexed her dating muscles.

"Okay, guys, you all did a good job for being the first team up. Now, you can go with Jennifer. She'll take some Polaroids of you and she'll give you a release form for your parents to sign. And again, good job," said Rod as he broomed us off. I think Rod didn't feel he had anything TV-worthy to work with from our trio.

I know I didn't feel like I did a good job, because I was as plastic as a Barbie with my answers. As we exited the auditorium, I saw the next group coming down. A big, fat, plastic voice inside my head told me to stick around.

It's times like this I wish I had a hidden camera somewhere or monitoring device, but I didn't, so I did the next best thing. It wasn't scientific. It was just pure snooping. I decided that I could run back behind the auditorium to the backstage where the stage crew normally hangs out and attempt to listen to the next group.

I had discovered this place when Bridge and I had put postcards out for Mase. And now I could discover what was going to happen next from behind the magic curtain. I peeked through the crack from the side of the stage.

For starters, Venus sat in the middle (what else would you expect), between Bart and Bridge. She crossed her freshly fake-baked legs and whipped her hair to the back. Then there was Bridge. Poor baby. She still looked a bit puffy after our *baño* banter but seemed to be genuinely excited as the video crew started tweaking the lights and microphones around her.

Bart, who was obviously short on camera etiquette, was smacking down a bag of chips and didn't worry one bit that his first interview might contain some graphic material between his teeth. Ew.

Again, Rod gave the meet-and-greet info, and then he got right down to biz, since he still had the three other grade levels to interview and that had to be at least thirty more people to go, by my estimation. My *zapatos* were weighing me down and my feet started killing me from standing there behind the curtain. Then that's when it struck me, or really my feet. I could use my Chica Speakas to record this interview.

I found a little box behind the stage to sit on and I turned on my recorder very quietly. I also looked at my Watchame so I could time this interview, because if it looked like it was going to last longer than twenty minutes, I'd have to stop the tape quickly instead of letting it shut off automatically *and loudly*.

Rod began, "So, Venus, how do you feel about being a finalist?"

Venus responded in the most fake sincere voice she could muster, "Well, because we all three hang out both on and off campus together, I totally feel like it was fate."

"Okay, and what about you, Bridget, or do you go by Bridge?"

"Bridget is fine."

"Okay, Bridget, we just interviewed your *best* friend and she said that you were *very instrumental* to her success in becoming a finalist. Tell me, how did you do that?"

I cringed on that question. There was a long silence. I just knew that Venus was giving Bridge some kind of stabbing look. I wondered if that was captured on camera or not. Then Bridge finally spoke.

"Oh, I know Luz from the science cluster, but really, I don't have that kind of pull around here."

Great. Now Bridge made me sound like I was one of those chicas locas that called you her best friend because you loaned her a pencil or something. I knew exactly why she said it, but it still stung.

"Bridge is just being modest," interrupted Venus. "And that's what it's like when you're up and coming in Gamma's more well-known or should I say 'popular' sects. You don't realize the degree of your influence."

That's really milking it, Venus.

Next, Bart started shooting his mouth off about being part of the Jocks and Locks group. He sounded like an arrogant punk, and I knew that Venus was totally uncomfortable because of the way she let out a little nervous giggle.

Venus then asked Rod if she and Bridge could leave because they had some really important Homecoming things they needed to tend to. *Yeah, right.*

I wanted to see what was happening now, so I peeked from the side of the stage's curtains. I saw Venus and Bridge gather their stuff and make a quick exit from the back of the auditorium.

Leaving my shoes behind, I ran to the side door to see if I could catch up with them. I knew Bridge would at least walk that way to the band hall where her mom always picked her up.

I could hear Venus chatting with Bridge on how well they did on camera. I also overheard her say to Bridge that they shouldn't get too close to Bart when he's acting like a jackass, because that could affect how things turn out for them.

Suddenly, I heard really loud footsteps running up. And then I recognized Adam's voice.

"Hey, guys, what's up?"

"Hey, Adam," said Venus.

"Hey, Adam," said Bridge.

"Why didn't you wait for me so I could interview with you guys?" asked Adam.

"Adam, don't be such a baby. It's no big deal. It's just the meet-and-greet session. Have you done yours yet?" asked Venus, annoyed.

"No, not yet," said Adam. I could tell that he wanted to talk more, but I could also tell by Venus's tone that she wasn't having any of it.

"Well, you'd better get going. Otherwise, you might be left out and wouldn't that be tragic," said Venus.

Just then I could hear a production assistant running down the hall calling for Adam.

"Sorry, we've got to go," Venus said, excusing herself and Bridge.

And that's when I heard the outside door open and the two of them leave, so I knew it was safe for me to swing open the door and get his attention. "Hey, Adam, we need to talk."

Adam, who was now following the production assistant, turned around and waved me off. I became so mad that he was blowing me off that I stepped out in the middle of the hall and yelled, "Adam!"

Not even turning around, Adam yelled back, "Later, I gotta go!"

As Adam went back into the auditorium, I tried to go back through the side door but it was *locked*. And my shoes were still on-stage behind the curtain while the interviews were still going on.

At least I still had my purse and backpack with me. I tried going back in through the front entrance, but there was some big burly crew guy named Monk who said I couldn't enter. When I told him that I had left something, he said I would have to wait until all the interviews were done. No sympathy in showbiz, I guess.

And if I waited until Rod got to the seniors, it would be at least another couple hours. Since I knew that my mom was probably waiting for me outside, I didn't have that kind of time.

My cell phone rang and, sure enough, it was my mom. I was ready to run outside, but knowing those stray shoes were onstage kept freaking me out. I had no choice; I had to go. I figured I would come by and pick them up in the morning. I just hoped no one would find them before I got there.

Like clockwork, my mom asked me how my day was. I told her, overall, it was great. I told her that my science project was already taking me to Regionals but only because I was the only one entering. She said it didn't matter. She still counted it as a victory.

I also told her that I was one of the freshman Homecoming finalists. She sounded very excited for me. But I told her there was one more thing. The dance and the regional science competition were both occurring on the same day. And since the competition was in Fort Worth (which was an hour away from Dallas) and wasn't going to be over until seven or eight, I couldn't make it to the dance in time. Even if I got home and dressed in twenty minutes (if that was possible), I would still get to the dance way after nine, and it ended at ten.

"So, what do you think you should do?" Mom asked.

"I guess I should finish what I started," I said, hating my answer.

"*Bueno*. Sounds good to me," Mom agreed too quickly.

"But, Mom, all the finalists get to be on TV in a video documentary. It would be a really big deal if I missed it," I argued.

"Maybe, Luz, you just need some new perspective."

"Mom, what are you talking about?" I asked, hoping she wouldn't try to act like we were in an *Afterschool Special* or something.

"How are you going to feel about this decision in one, five, or twenty years from now?" She was trying to be all profound.

"Are you serious?" I asked, thinking she was not so much serious as *delirious*.

"C'mon, Luz. Make a hypothesis—and I'm using your word here—to see how this one moment in time is going to affect the rest of your life."

"Gawd, Mom. That's pretty deep and philosophical to ask me while I have an empty stomach, y'know." I know I sounded bratty but I couldn't really concentrate right then.

"Yeah, it is. Now you just roll with it for a while, chica," Mom said now in her "girlfriend" voice, trying to mimic me. And then she continued in her total "mom" voice, "Just make sure you give your father and I plenty of notice on where and when we need to chauffeur you on that Saturday. Hey, why aren't you wearing shoes?"

I told her I would get them later since I was using them in an experiment.

Once we got home, it was good to be back in my room/laboratory. Shortie came running in to greet me. I gave him a big squish, because I was feeling victorious, but he spoiled it a bit when he licked me in the mouth. Oh, well, he loves me. I still couldn't believe that Bridge, Mase, *and* Susan made it as finalists. It was a scientific breakthrough with a little help from the PR department of Mason and Adam and their postcard parade.

And then to top things off, I couldn't believe that *I* made it. I mean, I thought about it a lot and I hoped I would, but when they actually announced it, it was simply unbelievable. How did it happen?

I supposed it was my sci-fi peeps who came to the rescue. However, I didn't think that there were enough of them to make that much of a difference in the ballot box.

Then I remembered the article that Jimbo had talked about. I pulled out the article that Swen had written about me. It was just a tiny blurb that didn't give anything away, but it still managed to make me look exciting and mysterious. I wondered if Bridge had read it, but she probably hadn't because she was so busy defending her life and her social status these days. My cell phone rang and I dug it out of my purse so quickly that I accidentally took a picture of myself.

"Hello?" I answered.

"I hear congratulations are in order," the voice said.

"Yeah, I guess so," I said sheepishly. "I'll have to deal with that later."

"Did you get to read the article?" Swen asked.

"I was just in the middle of doing that now," I said, smiling hard again.

"Yeah. I just wanted to get the ball rolling. You're okay with it?"

"Yes, totally. Thank you so much."

"Well, what are your plans now?"

"I thought I would get started working on my presentation for Regionals. And try to figure out how to put all this information together."

"Do you need some help?"

"Actually I do. But first let me gather up all my info and gadgets in one place," I suggested.

"Just say when, but let me know soon. I'm doing double duty also trying to cover the whole documentary story at Gamma."

"Got it," I said, trying to sound all official.

And then I remembered something. "Oh, Swen?"

"Yes?"

"Thanks for everything."

"No problem. Call me when you're ready," said Swen.

After I hung up the phone, I felt like I was floating in space and the air was more breathable and everything looked more, well, *shiny*. Then my phone rang again. I just figured it was Swen again, so I put on my flirty voice and said, "Did you forget something?"

And the voice on the other end said bluntly, "No, but you did."

"What?"

"Luz, what's up with leaving your shoes at school?" Adam laid into me. "The next time, you need to be a bit more discreet when trying to spy on people at school."

"It's not like that."

"It's *exactly* like that," Adam said, totally busting me.

"Okay, so you're right. So, what happened?"

"Well, I was almost at the end of my interview and I was talking about my ambitions of being a TV journalist when we all hear this beeping. And then the sound mixer says we can't go on until this problem is solved. So, they send this production assistant behind stage and she finds your shoes. I grab them instantly and tell them that I'll bring them to you. And then the next thing I know Rod is all fascinated with your shoes and asks me a million questions about you and your gadgets, and experiments."

"You didn't say anything, did you?"

"No. You had already stolen too much of my thunder. I just cut everything off by playing dumb."

"Well, Adam, that's not a stretch," I teased, hoping to find him in a better mood.

"You're walking on thin ice. Do you want your shoes back?" he asked.

"Yeah. Could you bring them by?"

"Yeah, but it'll cost you."

"It always does," I said.

And then I waited for Adam on my beanbag chair with Shortie falling asleep on my lap. I was a bit anxious to hear what was recorded on my shoe. I'm sure it would be interesting, to say the least.

Chapter

19

Adam arrived soon after our conversation. After we went back to my room, I turned on my favorite playlist of classic songs from the eighties, the stuff my mom used to listen to. It's sorta over-the-top punk music, but it really helps to put me in a good mood.

And for the most part I was—minus the part that my BFF wouldn't or *couldn't* speak with me. So, Adam would have to assume the role of Bridge, at least for today. Shortie made an emergency exit, since he doesn't care for eighties music.

"Here you go," Adam said, tossing my shoes at me from his bag.

"Yea! My Chica Speakas!" I exclaimed, catching them. "Have you listened to the tape?" I figured that he already had and waited for him to unload his usual snatchy comments.

"No, I've been busy."

I sat down on the floor and hit rewind. Adam looked around the room and hesitated a second before sitting by me.

"Too busy to snoop and spread gossip? You gotta be kidding me."

"Not really," Adam said without any expression at all. I wasn't quite sure what was wrong with him but something was definitely going on.

"Okay, well, maybe there's something good on here that will cheer you up to your ole evil self."

As I played my shoe, we first heard Venus and Bridge talking to

Rod. Adam and I both agreed that Bridge sounded really nervous, and it wasn't helping that puppet master Venus was pulling strings right in front of the camera. It was excruciating to listen to again.

But our moods did change for the better when we heard Bart acting like his normal butt-head self. And we could totally tell that Venus and Bridge were becoming uncomfortable and felt trapped like rats, or trapped with a rat, or an idiot, for that matter.

"It's really weird to hear a conversation like this that you weren't a part of," Adam said. "And then know that you talked to these people just seconds afterward. It's like rewinding the DVD of your life."

"Yeah." Then I thought I heard something important. "Let me rewind this. I want to hear what Bart was saying just after I left to catch up with you guys," I said.

As I rewound the tape, Shortie returned and said hello by tooting in my room.

"Shortie, get out of here!" I screamed. Shortie looked like his feelings were hurt and scampered down the hall to offend some other family member.

I wafted my hands at the stink in the air. "Sorry about that."

"I guess Shortie has been in the Snacktastics," Adam said.

"Not after I flushed them all," I said as I sat back down. Adam and I listened to Rod ask Bart a few more questions.

"Do you have anything else that you'd like to add, Bart?" asked Rod.

"Yeah. I can't believe that dude Mason and Jabba made it as finalists. I think somebody messed up bad, man."

"Now, why is that?" quizzed Rod.

"Because it was a *joke*."

"What was?"

"Yeah, I put their names down at lunch as a joke. I didn't think people would actually vote for them," Bart said sincerely, then continued, "'cause that Mason dude is weird looking and he's a mute. And, well, they don't call Jabba that for nothing."

"I'm not familiar with Jabba. Is that a nickname for someone?"

"Yeah, it's for that chick Susan, because she's all big and goopy like Jabba in *Star Wars*. I think it came out in your time or some-thing," suggested Bart, with his lack of any social graces whatsoever.

"Uh, thanks for the refresher there, Bart."

I paused my shoe for a moment and looked at Adam horrified.

"*Omigod!* All this time, Mase was mad at you because he thought you signed him up and it was Bart? I didn't even think he knew him," I said.

"I told you I didn't do it," Adam said.

"That explains the misspelling of Mase's name on the ballot. And can you *believe* Bart just called out Jabba's name in public? Now, she's definitely doomed to hear it to her face instead of behind her back for the next three years," I said, with my head in a tailspin.

"Yeah, and now that you've made her popular, it's only going to get worse for her."

"Thanks for the news flash, Adam. Now, what do I do?" I could feel the oxygen leaving my brain. *Must take deep breaths.*

"For starters, let's keep listening to your shoe," Adam suggested. I hit the play button again and we huddled in very close to hear since the sound quality of my shoe wasn't getting any better.

Rod continued with his interview. "Uh, Bart, what would you think if Mason and Susan did win as the Homecoming couple for the fresh-man class?"

"That wouldn't happen in a million years," assured Bart.

"But on the off chance, what if they did? What would you think about that?"

"I *wouldn't*, because I don't even think that would happen in a thousand years."

"Uh, a million is more than a thousand," Rod said, poking fun at Bart, who didn't even get it.

"Yeah. *Whatever*. I'm just saying that . . . Oh, man, you just wouldn't want to be around if that happened. Hell would break loose. I mean like total hell. Yeah. That's for sure."

"Would you be causing some of that hell that would occur?" asked Rod.

"Maybe," Bart said. "I suppose anything's possible."

"Okay, well thanks for your directness and honesty. We appreciate it, Bart," wrapped up Rod. "And, oh, before I forget, have you decided who you are taking to the dance yet?"

"Yeah, I'm going with Venus Hunter."

After that, we heard Rod yell, "Cut!" and then we heard the commotion of the next group getting ready to sit in. Since Adam had a strange look on his face, I paused the tape.

"Hey, Adam, why do you look so freaked out?"

"I'm just thinking . . . Did Venus say whom she was going to the dance with?"

"No, she just left with Bridge when Bart started acting stupid. Why?"

"Well, because I was in the next group with Susan, B-Dawg, and Jimbo, and after I announced how I was just so stoked about not just becoming a finalist but also having the opportunity to cover their project for the paper, your shoe went off and I panicked."

"Yeah, so what?" I said, not understanding why Adam was overreacting.

"Luz, in the middle of the frenzy of your shoe going off, I also told them *I* was taking Venus to the dance. Now I'll look like an idiot because Bart just said the same thing."

"Adam, no you won't. Bart's just shooting off his mouth. No one's going to believe him. If anything, he's the one who's gonna look like a jackass."

"I don't know. My investigative intestines tell me there's more to the story," Adam confided.

"Why don't you just confront Venus and find out?"

"I guess I have to now."

After we finished listening to the rest of Adam and the gang's awful interview, we just sat in silence. Mom offered to whip up some turkey burgers as a snack while we worked in my room. I could still tell that Adam had a lot more on his mind than Venus and this dance.

"Adam, so what's with all the weirdness lately?"

"What do you mean?" Adam asked, as if he hadn't realized he'd been acting like a freak for days.

"You've been acting really weird to me ever since Venus's party. And your phone's not working. What's going on?"

Adam stretched out his very long legs and brushed off the purple fuzz that was accumulating on his pants from my shaggy rug. Then he started to look intently at his shoes.

"Can you keep a secret, Luz?"

"Can *you*?" I stared at him with my eyes open as wide as humanly possible.

"Okay, that's fair. But I'm trying to be serious here."

"Alright. What is it?"

"I'm thinking about running away."

My body tensed up. "What?!"

"No, I'm just kidding."

I threw a pillow at Adam's face and made his glasses almost fall off.

"It's my mom. She . . . uh, cleans offices for a living"—Adam took a long pause—"and she lost her job last week."

I was about to bust Adam and say something real smarty-pants because I wasn't going to fall for another one of his jokes. But something stopped me long enough in my tracks to keep my mouth shut.

"Yeah, the deal is . . . the building where she works is being torn down and the company's relocating to Austin."

All of a sudden, I was getting a really weird sensation from this conversation. There wasn't any cutting sarcasm or giant pretentious words. This was the first time we were having a *real* conversation.

"I'm *so* sorry, Adam," I said.

"Yeah, so am I. I've been taking her to interviews and the employment office. It's been real fun," Adam said, trying to find his sarcastic self again.

"Adam, I feel like a jerk crying about my stupid problems when you have to deal with this. What can I do?" I asked, feeling totally helpless.

"For starters, Cinderella, you could stop leaving your wardrobe on the floor"—he picked up my Chica Speakas—"and work on that limited vocabulary of yours, and, well, we won't even get started on your fashion sense or baking skills," Adam replied, almost sounding like the ole Adam again. Almost.

I was going to tell him about how Venus got his Licky Sticky but it didn't seem that important anymore. Now everything seemed crystal clear to me why Adam worked so hard to be somebody with his clothes, his vocabulary, and his journalism skills.

But I didn't feel sorry for him. I felt sorry for me for being so caught up in my Gamma Glamma experiment and Homecoming that I had lost touch with my friends. And now I felt it was my responsibility to undo the madness that I had caused. I just wondered, was it too late?

Chapter
20

After hours of thinking—or dreading—I came to the conclusion that I couldn't—or really, I *shouldn't*—go to the dance, especially since I had put all my friends and their reputations in jeopardy.

Like Bridge, who was now terrified to talk to me because of Venus's threat to take away her only dream date to Homecoming. Or Mase who never wanted to be a lab rat or finalist in the first place, but did it for me and now was thrust in the kind of spotlight he dreaded.

But the part that truly made me sick to my stomach was what had happened to Susan. And since Bart had officially outed Susan as "Jabba," I could only imagine what her life would be like once this tag was broadcast to the entire school.

And then there was Adam, to whom I promised to deliver a date with Venus for Homecoming if he helped me, and he's more than done his part. And now I needed to do mine.

The only right thing to do was to pull myself out of being a finalist candidate. I figured this would at least increase everybody else's chance to win as well as help me keep my word to Dr. Hamrock and, now, most importantly, to Swen.

The next day when I went to school, I was a little taken aback when I saw all the camera crews everywhere. Some were following the freshmen. Other crews were covering the upperclassmen, just like the paparazzi do in all those glossy magazines.

And then there were even more camera crews shooting what's called "B" roll footage. I learned that that's just extra footage of random things to help tell the story of the documentary, like pictures of the front of the school, the sign of Gamma High, or our flying stallion mascot, the Pegasus called Peggy. Hideous, I know, but I guess they need Peggy to help tell the story.

The entire day was very surreal. I was just glad I dressed cute for the occasion. I wore my hair in two big buns on top of my head, and instead of putting in chopsticks, like some girls do, I put little antennas, and I dressed in all pink with a shiny silver vest with my silver boots. It may have looked a little Power Puff meets the SciFi Channel, but it did make me feel fierce. And I had a feeling I was going to need all the fierceness I could muster up today.

Throughout the day I looked for Mr. Stringer so I could let him know my final, fateful decision. Since he was working closely with the Student Council, I just figured I could tell him and then he'd tell the council, and then it would be over and done with. I just wanted it to happen pronto, except there was one problem—I couldn't find him all day.

Finally, I ran into him in the media room, where the production company had set up an office and also where they were editing. Mr. Stringer was on his computer looking at some lunchroom footage.

"Uh, hi, Mr. Stringer. I'm Luz Santos, one of the freshman finalists?"

Rod paused the scene and turned around. "Oh, yeah, you're the gadget girl—the one with the talking shoe."

"Yeah, that's me."

"Call me Rod. What can I do for you?"

"Well, uh, *Rod*, I was thinking that I needed to withdraw from being a Homecoming finalist and from the documentary and all."

"And why is that?" Rod said as he leaned back in his chair and cocked his head like I'd better have a good explanation.

"Well, because I have to . . . I mean . . . *I chose* to enter the science competition here at Gamma. And since there wasn't anyone to compete with me here, I automatically became eligible to enter the regional competition. And it just so happens that it lands on the same day as Homecoming. And it's on the other side of Fort Worth, which is, like, over an hour away," I explained.

I just rattled that last part off because I didn't think the production company was from here. I mean, I had overheard Rod talking in the hall about Texas and cowboy hats and boots and all. And it's not like that many people wear them here at school, but I thought it was still important to give him a geography lesson on the distance between Dallas and Fort Worth.

"So, you don't think you could make the dance," said Rod, bringing me back to my own so-called reality show.

"No, not really."

"I see. Well, for the sake of the story—and just so you know, the story is the *star* for *High School Rules*—not to mention all the students who voted for you, would you stay in for the duration of the shooting?"

I just froze.

"Look, I first want to portray a *truthful* perspective of who the students wanted as their freshman court. That's why I need *everyone* to continue to participate. Just stick in the race and you don't have to go to the dance. And then at the end of it all, we can still get your interview of why you wanted to withdraw."

"Okay . . . ," I said, not knowing what else to say.

"Luz, you should want to do the show because this not only is very compelling stuff but it's also *the story of your life*," said Rod, making an overly dramatic face.

I felt myself wanting to laugh, but instead I chose to bite on my lower lip. It sounded kind of crazy to me, because, well, my life wasn't *that* dramatic. Wait a minute—yes, it was. My friends' reputations were on the brink of being destroyed. I could fail science and be kicked out of the science cluster. And, oh, yeah, Venus could steal the man of my dreams. My head nodded automatically for Rod.

"Good, then we'll still have the crews following you so we can really get a clear picture of you and your life."

"Alright . . ." I said, still not quite sure of what that would entail. I left and headed to the cafeteria.

When I arrived, my biggest concern of the day was whom I was going to sit with at lunch. Little did I know, it wasn't going to be that big of a deal because there were going to be much bigger deals unfolding as the day progressed. As I walked up to Adam, he let me know right away that he was going to confront Venus. On that note, I decided I should lie low and hang with my sci-fi peeps at our table and watch from a distance.

I saw Adam talk with Venus for a minute, and she was all fake smiles and laughs until Adam confronted her. I couldn't hear what she was saying but, at the same time, I knew it wasn't good. I could see that she was saying something sarcastic because she struck a pose and started waving her hands (which she pretty much did on a daily basis).

But whatever she did say was definitely unexpected enough to cause Adam's face to drop. It was as if someone just told him that he forgot to wear pants or something, and then he just stormed off. And Bridge was standing by witnessing the entire train wreck.

Then out of nowhere came a camera crew of three guys rushing to Venus, and she started talking to the camera. Now I really wanted to hear what she had to say. But by the time I got up to the camera crew from the other side of the cafeteria, the press conference was over.

I tried to find Adam but he was already MIA. I even went to Adam's office (the girls' bathroom) to see if he dropped in to collect himself or something. Nope. He wasn't there. Just the usual bunch of chattering chicas. About that time the bell rang and I ran into the swarms heading to class and stumbled into Bridge.

"Do you know what just happened?" she said, on fire.

"I saw it but I was too far away to hear. What happened?"

Bridge pulled me over by a trash can so that no one would hear our conversation. "Well, Adam just came up and confronted V about whether she was going to the dance with Bart. And she said she *was*. She said she knew that Adam might not have money to take her to the dance and she didn't want to put him in that position because of his mom losing her job and all."

"Wait a sec, Bridge. I thought you weren't supposed to be talking to me," I said, scanning the crowd to make sure the Venus flytrap wasn't buzzing around.

"No, I'm *totally* talking to you now," Bridge said in her big-girl voice. "And when I asked Venus how she knew about Adam's mom, she said his mom used to clean offices for her dad's company, but now the company is relocating to Austin."

"Is Venus moving?"

"No. I know—*you wish*. Her dad's going to be commuting."

"Oh, that sucks."

"And when the video crew asked Venus what had just happened, she told them that at first she was going to go with Adam, but since his mom was laid off, she didn't want to go with him because he was probably hard up for money and all."

"You're *kidding* me," I said, feeling an extra twinge of venom.

"No, I'm not. I was in total shock when she said that, and I'm sure she realized that so she asked if she could have a 'take two.'"

"A 'take two'?"

"Yeah, like in the movies—a do over, another take. No one said no, so she just said, 'Anyway, I just didn't want him to feel bad, y'-know, about being poor and, like, having to come up with that kind of money for the dance. Like money for dinner, the limo, and every-thing else. I think I'll start a can drive for him or something.'"

My stomach started to knot up, and I pulled Bridge away from the sour smell of the trash can, which was also making me sick.

"So then Venus looked at *me* and said, '*That* sounded better, right? I didn't want to sound like a fake or like a bee-otch,' and then she asked me if she should have cried when she mentioned the can drive! That's when the cameras turned to me, and I felt so horrible, I ran off. I'm sure I looked like a big doof," Bridge said, then looked down at her cute little red ballerina flats.

"No, you did the right thing."

Bridge just leaned on some nearby lockers and held her books closely to her chest as if she was guarding her *corazón.*

"Luz, I'm done with this."

"With what?" I asked, not sure what exactly she was done with.

"I don't like feeling my life's under a microscope. I want out."

"What are you saying, Bridge? What about your date with B-Dawg?"

"Oh, no! I'll still go to Homecoming with him, of course, but I don't think I can handle being a finalist or a part of this documentary. It's *bad.*"

I was completely speechless as I looked at Bridge. Completely. But then I thought about our science project.

"What about the experiment?"

"Hey, you got me to finalist. That's got to count for something," Bridge said.

"C'mon, Bridge, it can't be *that* bad."

"Oh, yeah, it can. Those cameras are rolling on us all the time. Just like when you're taking your spy pictures. And you know what, Luz, we can look pretty stupid without even trying, just like everybody you take pictures of. I'm afraid we are all going to be crucified before the dance. And you know what else? I'm really beginning to think that we shouldn't have done the experiment at all, Luz. It's too high of a price to pay."

"Well, you know there's always a price or risk when conducting experiments."

"I don't have that kind of collateral, Luz."

"Well, maybe we can think of another experiment and change everybody's . . ." I started to say as thoughts swirled around in my head and my stomach started churning acid.

"Luz, get hold of yourself!" Bridge threw her hands in the air. "You're talking like a total freak! No more experiments, potions, gadgets, photos, or whatever. We just have to *deal,* like everybody else. I gotta go. I'll talk to you later." She started to turn to walk in the opposite direction.

"*You will?*" I said, suddenly feeling a wave of insecurity. I was hoping I wasn't losing my science partner, but, more importantly, my friend.

"Yeah," Bridge said over her shoulder.

"Are you sure you're not worried about the wrath of Venus?" I asked, just to make sure.

"I'm so tired of V that if I saw her right now, I would pull every strand of her blond hair out of her little pin head."

"You mean fake blond hair."

"Yeah, and that's not the *only* thing fake about her," said Bridge as she shook her bosom and rolled her eyes sarcastically.

And that's when we realized we were being filmed. How much had they heard? Bridge and I froze, and then she ran away and I walked in the opposite direction, hoping no one would follow us. For a second, it felt like an invasion of privacy. Isn't there a law about that kind of stuff?

As I walked up the stairs, I quickly realized that if they aired that piece of video, Bridge and I were going to be deep in caca. Again, since I felt like this was my fault, I felt it was my responsibility to fix it, and fast. But how? I decided to talk with Rod one last time.

I found him in the media center. His desk was filled with empty Styrofoam cups, while a pot of coffee was brewing behind him between stacks and stacks of videotapes.

"Hey, Mr. Stringer, I mean Rod?"

"Yes, Luz?"

"Look, I don't want to take up too much of your time again because I know you're busy, but I'm afraid some of your guys have recorded some footage that shouldn't get out."

"Luz, I have hundreds of hours of footage to go through," Rod said, putting another tape into a machine. "Could you be more specific about the footage you're talking about?"

"Well, for starters, Bart said he nominated Susan as a joke. I don't think she knows that she's referred to as 'Jabba.' And he called Mason a mute, which he totally isn't. And, uh, today, just a few minutes ago, your crew shot Venus and she mentioned that Adam's mom just lost her job . . ." I was waiting for Rod to take down some notes for editing purposes and stuff.

"And . . . ?"

"What I'm saying is, that information is really damaging."

Rod didn't seem to be bothered in the least bit.

"Rod, when you and your crew are done with this episode, the rest of the students here have to go on. And speaking for the freshman class in particular, we have barely gotten started here. And I feel like your crew is trying to ruin us or something."

"Really?" Rod said as he stopped what he was doing for a moment.

"Yes, *really*."

"Well, I'm really sorry you feel that way, Luz. But it's not about trying to ruin you and your friends. It's really just an honest snapshot of your lives. And that honesty is part of the price of being popular, being nominated, and agreeing to be part of the documentary."

"But not all the students I mentioned *asked* to be popular," I said, hoping I wouldn't have to reveal Project Gamma Glamma to him.

"Okay, what does that mean?" asked Rod. I could tell that he was getting a bit annoyed with my visit, so I knew I had no choice but to spill the frijoles.

"'Off the record,' there are some students who didn't ask to be popular—they were only helping me with my science project."

"Are you saying that you were conducting *an experiment* to make kids popular?"

"Yes."

"You're kidding me. *That's insane.*"

"Yes. I mean no! Yes, it's insane, but no I'm totally being serious here."

"Now why would you cook up an experiment like that?" Rod spun around in his chair and poured a cup of coffee.

"It's a long story," I said, hoping not to have to tell the whole thing.

"Oh, don't worry, I have time for this." Rod looked me straight in the eyes. "Because this is about you and *your life*. And this is a story that needs to be told. *Today*," said Rod, sounding overdramatic, like a used-car salesman.

Rod spun around again to grab his walkie-talkie from his desk. "Danny Jackson, can I have you come up to the media room? We have to pop off an interview. And bring Henning so he can boom. And make sure someone comes up here with some powder in case we're shiny." Then he turned to me and said, "If you're cool with it, then I'd like to put you and your story on tape." I just nodded weakly, not sure if I had any options at this point, but I was anything but cool or "shiny."

Chapter
21

I hoped that after downloading my entire science experiment, Rod would finally be more sympathetic to my plight and to everybody involved.

And I didn't mention anything about Bridge wanting to pull out as a Homecoming finalist or the documentary, because I hoped she was just overreacting, like she normally does.

Then I also hoped—okay, *I prayed*—that he would pull any footage that might make my friends look like total freaks. But for someone who prides herself in science and logical outcomes and such, I should have *known* better.

The next day when I got to school, the first thing I noticed was a TV monitor in the hallway by the gym playing a video segment on Susan. It started off cool enough, with footage of her Texas-sized mansion and all, but that pictorial scene was quickly overshadowed when Susan came on screen—as a *wizard*. It was pretty much downhill from there. The next scene sealed her fate, showing her out back feeding Frotastic, who was also wearing a matching wizard hat.

I wanted to walk away from the monitor, but then I saw J-girl. First, Susan showed the camera her drawing and then recounted the *entire* story—without emotion, mind you—of how J-girl saved all the other hobbits from the wicked Kimus.

The last shot was of Susan just staring into the camera through her giant spectacles like she was hypnotized or casting a spell or some-thing. It was just terrible. No, I take that back—it was *beyond* terrible.

I wasn't able to catch many more of these previews in the morn-ing, because I barely had enough time to get to my classes as it was. And there were at least forty different videos of all the finalists from different grades, so you never really knew who was going to pop up next, and on top of that, they had cut together other random mo-ments that showed us at our best (not). I just didn't want to stand there looking at every monitor and come across looking like I was all fixated on Homecoming, because I wasn't. Okay, maybe I was, but if anything, watching the spots just made me sad that I wasn't going.

However, I did get to see *my* segment. I was excited at first until I heard "La Cucaracha" playing as background music to desperately amp up my Latina heritage. At least for Jimbo's video they played "She Blinded Me with Science."

As I watched my spot, there was some random footage of me in my various outfits, which made me really rethink my wardrobe choices. I mean, wearing them day to day, I normally felt cute in them. But to see them now on a huge TV monitor, I began to feel stupid.

Just seeing my metal boots with memos swinging off of them or my crazy tutu really did make me look like a fashion-don't cartoon. And then when they cut shots of me in my whacked-out wardrobe with the reactions of kids from the science cluster, well, I wanted to curl up and die.

God, am I really this big of a loser? God, please don't answer that. That was just a rhetorical question.

As I stood in the hall watching my video, Adam walked up be-hind me and said, "Hey."

"Hey," I said. "Have you been checking out these videos?"

"Yeah, me and the whole student body."

"Well, that's great. That only confirms my fears that these babies are gonna seal our high school social death certificates."

"Well, there's such a plethora of them it's hard to catch every-thing unless you skip all your classes."

Plethora? Yea! Adam was using big words again. Life almost felt back to normal.

"Have you seen Mase's big moment yet?" asked Adam.

"Is he jumping over the bleachers?"

"No," Adam said and shook his head.

"Or jumping across the pool at the party?" I suggested.

"No."

"How about when he was going to jump over one of the school's short buses but got caught by Sargeant Fischer?" (The school cop.)

"No!" said Adam firmly, tiring of my guessing game.

"Then what, then?" I asked, becoming distracted again by the idiot box. It was featuring some junior named Chad Coats. Never heard of him.

Adam leaned down a bit and gave me a sharp little side hug. "Oh, well, I see someone hasn't been very observant lately. It's the video where the camera crew has cornered Susan and Mase together."

I could already tell this was going to take a while, and it wasn't going to be good. So, I started to walk to my locker and motioned for Adam to come with. "Okay, go on. Give it to me." I focused my eyes on the floor tiles. The floor was so shiny and clean, at least in the foyer.

"Well, they found them both in the lunch line and asked Susan if she had a date."

"And she said she wasn't going because she was going to watch *The Lord of the Rings*," I butted in, pretending I was so surprised.

"Are you telling this story?" Adam growled.

I gave him back the spotlight.

"Susan just said no. Then, they asked Mase if he had a date, and he said no. I mean, he just shook his head. Next, they asked Mase if he would ask Susan to the dance, and she was standing right next to him."

"Shut up." I punched Adam in the arm. "You're totally lying," I said, hoping he was.

"I know, it's lurid. But it's the truth."

"*Ugh!* Then what happened?"

"Well, I wish I could elaborate further but all they showed was the camera zooming in on Mase's face looking like . . ."

"A deer in the headlights?" I finished.

"You're psychic."

"No, just psychotic. What do you think happened?"

"Knowing our fearless friend, who despises confrontations, he said yes," Adam concluded without a doubt. When we arrived at my locker, I turned the dial to the lock a few times trying to remember my combination.

"Luz, are you in shock?" Adam asked.

"Yeah," I said, looking off down the hall into space, where it seemed safer.

"Move over." Adam pushed me out of the way and began fiddling with the lock. Down the hall, I saw two guys walking our way totally laughing in an evil Bart kinda way.

"This is why I pride myself on knowing everything," Adam said as he magically opened my locker and blocked my view. Something didn't feel right at all, and it wasn't the fact that Adam could break into my locker. I slammed it shut. Adam furrowed his brow at me with disapproval. I quickly spun all six feet four of him around and sheltered myself as I peered from behind him. Then I said, "Oh, my God, Adam, did you know about that?"

Walking toward us were two upperclassmen who looked like they were probably on the basketball team wearing T-shirts. But not just any T-shirts. One of them had on a shirt that said, "Alpaca (I'll Pack a) Vote for Susan If You Will." The other guy was wearing a shirt that said, "Hug a Hobbit, and Vote for Susan." As the guys passed us, I looked at Adam. I could tell that his wheels were spinning in overdrive.

"Do you think this is some kind of sick prank?" I said under my breath.

"It feels too blatant," Adam said as he continued to stare at the upperclassmen.

"Yeah. And those guys don't look like the crafty type," I noted.

"No, those shirts were definitely professionally done. They still had crease marks on the sleeves," noted Adam, with his investigative insight.

"Do you think it was Venus?"

"Anything's possible."

The bell rang and Adam said that he'd talk to me later. I tried to catch up to the guys with the shirts, but they had already ducked into their classes. I was scared. *Real scared.* I walked back to my locker and blanked out again as to what my combination was, and what I needed to get out of the locker. I decided to skip it and *just deal*, and I ran to class, ready to collect another tardy demerit.

I found out that Susan was absent today. I truly hoped she was sick and not freaking out about what was going on in school. It concerned me because today was Wednesday and the dance was taking place on Saturday. I wondered if she was going to go. I also wanted to track down Mase and get the rest of his story.

Throughout the rest of the day, I saw more and more shirts but they were for all the finalists, not just for Susan. That brought me a bit of comfort, but I still wondered who was responsible for the Susan shirts and why upperclassmen were wearing them.

At lunch, I found out that the art department for *High School Rules* had made up T-shirts for all the candidates and started to pass them out during the morning. There was no sign of Mase today except for his shirts. I saw a few versions of "Jump for Mason" and "Vote Extreme." They were kinda cute but seemed like some wardrobe supervisor was trying too hard.

Bridge came by my table and sat down. I was busy trying to get all my notes together for my science project. I was having a terrible time focusing, and I knew I was going to have to pull a few all-nighters to get this done by Saturday.

"Have you seen the shirts?" asked Bridge.

"Yeah."

"I haven't seen yours, but I saw mine."

I put away my notes. "Oh, really? What does yours say?"

"There are a couple of versions. One says, 'Take It to the Ridge for Bridge,' and the other says, 'Throw Out Some Digits for Bridget.'"

"That's sort of goofy but not too bad."

"Yeah. But I've seen some graffiti in the bathroom that says, 'Don't Fidget with Bridget.'"

"At least it doesn't say, 'Bridget is a Midget.'"

"Hey, don't put it out there."

"*Sorry*. Have you talked to Rod about pulling out of the documentary?" I asked.

"Yeah, and he just told me to stick it out until Saturday."

"Are you?" I asked.

"I guess," Bridge said, looking around at other slogans kids were sporting. "I mean, what terrible thing can happen in the next two days?" she added too casually.

I wanted to tell her that she shouldn't even be posing that knock-on-wood question right now. Because it's been my unscientific observation lately that when you ask for it, the universe just doles out a huge serving of crap.

I also wanted to tell her that I talked with Rod, too, and tried to pull out of the Homecoming Court election. And how I was *forced* to tell him about the entire Gamma Glamma experiment. But I didn't want to set off alarms. So, I just changed the subject to Adam. "How do you think Adam's taking the whole Venus thing?"

Bridge put her fingers in her mouth, ready to chew on her nails. "You mean what she said on camera?"

I shook my head at her not to chew. "Well, yeah, that."

"I don't think he knows about Venus talking about his mom on camera."

"He doesn't know *yet*. What I was really talking about was her not going to the dance with him," I said.

"I don't know. He told me he might ask someone from another school or he'll just go alone, but you know he's gotta be pretty burned. She's so freakin' toxic. Did you know she's actually collecting cans for him?"

My stomach dropped twenty feet. "Uh-uh."

"Uh-huh. She's housing the cans in her locker. And she copied our idea and made postcards that say, 'Can Adam.' I can't tell him. Do you want to tell him?"

"No, I think I'll wait a while so he can at least have a little time to recover between these bombs," I said.

In the middle of our convo a girl, a sophomore, I think, walked past wearing a shirt that said, "Absolute Adam." "Hey, that's cool," I said as I motioned with my eyes for Bridge to check it out.

"Yeah, that's better than some of the other finalists' shirts I've seen."

"Have you seen Venus today?" I asked, trying to keep posted on everybody's comings and goings.

"No, I heard she skipped today because she's out shopping for Saturday."

"Typical. And Mase?" I asked.

"No, but I know that he's been hanging out in the drama portable or sometimes with the stage crew guys in the auditorium."

"Oh," I said. "So do you have a dress yet?"

"Yeah . . . I do."

"You're not sounding thrilled."

"Well, I guess it's not what I thought it would be. I mean, now that it's here. I really wish you were going."

"I know. I wish I was, too. But I've made my bed and *I'm just dealing with it*," I said, letting Bridge know that I was taking her advice.

"How's your project coming along? Are you ready for Saturday?"

"Truth be told, not really," I admitted.

"Luz, the science department's counting on you. I mean, I guess. You're the only one."

"Trust me, I know. I've just been very distracted with all this documentary stuff."

"Well, you'd better get ready, because if you don't have a good showing at the competition, it's only going to be tougher when you get back."

"Thanks, Bridge," I said, well aware that it would go from *High School Rules* to *Survivor* after this weekend. It was going to be like episode one, first season, and hard-core.

"Well, I gotta go. I'll call you later," Bridge said as she got up to leave. And I just sat there looking at the rest of the cafeteria. I felt cold and a bit clammy. I hoped I wasn't coming down with something.

After lunch, I decided to go to the clinic and I found out that I did have a fever. The nurse asked me if I wanted to call my parents so I could go home. I decided that would be ideal especially if I needed to get the project up to competitive standards. Bridge was right. I was representing and so much more. And I needed to get my head in the game, even with a temperature.

My mom rushed from work to pick me up, and when I walked out the door, I spied a fellow freshman wearing a T-shirt that read, "Gamma's Glamma—Choose Luz." Normally, I would have thought that was hot. But a geek was wearing it and his colors were clashing. And the thought of Rod and his TV crew making fun of me, my friends, and my experiment made my temperature rise even higher.

Chapter

22

Thursday was a total loss. There were chills, fever, oh yeah, and vomit. I was hoping my day-pass home would give me a chance to get my Gamma Glamma presentation up to speed, but that hope ticked away with the hours I spent curled up near death under the covers. Finally, midafternoon my mom came home early and fed me some mild tortilla soup, and I found enough energy to crawl out and at least begin to organize my data.

I was surprised nobody (well, Bridge or Adam) called me after classes to dish me the new daily dirt. I hoped that nothing terrible had gone down, but I figured that they had their own busy lives to lead at the moment. And I didn't mind being free from the distraction of worrying about everybody else's lives.

Dr. Hamrock finally called to check up and make sure I would be good to go for Saturday. I reassured him that I was busy tightening everything up at the moment and that Saturday would be no sweat. But the sweat I was feeling wasn't just coming from my fever.

Friday I felt better. If I had wanted to, I could have gone to school since my temperature was back down, but my mom let me stay home again. She knew I really needed to spend the entire day, if not more, on Project Gamma Glamma.

I had all my gear and gadgets and data spread out on the floor of my room. I had the "before" and "after" photos of my subjects and had printed up pictures from everybody's cameras (Mase's were particularly arty) of the various cliques and groups that they each had penetrated, as well as a catalog showing everybody's "before" and "after" wardrobes. I also included the formulations and samples of the different scents that I had concocted, and I had recorded loops of the subjects' vocal transformations on separate tape players that could be activated by buttons under their pictures.

I also made sure to include the postcards that were, in a way, extensions of Mase's new voice. And, finally, I displayed the list of Homecoming finalists along with a last set of "after" pictures taken the day of the announcement. I thought it looked profound, but I still thought it needed something more; I just didn't know what.

I glued pieces of Gabber Gum and the White Away Right Away jelly beans along with their formulations to my presentation board, and that seemed to help a little. I didn't want to have my creations on a plate or something, because I wouldn't put it past someone to eat them just to sabotage my presentation. Yeah, it was an educational event, but for some participants this was a full-on scientific battlefield.

Midday, I took a catnap, or actually dognap, with Shortie. I fell into such a deep sleep that I had a dream that Venus was putting on her crown and speaking to the crowd. Just hearing her cackle woke me up from my slumber.

I wondered if my dream was just telling me that Venus and Bart were going to win and that it was just fate and the way life played out in high school. Shortie farted and I agreed, "Yeah, Shortie, that stinks."

It was around lunchtime when my cell phone rang underneath the display board. I just figured it was Bridge wondering where I was.

"Hello?"

"Luz?" Swen asked.

"Yes?"

"It's Swen. Are you at school today?"

Dang. I had completely forgotten about Swen—well, not really forgotten, but in the midst of illness and panic over my future in science and especially my fears over what damage my experiment might be causing my friends, I had forgotten to keep him posted on my progress.

"No. I was home from school yesterday with a temperature and other nasty stuff." I wanted him to know I wasn't faking but really didn't want to get too far into the details.

"Oh, I didn't know you were sick."

"I'm good now and my temperature is down so I'm working non-stop on my presentation."

"Well, that's good."

"Uh, Swen, I was wondering . . ."

"Yeah?"

"I was wondering if you could come over just to take a look at it. I mean, after school."

"You mean at the eleventh hour after I've been hounding you for days?"

"Uh . . . yes?" I said, feeling sick again, but only to my stomach.

I couldn't help it. I'd been spending so much time cleaning up mess after mess I'd invented or created that I hadn't had the kind of time I would've liked to have put into the project.

"Well, the only time I have is after school, but I can't really leave the campus since I've got to do interviews with Rod and his crew for the paper."

"Then how about I meet you in the media center after school. And I'll just wait for whatever time you can give me," I said, feeling bold—no, just feeling *desperate*.

"Sounds like a date," Swen replied.

Date? Hearing that stabbed my heart. No date. No Homecoming. I could barely focus.

"Great, I'll see you at the date. I mean, media center." One day I am going to make a way-back machine that only goes back like five minutes so that when you say something superstupid you can have a "do over" or a "take two." The fact was, I couldn't wait to see him and give him my own in-depth interview on how much I am over documentaries. Unfortunately, there was no time in my schedule to be bitter right now.

I had to call my mom and she left work early again to take me back to school. As soon as I walked inside and down the hall, I ran across one of the TV monitors and caught the footage of Venus in the lunchroom waving her hands. I didn't bother to stop and listen since Bridge had filled me on the horror of that episode.

I especially didn't want to hear her announcement to the world about Adam's mom's employment status. I heard a few kids down the hall laughing and I couldn't tell if they were just laughing-laughing or if they were making fun of Adam. After that I found postcards on the hall floor of Adam that said, "Can Adam" with a picture of a can over Adam's mouth. I could only imagine what kind of day Adam had endured.

Honestly, I didn't really want to know right at this moment since time was not on my side. I shuffled as fast as I could upstairs to the media center. And that's when I passed a flier taped on the wall that read, "Tell Fridge Joiner to Eat It." And it had a picture of Bridge eating a turkey leg at the state fair when she was like twelve or thirteen and wearing extra large "missy" sizes. It wasn't flattering, to say the least.

In a panic, I set down my bulky display and ran down a few hallways and checked a few bathrooms including the boys'. Nasty. I retrieved five fliers in all. I looked at my Watchame, and even though I wanted to continue to scour the school and confiscate any more hate propaganda, I knew I needed to get back to the media center and to my project.

I was sweating and I could taste the salt from my upper lip as I walked in to the brightly lit room. The center was humming from the aged fluorescent lights and computers in the room. And that's where I found Swen, tapping away at supersonic speed at his computer. A few people from the Student Council and the video crew were rushing around grabbing last-minute decorations and equipment to take to the gym, where everyone was getting ready for the Homecoming festivities.

While I was looking for a place to set down my heavy and awkward-sized Gamma Glamma display, I saw what looked like a very important box. And it was. It was the box that contained the freshman king and queen crowns. They were kind of gaudy looking, but because they were shiny and made of metal, they called my name.

I very carefully picked one up and scanned the room. No one was really around now except for Swen, who, sadly, hadn't noticed my existence yet, because he was still typing a million miles a minute. *Oh, whatever, just do it,* my thrill-seeking cerebral neural network told me. I placed the crown on my head. I just wished I had a mirror. I tried to look at my reflection in a nearby computer that wasn't on.

"I see you like shiny things," said Swen, peeking over his computer and causing me to jump.

"Yes, I like shiny things and metal."

"Well, when you win Regionals maybe you'll get crowned 'Queen of Science.'"

"Yeah, maybe with a satellite dish."

Swen walked over and shook his head. I opened up my display and asked for some constructive criticism. He just stared a long time at the before and after pictures, my visual aids, and covered his mouth with his hand and thought and squinted his eyes. As I stared at him, I hoped he would help me and didn't think that I was stupid or that this project was a failure. Finally, he spoke.

"Was the project successful?"

"What do you mean?" I asked, already feeling defensive.

"Do *you* think this project was successful?" Swen asked again.

I stammered, "Uh, I mean, I took three subjects and changed elements of their self-presentation to gain admittance into new peer groups and raise their social status, and using that criterion I proved my theory. They even became Homecoming finalists."

"But was it *successful?*" Swen pressed. I wasn't quite sure what he was getting at, but I tried to answer him as best I could.

"Well, from a scientific perspective, yeah, it was, but personally speaking and between you and me, it's been nothing but a complete disaster and it's getting worse by the minute."

My brain flashed me pictures of Adam's can-drive postcards, a missy-sized Bridge, and Susan in a wizard's hat. "With the Homecoming nominations and the documentary exposure, it's kind of been creating public humiliation and emotional scars and maybe even permanent damage to our high school cred the next four years. And these weren't just test subjects. They're *my friends*."

"Then I think you need to include that in your conclusion," Swen said.

"What?! You think I need to say that my project is a failure?! I'm sorry, but you don't really win that way."

"It will be more poignant if you show off the impact of science through your experiment and presentation."

"What do you mean, the impact of failure?" I said, feeling kind of hurt that he was giving me lousy advice.

"Look, Luz, I've been trying to help you for weeks, and at the last minute you come and want my help? I'm telling you if you detail the *entire truth* about this project, warts and all, it becomes compelling. If you don't, it becomes sci-fi plastic surgery," Swen said, holding back no punches.

Omigod. I can't believe he said that. He wants the truth? How about that all I wanted to do was go to Homecoming with him? How about that I never wanted to do this stupid experiment in the first place but I only did it so I wouldn't fail out of the science cluster, and then later because I wanted to help his uncle keep his job. I tried to hold my tongue but it was hard to do when it was on fire.

"Do you want me to tell the truth or win?" I asked.

"I want you to do both."

"I don't get it."

"Well, I thought you would. You *seemed* to have a conscience."

Seemed to have a conscience? Oh, that was great! I took a moment to gather my thoughts, but I kept visualizing emotional fuel rods sliding into my core and approaching critical mass, at which point there would be a total nuclear meltdown. So, in a word, I was a ticking bomb. I kept telling myself, *Por favor, don't explode!*

I literally held my mouth and took a deep breath, hoping that the extra oxygen to my brain would cool things off a bit. And, finally, I responded to Mr. "I thought you had a conscience."

"Well, Swen, I have a lot of things lately but right now time isn't one of them. I think the best thing for me to do is to go home and keep working on this. I know you're busy. Thanks for your time." I spit all this out knowing I sounded very sarcastic. But I couldn't help it.

I immediately gathered up all my stuff, which wasn't hard to do since I was still really mad, but I was trying to act cool and I wasn't about to cry. Even though I wanted to. As I began to make my grand exit, I turned around and gave Swen a courtesy smile good-bye.

"Uh, Luz, do you still want me to pick you up at five for Regionals?"

"Yeah, I guess," I spit out quickly because I had a lump in my throat and tears were forming in my eye ducts and I still wanted to see him even if he thought I didn't have a conscience.

"Um, Luz?"

"Yes?" I squeaked.

"I think it might be a good idea if you didn't leave with that crown. You know how uptight those Student Council guys are."

Heat built up into my face, causing it to turn bright red. I set my presentation on the floor and returned the crown to the box. Here I had been arguing about having a conscience and telling the truth and I was wearing a crown. A crown! What an idiot! Maybe the fever was returning.

As I ran down the stairs, I passed the gym. And I just had to torture myself further and see all the decorations that I would miss. I poked my head in and saw about three video crews running around shooting all the Student Council members, who were hanging streamers and tying down a giant balloon arch by a small stage that was draped with curtains that had been created especially for the dance. It was sooo beautiful. I thought about Bridge and B-Dawg dancing under the disco ball of lights.

From behind me I heard a familiar voice that grated on my last nerve.

"Do us proud tomorrow."

I turned around with all my belongings (which were getting really hard to hold).

"Excuse me," I spat back.

"I said do us proud tomorrow." Venus grinned as she walked in with Bart. I couldn't say anything. Not because I didn't have a snappy comeback but because I was in shock at the sight of the two of them. Venus was wearing a wizard hat and Bart had masking tape over his mouth and a T-shirt with "Toot for the Mute" written with a marker. I watched them walk up to a group of cameramen.

Those two were dissin' Mase and Susan to get media coverage. This was truly evil. It was so unfair. I set my stuff down because my arms were about to give out.

My forehead was hurting, and as I rubbed it with my hand, I discovered all the tiny indentations on my forehead still left from the crown and then thought about the future. Even though Bart and Venus were evil and shallow, would they still win because the media loved the show they put on and no one would ever think to challenge them? Would the obvious truth about these two be appreciated by the masses? Then it hit me like lightning. The truth was going to set everybody free because now *I would be science with a conscience.* And I couldn't wait to get home and get started on my latest experiment.

Chapter

23

I decided that first thing after my mom picked me up and brought me home, I would rewrite my final summary to encompass the whole truth surrounding Gamma Glamma. Well, except the fact it was originally planned to die on the drawing board because I wanted to go to the dance.

What I did include was the fact that my participants didn't exactly volunteer to take part in the name of science. Rather, they did it for me. And the experiment *did* work, at least in the short term. Bridge, Mase, and Susan became popular and achieved much higher social status within new peer groups, to the point of being elected freshman Homecoming finalists.

But from a long-term standpoint, I was still discovering how this experiment was going to impact their lives. For instance, at first, Bridge wasn't sure what to do with her new power but still didn't want to lose it, so she chose to pay the price of bowing down to Venus.

Then Mase, who had preferred being by himself, was now continually bombarded with groupies and people who would cling on just because he was popular. And, finally, there was Susan, whose very existence was at one time not even acknowledged by most of the student body. But now that she had some celebrity exposure through the power of television and she had risen to become a target of the popular kids' ridicule, she was at risk of a social public stoning with her freshly revealed nickname of Jabba.

So, in conclusion, did I accomplish what I set out to do? Well, kinda. But I learned so much more than that. What I discovered wasn't a quick fix to attain popularity, but something entirely different—that we, as scientists, need to be always mindful that whatever we do, create, or invent has long-term effects that we may not foresee. And if we want to respect the legacy of those great thinkers who came before us, then it is important to practice our science with a conscience—an awareness and concern about the consequences of our actions. I have to admit my conclusion felt a bit after-achool specialish but it was *the truth*. Wow, what a concept!

It was weird. I felt proud. I felt lighter because I was telling the truth about my project. I didn't try to give it a makeover so it would sound better or more successful than it was. That was pretty cool, telling the truth. Everyone should feel that good about telling the truth. And now, everyone would!

Seeing Venus and Bart earlier had gotten me to thinking. They were more than likely going to win tomorrow. It was almost an overwhelming statistical probability. I wondered if they would tell how they got there. Would they say they won because of bullying and intimidation? *Yeah, right.* But wouldn't it be refreshing for the entire student body to have the opportunity to hear how they *really* won? It would be so juicy, or memorable, to say the least. And I wanted this year's Homecoming to be memorable for all, even if I couldn't be there myself.

So I decided (against advice, of course) that I would try one more invention. Bridge would kill me if I asked her to help me (and she was probably way too stressed out about getting ready for the dance), so I would attempt this one solo. I decided to tinker with the idea of engineering electrodes to emit certain wavelengths of microvoltage energy and induce specific neural patterns in the higher logical regions of the brain—just like truth serum. It would kinda be like superacupuncture on the ole *cabeza*. It wouldn't hurt at all; in fact, it would make the wearer very, very relaxed. So relaxed that the person just might start talking freely and *truthfully*.

The only thing that I had to consider was the fact that I needed to make the electrodes really, really small so that I could mount these little ticklers to the inside of the crowns. I had to use the best wires and batteries and other components I had available. I'd have to rip apart other gadgets to get what I needed to make sure this invention would rock.

It took me all night with no break for a nap. By morning I had a matching pair of tiny truth extractors. I was so excited and I couldn't resist calling my new invention the "Truth B. Told." Now I needed to test them out, but on whom? As usual, I knew I had to be my own guinea pig. I also decided to have one of my Chica Speakas record whatever I would say so that I could review it.

I placed the loose set of wires on my head and they kind of tingled, but not in a bad way. The sensation felt like when I use my mom's chamomile and mint shampoo.

I stood in front of my dressing mirror. I looked normal except for the dark circles under my eyes but, hey, that came from lack of sleep. I talked softly and began to tell the truth.

"My name is Luz. My best friend is Bridget Joiner. I wish I could go to the dance. I wish I didn't have to go to the science competition. I wish Swen would see me as a girl instead of a science project. I hope nothing bad happens to Susan and Mase tonight. If anything happens to my friends tonight, I won't be able to forgive myself and that's the truth for sure." Well, everything seemed like the truth so far.

I sat down on my bed and thought, *What's a question I can ask to make sure I can tell if I'm telling the truth?* I looked across my floor, strewn with wires, pliers, and aluminum, and then my silver boots. It made me laugh because it didn't matter if I was a scientist or a fashionista, I was always drawn to things that were metal, bright, and *shiny*.

And then that's when I had my Einstein moment. I stood up and tip-toed to my mirror with my truth extractors on. I looked in the mirror and I whispered as quietly as I could, "Am I jealous of Venus?"

I didn't even have time to think about the answer because my mouth said, "Yes" for me. *Wow. It really and truly does work!* It was kinda creepy hearing my own voice telling me the truth.

One thing I knew I couldn't lie about was the fact that I was really, really tired. It was already ten in the morning and I hadn't slept. Swen would come for me in about seven hours and I still needed to rush to the school and hide the electrodes in the freshman Homecoming crowns. I hoped Swen wasn't mad at me for acting like a little brat yesterday, although it felt like that had happened eons ago.

I was so tired, so sleepy that I thought I would lie down for just a minute and then wake up and start getting everything, and myself, cleaned up. A minute of sleep wouldn't hurt. Yeah, it wouldn't hurt at all.

Chapter

24

Well, that little minute of sleep didn't hurt; however, the other six hours and fifty-nine minutes I overslept did! I woke up to my cell ringing. It was Swen.

"Can I speak to Miss Gamma Glamma?"

"Hi . . ." I muttered, sounding a bit groggy and hoarse.

"Were you sleeping?"

"Not at all! I'm just trying to get everything together." Actually, I *was* trying to get myself together at that moment.

"Do you want me to come in and help you carry stuff to the car?"

Come in? Omigod, he's here.

"No!" I screamed.

"Alright, alright. No problem. I don't think I ever met anyone who has turned me down more times than you," joked Swen.

"Oh, yeah? Uh, could you give me about five minutes and I'll be right out."

"You got it."

After I got off the phone with Swen, I wanted to die. Not like I normally do from just hearing the sound of his voice, but because he was here to pick me up and I wasn't ready at all. Panic struck my heart. My mind could not absorb the fact that he was here. I couldn't believe I had overslept so massively. How could I have been so stupid?

I ran through the house like a chicken with its head cut off, which is gross if you think about it. I mean that poor headless chicken's nervous system going full blast for no reason whatsoever. Maybe I was more like a robot chicken. "Luz, get out of your head—you're late!" I had to scream out loud to myself in my mean voice. Thank God no one else was around to hear me.

My parents weren't home because they had a series of errands to run. Mom told me this last night before I went to work on my latest and greatest invention. She said to call her from Regionals and let her know how I was doing. My parents actually wanted to come tonight, but I would have felt really stupid around Swen if my parents were around. I am so thankful they respected my wishes.

However, even with my parents not around, I still felt like I had masterminded looking pretty stupid around Swen. Like a truly mad scientist, I grabbed every gadget in my room and chunked them all in my backpack.

I only had enough time to brush my teeth and wipe on deodorant. I put on my test tube T-shirt, a pair of jeans, my silver boots, and my emergency bed-head green trucker hat that said, "I Brake for Science." So much for *Gamma Glamma* now. As I was locking the door, I heard my phone ring. I had left my cell phone in the house. I felt sick to my stomach. I felt rushed. I knew those five minutes I had asked for were more like fifteen or maybe even twenty.

Swen got out from the driver's side of the car and quickly rushed to my aid.

"Hey, Luz, are you okay?" he asked as he looked at me like I was some accident victim.

"You want *the truth*, Mr. Swenson? No, I'm not okay," I stammered. I dumped my science display in Swen's willing and always strong hands as I ran back in the house.

"I need to get my phone."

As soon as I made it to the car I had to run back again, for the second time, because I realized that I had left the front door unlocked. My parents would've killed me for that. As I jumped in the passenger's side of the car, I saw my missed call. It was Adam. He must have finally got his phone turned on. I'd call him later. I strapped on my seat belt. I could feel my heart beat a gazillion times a second. I just stared straight outside the windshield. I still wasn't fully awake yet.

"Sorry, I overslept," I confessed.

"No worries," said Swen, who probably knew I was pretty embarrassed.

"Um, can we swing by Gamma?" I asked.

"If we do, Luz, you're going to be late for registration and that will disqualify you."

"Yeah, I guess you're right." I tried to breathe.

Then for a split second, I thought maybe there would be some magical way to get my truth extractors back to Gamma. Okay, maybe not. Maybe I had just wasted a precious night on my ego and my inventions. There would be no time to deal with that or the setting free of the truth tonight.

"Okay, then, let's gas it," I said.

Swen looked at me and made a small motion to my hair. "You might . . . wanna do something about that. . . ." Swen pulled down the visor to reveal a mirror to me.

I looked in the mirror. My hair, which was still really long, was pretty much a bed-head nightmare, but what made it worse was that I had skillfully managed to spread toothpaste in it. All I could do now was comb my monkey hair out and scrape off the toothpaste with my nails.

Swen and I didn't really talk on the way to Fort Worth. I think I must have really looked like a mess. I was still nodding off and it didn't help that the sun was blasting through the window and making me even sleepier.

My phone rang and it startled me. I didn't look to see who it was. I figured it was Bridge, to tell me good luck. I felt like such a bad best friend.

She was probably getting ready right now putting on some cool eye shadow, and I didn't even call her to say have a good time or anything.

I didn't even know what dress she was wearing. What purse she was going to take. And had she the guts to ask B-Dawg to color coordinate with her? Was she going to wear her hair up or down? What would she do if B-Dawg tried to kiss her? There were so many things I didn't know about our—I mean *her*—biggest night.

It made me sad and sick (probably from not eating) to think about it. I just put my phone on stun, at least for the ride, and set it down in Swen's cute cup holder.

When we finally got to the convention center it was a complete nightmare. The parking lot was jammed with cars, trucks, and buses. From a distance, it looked like there was a rock concert going on until you got one look at the kids, their parents, and their accessories.

"Looks like we should have gotten here a lot earlier," said a concerned Swen.

"I would have still been sleeping," I tried to joke. It went off like a lead balloon. Swen was carefully avoiding collisions with the zooming cars and science geeks that were running between cars.

"Well, why don't I drop you off here and then I'll find you inside." Swen stopped the car in front of the building.

"Are you sure?"

"Absolutely."

"I feel bad for making you have to wait. You already had to wait twenty minutes at my house for me."

"*Thirty*." Swen motioned for me to get out of the car.

"Sorry."

"Just teasing," Swen reassured me as he cracked a smile. "You'd better hurry and get in line for registration."

I jumped out and gathered up my stuff from the back of the car and started trucking to the front entrance of the convention center. The walk seemed to take forever. As I made my way inside, I had a feeling that I was forgetting something. I did a quick mental check. Did I leave the iron on at home? No, it was obvious that I hadn't used one today. Did I lock the front door? Yeah, I did. Then my stomach growled really loud at me. Maybe I just needed to eat, I thought.

The line moved really quickly and felt like the lunch line at school. When it was my turn to register, a lady gave me a map of where I was going to set up, a badge, and a gift bag of some sort. Normally, I would have loved the gimme bag, but it was just one more thing to deal with and I was all dealt out.

Walking into the gigantic ballroom, I felt an immediate chill, because they'd set the AC below zero here. As I made my way down to my setup area, which was the farthest corner of the ballroom (just like where I sat in the lunchroom—by the fire exit), I passed many of my fellow competitors with their parents. I kind of wished I had let my parents come.

My dad would have been carrying my display for me because he loves this stuff. He works for the Museum of Natural History and he's in charge of all the touring shows that come through Dallas. And my mom would have made me eat at home or at least would have given us "special permission," as she calls it, to eat something that has "no nutritional value whatsoever," which we would have picked up at a drive-thru.

But they weren't here. And now, without them, I felt like an orphan of science. But I didn't have time to boo-hoo about it, because I needed to get my display up. It took me about four minutes and fifty seconds. That was it. It was definitely a little anticlimactic after I had done all that work. I had devised all these inventions and potions, put my friends' reputations on the line, and in the end, it had taken me less than five minutes to prop it up on a cheapo convention table. I didn't know what to think.

Next to me, I saw a chubby boy in black stretch pants and a beige pullover shirt with his mother setting up his (aargh!) exploding volcano. Who does that anymore? Oh, well, I guess the bonus is that he makes my project look a wee bit better.

As I stood back to look at my presentation, I crossed my arms to stay warm. I heard my competitor's mom say they were going to have judges walk around for the first hour and then it would be open to the public after that.

I just hoped that when Dr. Hamrock showed up he would be proud of what I had done for Gamma. And if he didn't like it, well, I didn't even have the strength or the stomach to think about it.

As I made my way back outside the ballroom in search of a baño and a snack machine, I gazed at all the other projects totally loaded up with smoking beakers and computer monitors and such. They were really tricked out. *Oh, well, there's always next year, right?*

And among the sea of boy geeks, this girl geek could find a bathroom and at least comb her hair and apply lip gloss and find her "scientific eleganz" and Gamma Glamma.

The first thing I noticed when I entered the restroom was the overhead icky fluorescent lighting that came on. Whoever invented that type of light source should be shot. When I looked in the mirror at my greenish complexion, I discovered that I had eye crusties in both my eyes and still had crumpled sheet indentations on my cheek. I don't think I noticed it earlier in Swen's car because the toothpaste horror weighed in so much more at the time. And I can't believe that Swen hadn't said anything. Was he that much of a gentleman or was he driving around legally blind?

I pumped some pink industrial bathroom soap in my hand and began to wash my face. It was hard to rinse, though, since it was that kind of sink where you have to turn the knob and hold down or else the water flow would stop (in my opinion, another very bad invention). With one hand I turned on the sink, and with the other hand I scooped up the water to rinse my face.

"Here you go," spoke a voice as I was handed a wad of scratchy paper towels. I wiped my face down and opened one eye slowly. As I looked in the mirror, I was stunned to see who was behind me.

"Por favor, tell me you're a mirage," I begged.

"Okay, I'm a mirage. Good word choice."

"Adam, what are you doing here? You just can't barge into every women's lavatory."

"Another good word choice."

"Shut up. What's going on here? Why are you here?"

"Didn't you get my phone messages?" asked a surprised Adam.

"No."

"What about my text messages?"

"No," I repeated.

"Señorita Sci-Fi, where *are* your instruments? Where's your phone?"

I hurriedly felt my back pockets. I shook my backpack. I opened it up, but there were so many wires and so much crap that I'd tossed in when I was leaving my house, I didn't want to start digging. As my eyes burned from cheap industrial-grade soap, I wanted to know what Adam was doing here.

"I don't know. I don't know. What's going on? Why are you here?"

Just then an elderly woman walked in and screamed at the sight of Adam. We both figured it was our cue to continue the convo outside.

"Is this about Venus telling the TV crew about your mom?"

"No."

"The can drive?"

"No, that was, like, so Friday. I'm over it. A couple of hours ago, Bridge called and told me that B-Dawg canceled his date with her right before the dance. Bridge went to the school to look for Venus, and she found her and got in a lot of trouble. She blamed Venus for his canceling the date because Bridge had stood up for me. Venus put her hand in the air like she does and so did Bridge. And then Bridge accidentally scratched Venus's face."

"Please tell me you're kidding."

"No. Bridge tried to apologize and check on V's face but that's when V pushed her off and gave Bridge a *black eye*."

"What?! No! Tonight is the biggest night of her life! I need to call her. I can already hear the vicious rumors Venus is spreading about Bridge now."

"No, I'm afraid Miss Hunter is really not wasting her energy shooting off her mouth right now."

"How do you know?"

"Because Bridge pushed Venus off and gave her a *fat lip*."

I felt like crying and it wasn't hard to do right now since my eyes were still stinging from the soapy residue.

"What do you want us to do about Bridge and Venus?"

"Nothing. That was just the daily dish. I'm here about Mase and Susan."

"What about them?"

"I heard they're going *to win*."

"No way!"

"Way, José!"

"Shut up! I don't believe it. Venus would never let them win."

"I'm not so sure. But I do know that Venus and Bart are going to do something to them tonight."

"Now, how do you know this?" I asked, even though I know Adam is such a supersleuth about these things.

"When I was in the media center 'working,' I watched Rod looking at the footage where Venus and Bart were dressed up with the wizard hat and the 'Toot for the Mute' T-shirt. Well, the reason that they got a lot of coverage was that 'they added drama' and he said how he couldn't wait to see them react if Mase and Susan won. Then I heard one of the cameramen tell Rod he was going to follow V and Bart to the balloon store. My investigative gut started screaming to me that they were going to do something tonight."

"Yeah, why would they go to the balloon store if they aren't on the Homecoming decorating committee?"

"That's where I'm leading. I need you to help me stop them. You and I can take it on the chin and Bridge can even take it in the eye. But Mase and Susan can't."

"Adam, I can't leave. I just got here."

"So?"

"I'm representing Gamma. If I leave, I don't know if I would be disqualified or not, but I would probably fail Dr. Hamrock's class."

"Hmmm, let me think . . . science project or having my innocent friends be destroyed at the dance and on national TV. Uh . . . yeah, Luz, where's your conscience? Is it on your display board?"

"Ow! Alright, Adam. Give me a minute to get it together."

I scrawled a small note to Swen on a paper towel that I had an emergency come up and I gave it to the boy with the volcano.

Then Adam and I quickly weaved through the parents, students, and displays to make our way to the parking lot. It took us a minute to find Adam's car, and then when we did try to peel out of the parking lot, it was fruitless, because there were cars still inching around trying to find parking spaces.

Finally, we broke free, and as we drove away, I looked at the convention center growing smaller and smaller in Adam's sideview mirror. I felt bad. *Really bad*. I figured I would call Swen when I got to the dance.

I just hoped that he would understand and not totally hate me. I also hoped that Dr. Hamrock and Swen would realize that this was just an extension of Gamma Glamma, that it was actually going to be an attempt at "science with a conscience" *in action*. And I hoped it wasn't going to blow up in our faces.

Chapter

25

On our hour long ride back to Dallas and back to Gamma High, Adam and I formulated our plan of action. If we were right, the only thing Venus and Bart would have time to do was set up a few water balloons and get dressed before the dance started.

And since the dance was in the gym there wasn't a lot that could be hidden. So it made sense that the only place you could hide the balloons would be from above the temporary stage where the lights and curtains had been hung. No one would notice Bart coming and going from the gym since he was, in fact, a jock and a gym rat. And no one would say anything to Venus because no one ever says nada to Venus.

The sun was setting and the sky was turning from that pretty pink to a dark blue as we drove into Gamma's parking lot. When we got out we could see a few well-dressed stragglers hoofing it to the gym. I grabbed my backpack, and Adam and I followed in hot pursuit.

With the music thundering and the dance in full swing, Adam and I walked right in since there wasn't anybody manning the ticket tables.

Even though the lights were dim, I could tell that everybody looked amazing. The Dramaticas were in their corner wearing black pleather and velvet while the band girls dressed up in green taffeta to show their school spirit. The sci-fi gang, who were mostly dateless boys, flashed their style with khaki pants, white short sleeve shirt with skinny ties. And never to be out done, the J+L posse came paparazzi-ready, with the guys in suits without ties and girls with slinky dresses, fake tans and lots of body glitter All these beautiful people, regardless of clique or class, made me wonder what fantastic outfit I would have chosen to wear on the biggest night of our lives. And even for a stinky ole gym, the smell of perfume, cologne, and corsages almost made me forget we were on a mission. That was until Mr. Sekin said that they would be announcing the court in about five minutes and then they would start the dance contest.

"Let me remind you students to ease up on any dirty dancing since we *are* representing Gamma High with a TV crew present," Mr. Sekin ordered in his brief moment onstage at the mic.

"Is he serious?" I asked loudly.

"Hardly," Adam said. "You can't expect to have a dance with bumping and grinding music and a bunch of hormonal students desperately grasping for their fifteen seconds of glory and not have some dirty dancing."

Adam and I rolled our eyes at each other, and then Adam grabbed my hand and led me through the dirty-dancing couples toward the back of the stage. Once there, it wasn't hard to hide by blending in with the video crew and the pandemonium.

Being so close to my fellow freshman Homecoming finalists and the deafening speakers, I could feel my heart start racing as I tried to take it all in. I first saw Susan, who had this long dark purple gown with a gold sash that looked like she had pulled it from the wardrobe trailer on the set of a Harry Potter sequel. She looked, yet again, like a wizardly wonder. Her hair was twisted in a French braid and she had on her Coke-bottle glasses. Didn't she remember anything I had shown her? Well, I stood corrected, she did eat just the right amount of White Away Right Away jelly beans to give her cheeks a healthy glow tonight.

Next, I spied Mase, who looked exactly the same as he normally does except he had on a black leather jacket over his T-shirt and classic checkered Vans. He looked a bit uneasy. He was chomping on a wad of gum, but I knew it definitely wasn't Gabber Gum because he still wasn't saying anything.

Traci Armstrong was dressed quite fem tonight in a pale blue sleeveless satin dress that showed off her well-toned arms and brought out the blue in her eyes. She wore a stunning updo. And equally stunning next to her was my buddy Jimbo. Nothing unexpected. Jimbo came in a pair of beige slacks, a short-sleeve shirt, and a tie. *A bow tie.* And that brought a smile to my face.

My smile crumpled when I saw Miss Hunter strutting around with a richly tuxed Bart. Venus had chosen a black dress that was cut so low the rating wasn't even PG. I guess she picked this dress to help detract from the scratch on her face, which was heavily covered up with concealer, and her fat lip, which was grossly overglossed.

My heart started beating even faster when I thought about her and Bridge getting into a catfight, and I kept trying to take deep breaths to calm myself down. It did appear to work for a moment until I saw Bridge.

She was draped in a gorgeous cotton-candy-colored strapless cocktail dress. The top of the dress was fitted and the bottom was beautifully puffed out like a ballerina's gown. I just knew that Mrs. Joiner was proud of Bridge's wardrobe choice. What I was most proud of was that Bridge hadn't even tried to cover up her black eye. Even with it she looked gorgeous. That was fierceness in fashion. *That* was Gamma Glamma.

"Can I have all my freshman finalists come up to the stage at this time," ordered Mr. Sekin backstage. The crowd started cheering over the music.

My eyes were still affixed on Miss Joiner when Adam grabbed my arm.

"Luz, heads up. Are you ready to do this?" barked Adam.

"*Listo!* Yeah, I'm ready!" I shouted back.

"What did you say?!" yelled Adam.

"I said I'm ready to do this!" I screamed.

It was hard to hear because of the thumping beats that continued to pump through the speakers. And it was even harder to read lips since it was dark, not to mention the camera crew kept jumping between Adam and me to get new shots. It was completely nuts. Adam still looked puzzled and I just gave him a thumbs-up.

Suddenly, a crew guy trampled on me. "Hey!" I said, totally mad that he didn't look where he was walking.

"You're in a high-traffic area, kid," grunted the grip as he stepped on the stage.

When I stepped to the side and out of the way, nothing could prepare me for what was going to happen next. Bridge spotted Adam.

"Adam!" yelled Bridge excitedly. "Adam, come *here*!" Bridge yelled again.

This time Adam heard Bridge, and for a moment Adam froze when he saw how beautiful Bridge looked. He looked around nervously but couldn't see me.

"Adam, hurry!" Bridge motioned as she invited him up on stage. Adam followed Bridge's command reluctantly, especially since all he was wearing was a T-shirt, a pair of plaid shorts, and his sandals. The crowd let out a roar.

"Adam!" I yelled.

It was pointless. There was no way he was going to hear me now.

The lights were dimmed even further and a very bright spotlight came up on the stage as Mr. Sekin approached the microphone. The crowd started to simmer down just enough that I thought this would be my chance to get Adam's attention. And I was just about to yell when something shiny caught my eye. The crowns. Not just any crowns but the *freshman* crowns.

I still had my backpack and I quickly dug through it while spilling my science gear, gadgets, and other random personal belongings backstage on the floor. Retrieving the truth extractors, I shoved the electrodes and power supplies as far as I could into the upper part of the crowns and quickly wired them in. There wasn't time to dally, and at this point, I didn't really think Mase and Susan would actually win.

But I wanted to be prepared and I wanted Venus and Bart to be prepared to tell the truth. And with small flicks of the tiny little switches, I turned my latest devices on.

"What are you doing?" interrupted some boorish production assistant from the TV crew.

"I was just getting these ready for the presentation," I lied. I know, I was supposed to be telling the truth now, but really, I *was* getting them ready for the presentation.

"Excuse me, but when you go to school and study film, then maybe you can take over my job. But until then, hands off the props, sweetheart." And with that the production assistant jerked the crowns from my hand.

Must remember to never go to school to study film. What freaks! I thought.

Suddenly the music stopped and Mr. Sekin tapped on the microphone.

"I would now like to announce one more time your finalists for the freshman Homecoming Court!" The cheers were deafening.

One by one Mr. Sekin began calling names. He first started with B-Dawg's name and mentioned that B-Dawg couldn't be present due to a wrestling injury but wished him a speedy recovery. The crowd responded by clapping and cheering, "Woof! Woof! Woof!" I saw Bridge give a piercing glare at Venus, who simply responded by showing off her shiny fangs.

My name was called next and Mr. Sekin announced I was representing Gamma at the science regionals and wished me luck. Yeah, I was going to need all the luck I could get, especially since I was practically standing behind him and I could only imagine what Swen and Dr. Hamrock were thinking back at the competition. The crowd continued to cheer and I did hear a few kids scream in unison, "Geek! Geek! Geek!" It was a magical moment, but I had to slap myself out of it.

Mr. Sekin finished calling everyone else's names and now it was time to announce the winners and activate our plan. All I knew was that if on the off chance the winners were Mase and Susan, Adam and I would push the duo away from where they were standing and into safety. I just hoped that Adam hadn't forgotten our mission and was ready for whatever was about to happen.

Luckily, Adam was in the absolute perfecto spot on stage, right next to Susan and Mase. If need be, Adam and I could bum-rush them from their left side toward Venus and Bart.

"And your freshman winners are Susssan Seeeammmus and Massson Milllaaammm," Mr. Sekin announced.

Slow motion. I had never experienced an actual slowing down of time in my life, but now I had and it was quite horrible. That's when I screamed, "Gooo Adammm." I charged up the stairs and rushed toward Susan. Adam apparently had a delayed reaction and did nothing. I flew on to the stage, and due to my short stature, I lunged at Susan's legs. Susan stumbled on her wizard wardrobe to her right and Mase tried to hold her up (like he had done with me during my hair disaster).

Then Adam decided to take flight and leap in like a large awkward ballerina and tackled Mase, who flew another two feet to his right and toward Venus. We were all like a giant ripple of ugliness. And Venus and Bart quickly stepped to their right and back and out of our path of destruction.

Susan and Mase were startled, to say the least, and had no idea of what (or who) had hit them. When Adam and I stood up and tried to help them back on their feet, that's when they were hit again, this time with the falling water balloons. Susan yelped, unable to see anymore through her wet spectacles, and Mase didn't need to speak. I could tell he was furious. The crowd started roaring with oohs and laughter.

"What's going on here?! Are you two responsible for this?!" Mr. Sekin screamed.

"No!" Adam screamed back as he picked up his glasses from the stage. It took a moment but then Mr. Sekin noticed me.

"*Luz Santos*, why aren't you at Regionals?"

"Uh, I can explain . . ."

"You can do all your explaining in the Youth Action Center," barked Coach Smith as he jumped onstage and grabbed Adam and me by our arms.

And that's when Mr. Sekin got back on the mic. "Okay, everybody calm down. Let's get this show on the road. Your Homecoming freshman representatives are Susan Seamus and Mason Milam."

The crowd gave a deafening roar and Adam and I looked at each other in complete shock. Then as we were being hauled to school jail I started to laugh. But then I remembered that Mase and Susan were about to be crowned and I got worried that since they were now wet they might get shocked or something.

I yanked myself away from Coach Smith's grip and passed Adam as I ran back toward the stage. The Student Council members crowned Susan and Mase, but nothing happened—I mean, like electrocution or anything. I stood there completely frozen.

"Susan, would you like to say a few words?" asked Mr. Sekin.

Susan nodded, then walked up to the microphone and said more than a few.

"Uh, thanks for voting and choosing us. This is part of Luz Santos's science experiment, and she said if she could just change a few things it would give us the edge to make us popular. I guess it worked. I didn't really care about winning; I just wanted the extra credit so I could win valedictorian in three years, which is way more important than this dumb contest." The crowd then let out a series of oohs and boos.

Por favor, Dios. No, she didn't just say that! I thought. We are all doomed. And just as I was going to go up there and yank her crown off and hopefully pull the plug on the speech, Venus beat me to it.

"*Omigod!* You don't even deserve to win!" Venus screamed in Susan's pudgy face. "You and Bridget just cheated by, like, using your little secret freak-of-nature science experiment to lie to the student body. You're a bunch of freaking liars!" And then Venus yanked the crown off Susan.

The fickle crowd began to roar and cheer. And this is *exactly* what I had been afraid of.

I wasn't sure what to do next until my very special little friend Venus helped me out—she placed the crown on her own head and grabbed the mic.

"Y'all really deserve better and I just want you to know that in light of this corruption, I will accept being your freshman queen and want to personally invite each and every one of you to a victory celebration at my house next Saturday."

I was glad the crowd was cheering so loud because Coach Smith had to give up his search for me to control the crowd. That gave me my chance to climb up onstage by Venus's side.

"Get away from me, liar," Venus hissed.

As expected, the crowd booed me. It took all I had not to mouth back. I just stood my ground and spoke into the mic since I just had a few questions for our new queen.

"Venus, as our new freshman queen, can I ask you a few questions?"

Venus just glared at me with a cock of her well-waxed eyebrow. I knew it was on.

"Venus, isn't it true that you had a party not because you liked anyone but because you wanted to buy votes?" I asked as I looked at her and then into the crowd. A confused Venus looked out into the blinding spotlight.

"Uh, yes?" Venus couldn't help but confirm. The extractors were on and so was I.

"And isn't it true that you had no plans of letting Adam Bellows take you to the dance and that you were just using him to be a thorn in my side?"

"Well, yeah," a glazed Venus said, unsure of what was happening to her.

Now Coach Smith jumped back on the stage but Mr. Sekin held him off. I knew I had better wrap things up quickly.

So I leaned into the microphone and said, "And yes, it's true that I helped to enhance Mason, Susan, and Bridget for my science project, and that helped get them noticed. But it was all of you in the student body who chose to accept them into your groups, and when the TV crew started doing their coverage, the rest of you really got to know and like Mason, Susan, and Bridge. And then you voted for them. And isn't it true, Venus, that you couldn't stand the fact that somebody was more popular than you?"

Tears started to well up in Venus's eyes. I started to feel bad. No, that's a lie. I enjoyed every second of it.

Venus said, "Yes." The crowd gasped.

I continued, "And lastly—I'm almost done, Mr. Sekin, I swear—

"isn't it true that you only liked Bart and let him take you to the dance because he'd do anything you say? And didn't you both conspire in this vicious balloon attack on Mase and Susan?"

"Don't answer that Venus!" demanded Bart.

Unfortunately for Venus, she was on a roll, and when she said yes, Bart lunged at her and knocked her down. For a moment, I thought that he was going to beat her up. But then Adam jumped in and Bart punched him and then Bridge jumped on Bart's back kicking her pink kitten heels like she was riding a bronco.

That's when the houselights came on. Party over. The cameras were still rolling and Coach Smith and Mr. Sekin had Bart in a headlock. The crown was off Venus's head and she was crying uncontrollably. I think it was because it was the first time she felt human in, like, her whole lifetime.

Traci and Jimbo were talking with Susan to make sure she was okay. Bridge was checking on Adam's new matching shiner and was screaming for ice. And finally, I realized that my stomach was screaming because I hadn't eaten all day long and I just needed to sit down backstage, where no one could notice me.

And then that's when I heard a voice on the microphone. I didn't try to see who was talking because I figured it was some parent who was chaperoning or something. It was anything but.

"I want to say something," the deep voice said. "I just wanted to say sorry to my friend Adam Bellows, since I found out through the magic of television that he didn't nominate me, and I didn't want to be nominated. And Luz Santos, wherever you are, I thought your science experiment was dumb at first, but I did it because you've always been cool to me. Yeah, I got to be popular or whatever. But you hooked me up with some good friends, especially in the stagehand department."

From back in the corner of the gym, a crowd of Dramatica Gamma stagehands chanted, "Mase! Mase! Mase!"

Mase continued, "Uh, so that's how we knew about the balloon sabotage and moved them out of the way. But since Adam and Luz performed some extreme moshing, they pushed us back *in the way*. 'Thanks,' *guys*. But anyway, I'd like to pass the hat—or crown—to

Adam Bellows. I'm not into kingmanship or anything unless it's the king of the buffet."

Even with the sobering gym lights on, the crowd started cheering. I was soooo incredibly happy! I mustered all the strength I had and went over to Susan, who was about to put her crown back on. I ripped the extractor wires out before there were any more unnecessary revelations. And then I found Adam and cleaned out his crown before I placed it regally on his head.

Mr. Sekin escorted Venus and Bart away and asked Adam (with his crown, of course), Mason, and I to come down to the Youth Action Center and divulge all the details of this whole drama-rama. And then, Mr. Sekin turned the emcee duties over to Coach Smith.

And because Coach Smith is an athletic director and not an entertainer, he shouted out the names of the rest of the Homecoming Court like it was roll call for the marines.

As we walked outside the gym, we could still hear him ordering that the lights be dimmed again and the music started up and reminding our fellow classmates that he didn't want any stray Gamma Stallions (yes, we are Pegasus horses, but a horse is a horse) wandering around on campus after the dance was over.

Yes, he was a bit of a buzz kill but at least he got the party started again. After Adam and I recounted the entire Gamma Glamma epic to Mr. Sekin, we were finally allowed with Mase to return to the dance. As we entered the dimly lit gym again to the pulsating music, it was impossible to see any negative impact our freshman class drama had had on the overall festivities.

Adam, Bridge, and I sat down together after visiting the buffet and chowed down on chips and salsa and cheap fruit punch.

"So, we have a lot to talk about," Bridge joked to me as she smelled her wrist corsage made out of baby roses.

"You're not kidding."

"I'd ask you if you want to spend the night but you look tired."

"And you look fabulous. Maybe next week." I looked at her swollen cheek. "Does your eye hurt?"

"Only when I touch it."

"So, don't *touch* it then." I smiled.

"You're hilarious," Bridge said. Not realizing how sensitive her cheek really was, she crunched hard on a carrot stick and winced in pain.

"I'm surprised Betty let you out of the house without trying to cover up that shiner," I said.

Bridge nodded.

"If you want, I'm sure I can make some type of ointment that can help accelerate the . . ."

"Luz! Stop! You're delirious."

"No, I'm a scientist and . . ."

"So am I, and . . . as your best friend I'm telling you that parading this black eye here tonight is my most important Gamma Glamma invention ever and it's called courage."

She definitely gave me a lightbulb moment. "Dang, Bridge, that's really horribly sweet and profound."

"And you know what I call my black eye? 'Shiny,' " Adam said, now back to his sarcastic self.

"You know, Adam, I never realized how brilliant you are," Bridge said as she leaned in lovingly from her chair and put her head on his shoulder.

"Really?" Adam said, quite taken aback.

"Yeah. Even with all our world and mad science falling apart you still managed to copy what I'm wearing for Homecoming."

"Yes, I *am* brilliant." We all laughed and gazed at the couples who were practicing their dirty-dancing skills on the gym floor.

Then, for a while Adam and Bridge compared the swelling of their shiners until Bridge's phone rang and she jumped and ran out of the gym so she could hear—especially since she saw the call was from B-Dawg.

Mase came by our table after Susan dumped him. She said she wanted to hang out with Hector the oboe player who came alone to the dance. And truthfully (even without the "Truth B. Told"), Susan explained that she only said yes to going to the dance with Mase because they were on camera. And even though Mase was alone, he was relieved.

Once again the word traveled faster than the speed of light, and in an instant a gaggle of drama mamas were ready to escort Mr. Milam, the newly crowned "King of the Buffet," during the last hour of Homecoming.

So now it was just Bellows and me, resting our heads on the table, and then one of those songs started playing. And I don't even know the name of it. You just hear it at the end of every teen movie where the girl is teary eyed and pathetic and then her dream luva shows up and they dance at the end and the credits roll. Yeah, it was that song.

So then Adam said, "Wanna dance?"

"I guess so," I said, feeling unsure whether I wanted to or not. I must have looked pretty sour faced.

"You don't *have to*," Adam snipped.

"I know. I'm just torn. I want to, so I can say I did, but I'm exhausted." I put my head in my hands on the table, but a determined Adam grabbed my hand and dragged me to the dance floor. Since I'd long since pulled my boots off (because in my hurry to leave the house I hadn't put on socks before I put my boots on and now I had blisters—again), I was now barefoot. Even in my trucker hat I only came up to Adam's stomach. We danced for exactly two seconds. Adam threw my hands down.

"You're right, I'm exhausted too," said Adam, yawning.

And just as we turned around to head back to our table to observe and sleep, and maybe not in that order, Swen materialized out of nowhere and stood before you-know-who. And he was smiling. *Thank God.* We all just stood there in the middle of the dance floor looking at each other and doing nothing. It was rather awkward.

Finally, Adam broke the weirdness by yelling over the music through his cupped hand, as a small megaphone, "Did you want to cut in?!"

"No!" Swen hollered as he shook his head.

"What did you say?!" Adam screamed as he scrunched his face as if that was going to help him hear better or something.

"I said no!" Swen repeated, using both his hands to make a bigger megaphone.

"Alright! Well, then, I'll leave you two alone anyway since my investigative gut tells me that you want to discuss the girl's sudden disappearance from Regionals.!" Adam used his hands like sign language to make sure Swen understood what he was saying before he disappeared into the crowd, covered in reflections of twinkling disco ball lights.

I know this is not just improbable but completely dumb, but even with me looking like a barefoot science trucker who now had queso and salsa breath, I did kinda hope that Swen would ask me to dance. You know, just like in the movies. I mean, that stupid song was still playing and the dance was almost over. But he didn't. So, we just moseyed back to the table where I had been sitting with Adam, and now it was Swen and I observing all the hormonal urges bumping and grinding on the dance floor.

"I can explain everything. How did you know where I was?"

"I'm a journalist, Luz."

"You're good."

"I'm even better with your cell phone, which you left in my car." Swen reached in his back pocket and pulled out my cell phone.

"So, that's where it went," I said, having a momentary flashback.

"Yeah, I hope you don't mind that I answered it when your mom called."

"*Omigod.* What did she say? What did you say?" I asked, feeling a bit freaked out.

"Well, she called before I realized you had escaped Regionals. I told her that I had dropped you off and I was looking for parking."

"What did she say?" I asked, because I had to know.

"She said to call her when you had a chance. She told me to tell you good luck and that she loved you."

Normally, I would be terribly embarrassed by this, but I think I was just terribly exhausted. I turned once again to all the happy couples on the dance floor, who totally looked to be in love. Another thought made me jump.

"So then, how did you know I was here at the dance?"

"After I talked with your mom I saw that you had an urgent text message from Adam and I read it. After I read about Mason and

Susan being in trouble and then you being MIA, I figured you would come back and help them since you *are* science with a conscience." Swen smiled.

That was the best news all night. It almost could have ranked up there with him saying he loved me, but he didn't. We talked (and I explained) for what seemed like hours, but I know it was only minutes because the dance was almost over. And then I fell asleep at the table.

After what was supposed to be the biggest night of my life, Swen took me and my boots home, and the scary thing is I have no recollection of it. He said I was pretty loopy (due to weeks and weeks—well, two weeks, anyway—of lack of sleep). Apparently, I had asked him if he hadn't been covering the science competition would he have asked me to Homecoming. He had said no. When I had asked why, he had said that he didn't know how to dance.

I do remember one thing though. He looked at me and I looked at him while we were sitting in the car and he *did* lean in this time just like the magazines said it would happen, and it was beyond chemical. It was *muy mágico*! I would have called Bridge to report the news, but as soon as I got to my room I fell asleep on my beanbag chair with Shortie.

Epilogue

Today, Gamma is a whole new world. Mase now talks a smidge more than he used to without the Gabber Gum or my "Truth B. Told" crown or any other artificial aid, and Adam is now a special investigative reporter for the *Gamma Gazette*. Not only did Bridge's eye heal, but so did her heart, especially after she found out that B-Dawg really had pulled a groin muscle and had actually asked her to the dance on his own accord. And now he's invited her to attend his cello recital.

Jimbo and Traci have been breaking clique boundaries and are dating. People have been calling them the "hybrid couple." And even though I lost Regionals, the science department got major press when the documentary aired. Rod even gave me a "special thanks" at the end of the documentary. Can you believe it? The science department was championed for helping to invent "Science with a Conscience" and has been awarded quite a bit of funding.

Oh, and as far as Venus and Bart, well, they are now responsible for cleaning and maintaining all the new fish tanks that have been purchased by the department. Bart got suspended for attacking Venus and doesn't get to do anything sports related until next year.

Dr. Hamrock must really love his fish because he bought fourteen tanks. But I think the most amazing thing that I've learned this year so far came from Susan. I found out that she knew all along that people called her Jabba and she really didn't care. In fact, she had thought it was so funny that people spent that much time thinking about her that that's why she created her superhero character. J-girl actually stands for Jabba-girl!

And these days, Susan has returned to her old hairstyle and clothes, because, well, she actually *likes it*. However, she did request that I make more jelly beans because she says she likes to look Latina, like me (even though she's redheaded and freckled!).

I can't believe it's almost March. Now that the Student Council has just announced that a Sadie Hawkins Spring Fling Dance is coming up, Bridge and I decided that we want to have spiral curls for that dance and we've started to develop a formula for that but we are only doing testing on weekends. As a surprise for Swen, I'm working on some electronic rhythm *zapatos* for him so that when he takes me to the dance we can actually dance. I mean, I'm Latina and dancing is like breathing for me and I really need to shake my Gamma Glamma this time and represent. I wonder what shoe size he wears?